I0699670

To the American education system.
Without it, I would've never had this story.

And to One, Two,
Three, Four, Five, Six & Seven!

Contents

The Diary of a Sugarbaby

I

Shopping

1

The Red

Nobody actually believed what was said on the news that day.

People went to work as if they heard nothing at all. The only difference was Elders stood prouder, and Minors stiffened.

I am a Minor, and I, too, could not believe the news that day. It wasn't until I was taking my morning commute that I saw an Elder—who looked to be in his 50s—walk up to a Minor and request her companionship.

The Minor was a white, collegiate girl in her 20s who, from the looks of textbooks in her hands, was en route to campus. She was unequivocally beautiful—blonde hair, slender body, intelligent eyes. It was no wonder the Elder gunned for her.

She politely denied his request.

She may not have heard the news or, like everyone else, did not believe it.

As the train slowed, the Elder pulled out a scarlet necklace from under his shirt. At the end of the necklace was a tiny pendant—a compact case with a red button inside. He flicked it open and pressed the button. When the train halted, a group of soldiers in red camo swarmed in through the doors and followed the point of the Elder's finger.

It happened so quickly.

The Red engulfed the girl. Her books were flung across the floor. Her scream pierced the air.

One soldier had the Minor by the hair. Another held her hands behind her back. They ripped her from the train and shoved her onto her knees. Tears were welling in her eyes, and a cloth was jammed in her mouth.

She stared up at the soldier facing her. The girl's pleading eyes moved up the barrel pressed into her forehead. The soldier pulled the trigger.

Blood splattered everywhere. The Minor's body went limp.

The doors closed, and the train continued.

Everyone on the train was so stunned no one spoke. All I heard was the train moving along its tracks.

From that moment on, oh I believed.

2

Minority

*T*hey were the cruelest during the first few days after the Bill was ratified. They wanted to show that They were serious, that we must obey, and that if we rejected an Elder, They would make an example of us.

The moment on the train was one of many. Many, many lives were lost during those first few days—several thousand in Philadelphia, close to a hundred thousand in D.C., and a quarter of a million in New York City.

I could be next.

Before our phones were disconnected and confiscated, I read an article about this one Minor who was executed in her practice after rejecting companionship with one of her patients.

It happened everywhere, in all public spaces, even in front of children as though to tell them, *When you turn eighteen, this could be you, so don't try anything smart!* Might as well show them while they're young, right? Show them what it means to not follow the Law. Show them that their bodies belong not to themselves but to *Them*.

Not every child would endure Minority, though. For the right price, you could be exempted from the civic duty, which the Divided *swore* was henceforth obligatory.

Obligatory, my ass. Only the super-rich would wiggle out of a law created to suit their kind.

When bodies piled up, and people began accepting the Law, we Minors—the poor, the middle class (if there ever was such a thing), and even the lower rich—went into hiding.

Unfortunately for us, Elders came seeking.

3

Autonomy

I have five siblings.

The two oldest are thirty-seven and thirty-eight years of age. They lucked out and never had to be a Minor. They don't know what it's like.

The year the Bill was ratified, they were instantly inducted into Elderhood.

I don't think my older sister, Goldie, would like it very much. Of course, Elderhood is far better than Minority. They have more freedoms, like personal autonomy, companionship, polygamy, and the freedom of choice; the freedom to choose whomever they want to screw.

But still, I don't think Goldie would enjoy having total control over a Minor's life and body and fucking someone who doesn't want to fuck her.

My older brother, Silv, I don't know very well. He's the conservative one of the bunch and lives in the south of the Divided.

Our region of the post-United isn't actually called the Divided. Imagine what the rest of the world would think! No. *I* call it the Divided. You might find the name unimaginative. I find it appropriate.

Anyway, I don't think Silv would rape someone. But to have autonomy over a Minor… maybe.

I could be wrong about the rape. Many people who I thought were better than that still did it.

When the Law allows you to do something, more people do it than you would expect.

4

A Liar, a Cheat, & a Thief

I *have never believed in what people call unconditional love.*

We maintain relationships for personal gain and emotional support. I had friends from whom I benefited; I'll be honest. I think everyone does. Most people would deny it though.

Oh no, I'm a good friend! I have friends because I love them, and that's that!

I never said we didn't love our friends. We can love someone for sure. But that love is still conditional. We only love when we feel like we need it. We only love when it's convenient for us. We only love when they treat us right.

Unconditional love shouldn't exist anyway. To love someone unconditionally, we must love them regardless of their actions, allowing them to cause us distress and harm. No one should be that self-loathing.

Some may say I am a pessimist, a nihilist, or a child of divorce.

All is true.

Though I will say, of all loves, I imagined parental love to be the closest to unconditional.

Then I grew up.

When I was sixteen, my father packed my things into a suitcase, threw it on the doorstep, and told me never to return. I know. How unique, right? A father throwing his kid out on the street? Never heard that one before.

I was the farthest thing from a delinquent. Unlike my older brother Nickel, I never busted up cars or robbed liquor stores. No, I was a good boy. Boy? I hate that word. I was a good *child*. I never got arrested or grounded. Never took money from them. I had straight As and was in every club and sport. I graduated with the most community service hours. I didn't even know someone was calculating that shit. I just liked being a part of a community. The worst thing I did was steal a pair of sunglasses from a department store.

So why did my father throw me out of the house?

For wearing the occasional dress and earrings. Isn't that funny? At that age, I normally wore "boyish" clothes. I wore whatever my older siblings handed down to me. I couldn't afford anything more. When I got my first job, I started going to thrift stores and playing with fashion. Most people don't see fashion as an art. They see it as their identity. Not me. I just wanted to be creative.

My father said he threw me out because I used his car to get sushi instead of Chinese take-out. The sushi bar was a mile away from the Chinese place. Though this was true, this was also the day after I came home wearing a dress.

My father was an exceptional yet obvious liar. I know that's paradoxical, but I myself am a liar. The way he lied was very specific: he used small, innocuous truths to mask bigger, more deplorable truths. In other words, he used this truth about me using his car to lie about his queerphobia to make me the bad guy.

I was never mad or sad about being thrown out. Honestly, I never liked living with my father. He made me and my friends—particularly my girlfriends—feel uncomfortable. He was bigoted in every way. He was mean, cruel, and rude. A liar, a cheat, and a thief. He was a terribly repressed man.

I wasn't surprised I was thrown out either. He once got in a fight with my mother, claiming I wasn't his child. He said she had cheated on him with some Latino guy in what was once called Virginia. But if you put me in a line-up with my siblings, it's obvious I share their blood. Regardless, he was the one who had raised me. So, does it really matter?

I am who I am.

Before Minority, I had always been my authentic self. I was a genderfucking loner in a rural, conservative world that shamed and rejected me. Despite all the adversity, I held my queerness like a dream worth returning to.

Some people admired my courage.

Others glared.

Pride is a privilege and luxury queer men of my father's age never knew. Their privilege was white and wealthy, cisgender and male, passing, abled, and Christian-American. Their luxuries were fast cars and lake houses, weekend "business" trips, sunkissed skin, food, water, and shelter. He was proud of himself for having these tangible things, but he never had pride in the other sense of the word.

If he had all that, why would he ever choose *pride*?

5

Propaganda

*E*very Sunday, the Red force Minors out of bed at the crack of dawn naked and barefoot.

They march us to Center City toward a circle of bonfires and force us into lines like nurses at a psychiatric hospital. Instead of dishing out pills, the Red hand each of us a pile of media and art—vinyl, CDs, news articles, cellphones, magazines, books, what have you. We then use those piles to feed the flames.

On one particularly beautiful, horrible Sunday morning, I was given a Margaret Atwood novel, a couple of love poetry books, a few issues of *The New Yorker*, a Lauryn Hill vinyl, and a box of iPhones.

I eyed the iPhones. I badly wanted to slip one into my pocket so I could later call my siblings and friends and find out where they were and if they were alright. It would be a futile attempt. Not worth the beating. The phone would surely be out of charge and without service and Wi-Fi. Not to mention, the Red have eyes everywhere.

We moved in a single file and formed circles around each pit. The Red ordered us to toss in our piles. I threw in the books and magazines and watched the flames engulf their pages. Their words and voices became instant ashes. The vinyl and phones took their sweet time melting into lumps, mocking me.

The Divided made us do this every Sunday to condition us never to read or listen to profanity again. Literature and music gave us ideas and told us stories. Ideas that go against the Law and stories that make us dream and yearn. No, no. That would not do. Those thoughts would have to be burned out of us.

The only reading Minors are given is *The Monthly*—a monthly news pamphlet about two pages long. The pamphlet provides "global news." In other words, fabricated lies and horrendous, exaggerated truths.

The Divided issue the pamphlets to teach us that we have it better here than anywhere else in the world, that companionships are far better than wars, epidemics, homelessness, poverty, and famine.

Though I am sure it is fake news, I would never say so out loud. If I did, I'd be charged with slander. The ramifications of slander against the Divided would be rape by twelve Elders. The twelve Elders would be selected at random, like jury duty.

6

The Ameriqueerocide

I found myself daydreaming, staring into the flames.

I imagined what it would be like to simply walk in and embrace the hellish death. Would it be quick or drawn out? Would I experience pain worse than what I know? What does death look like, and would I be free?

Of course, the Red wouldn't allow that. The tracker in my thumb would tase me before my toes ever found the bed of embers. Sometimes, if I get too close to the fire, I feel prickling in my hand. The trackers are essentially our shock collars.

Falling forward into the fire would rely on luck. And even then, I might not die. I'd be disfigured, yes, but the consequences of attempted suicide are much worse than death itself.

I once saw a Minor—who always had bruises scattered along his body—try jumping into a pit. The fire was extinguished instantly before he even landed. He flopped onto the ground, confused about where the fire had gone. When reality sank in, he looked more scared than he did before he had jumped. He was dragged away that day, kicking and screaming, naked and afraid.

I never saw him again.

As the Atwood novel burned, I met eyes with a handsome, Black boy across a pit.

Minors are not allowed to converse, but I knew his name was Raphael. At least, that's what his Elder called him.

Every Sunday, Raphael and I made eye contact. His gaze always lingered on my ass and mine on his giant cock.

Why must we do this ritual naked? Because the Divided liked it. They had power over us and got off on it. It was another way to embarrass us, make us vulnerable, and weed out the queers. If you get hard looking at other guys or wet looking at other girls, you were labeled and put on a list.

I was already on that list. After the Bill was ratified, the Divided found our internet histories and health records.

And then came a mass genocide of queer Americans. This period would later be called *the Ameriqueerocide*. I don't know what the estimated death toll was. It's still climbing, I'm sure. Historians will know one day. If queer erasure persists, then perhaps not. All I know is that trans men and trans women were the first to go. Then, anyone non-binary or genderfluid. When I heard, I burned all my dresses, blouses and anything else that skewed fem.

Gay men and gay women were next. Gay men were targeted more because no matter how masculine they were, they were still seen as weak and gross. Gay women, on the other hand, were only targeted if they were butch. Fem lesbians were a kink fetishized by straight men.

Other minorities were targeted next. Bisexuals, Pansexuals, Arabs, Latinos, Black Americans, Asian Americans, Indigenous Americans, Jewish Americans, Disabled Americans, Pacific Islanders, Immigrants… There was so much bloodshed. Most of it—unsurprisingly—happened in the south of the Divided.

The Divided told the rest of the world They had successfully rid their lands of the entire LGBTQIA+ community, which They inaccurately simplified as "the gays." Not even a community, just "the gays."

Some countries wanted to know how They did it. Others debated with the Divided but never intervened or came to our aid. They feared the Divided's nuclear arsenal, one of the most formidable in the world.

But the Divided had not successfully killed off the queer community. We still exist, and the Divided know. That's why They kept *the list*.

How did we all not go extinct? Well, fortunately for us, those in power liked to have options. They wanted to seem pure and sinless to the rest of the world. But at night, They would welcome a gay, Black boy or a trans, Asian girl into their room and fuck them raw.

Those companionships, my companionships, were always discreet. A secret known only between an Elder, their Minor, and the Divided.

It was illegal to be out and proud.

That's why I willed myself not to look at Raphael. I could not daydream. If I got a semi in public, I'd be whipped until I bled.

7

New Kid

*W*e moved a lot when I was a kid.

My parents never traveled abroad or met people from other walks of life. They saw no reason to. But they dragged us all along the East Coast. Massachusetts, Virginia, Florida, New York, Connecticut, Pennsylvania, elsewhere, nowhere. They never stayed in one place for too long. They ran from their pasts and buried their mistakes. They dropped their friends and tore up roots just to keep their gardens pristine. No, not pristine. Empty.

The less responsibility, the better.

I never quite know what to say when people ask me where I'm from. I could say I'm from Hershey, Pennsylvania, where I was born. I could say I'm from Pulaski, Virginia, where I spent most of my childhood running around with my siblings and reading books in trees. Or I could say I'm from Clearwater, Florida. We lived there until a tornado drove my family back to my mother's home state of New York. New York was where I was called faggot for the first time, where I learned I was the smartest in my class, and where I accepted that, despite every uplifting novel I read and every heartwarming movie I watched, nothing ever truly matters.

Nowadays, I never get asked where I'm from. I miss being asked. I miss talking about myself. But, at the same time, I am grateful I am never asked. My past is a can of worms.

Before middle school, I never minded being the new kid. I had white privilege and wore glasses and hand-me-downs. My curly hair was gelled back. I was the nerdy type, but not nerdy enough to stand out and get harassed. I was nondescript. And as someone who had yet come into themself, hiding was important.

Then, we moved to Connecticut, and I entered high school. I had just gotten contacts and learned how to style my hair and wear clothes that complimented my figure and accentuated my identity. My muscles started to form, and my handsome features started to show.

And suddenly, everyone paid attention to me.

My first day at the Connecticut school was chaotic. I remember walking into the cafeteria and being engulfed by the girls like a phagocyte. Around sixty to eighty girls ushered me to the center of a long cafeteria table and squeezed beside me on the benches. It was a game of musical chairs. Those who couldn't find a seat sat on the ground, hovered over my shoulder, or plopped themselves right onto the table. At first, I thought, *Wow, a big, close-knit group of girlfriends. We love that.*

But no. Turns out, everyone just wanted to know everything about the new kid. Not me. The new kid. I was an object to them. Something they could pull apart with their fingers.

As an extroverted introvert, I liked being desired but was still incredibly overwhelmed.

I ended up leaving the cafeteria entirely and finishing my lunch in a bathroom stall—typical new kid move.

I wish I had pulled a dick move and told them all to fuck off, like my older brother Nickel.

I shouldn't be complaining that everyone wanted to be my friend. It's usually the opposite for most new kids. But when you have no friends, you have time to find that one gem. That's what I wanted. Some*one* who knew everything about me. Some*one* I could confide in. Some*one* who was simply around.

Being a kind person though, and a naïve one as well, I allowed everyone to have a chance at being my friend. But to welcome everyone into your garden is to let in snakes.

There was this clique of seven good-looking kids in the honors classes. They were exceptionally intelligent. I remember reading some of their papers and thinking, *Damn, I'm not the smartest one here.*

They were nice kids, too… at first. They sucked me into their folds, and I considered them friends. But I soon learned how superficial and mean they all were. They used to form group messages and gossip about how I dressed and shaved my armpits. They speculated about my sexuality as though I were nothing more than a sexual prize, as though they had nothing better to talk about, as though the way I presented myself determined my sexuality.

There was one person in the group I quite liked. She was the one who showed me the messages. At the time, I took it as loyalty. In retrospect, she was probably just stirring the pot.

After seeing the messages, I started to disassociate myself from the group. It wasn't easy because we were in all the same classes, sports, and clubs. It took me until senior year to find people I genuinely liked.

When it comes to friendship, I look for depth. I don't care about the brand you're wearing, only how you feel in it. I don't care how much money your family has in the bank, only the passions you invest in.

After a year of being friends with that clique, I learned the twins in the group had an older brother. I remember being so disappointed in myself for not knowing this. Family is fundamental information you should know about a friend, at least to me anyway. I want to know every layer of a person. I want to know about their families and loved ones, their backgrounds and childhoods, their heartaches, traumas, cultures, and traditions. I want to hear their favorite music and read their favorite books. I want to see their strengths, flaws, and quirks. I want them to tell me their dreams and fears, beliefs and opinions, and what makes them happy and sad. That's the shit that bonds two people.

I found what I was looking for, eventually.

I found depth in Chavos. She was a highly articulate and introspective person, even back then. I vibed with that. We bonded over Beyoncé and Oreos with peanut butter. She taught me how to make empanadas. Some of my favorite memories with her were when we sat in the local McDonald's parking lot and talked for hours.

Our peers thought she was a bitch because she had a resting-bitch face. What they didn't see behind her RBF was her anxiety and propensity to overthink. She was also into fashion and one of the only Puerto Ricans in the school so it could've been a case of stereotyping. But she never did anything to earn the label of bitch. In fact, she mostly kept to herself. A remarkably independent woman. Men—and many women too—fear that in other women. Fucking stupid if you ask me.

She always compared herself to others, even later in life. I always told her she was different and far better than everyone else. She never listened to what I said, or at least found it difficult to believe that someone thought so highly of her. She only listened to herself.

While I found her obstinacy irritating, I admired her conviction.

I also found depth in Rupiah.

Rupiah was chaotic, and I loved that about her. She and I bonded over philosophical poetry, spirituality, tarot, and astrology. She was the Aries to my Sagittarius, we always said. Our shared moon in Cancer, we mused, gave us our synchronicity, similarities, and total understanding of each other. Astrology was a way for us to be vain, to talk about ourselves, to be cognizant of our shortcomings, and to celebrate our come-throughs.

We were total stoners. We'd go on long drives on Connecticut back roads and bump to R&B music or scream to some angsty rock song. We'd rip a bong by the lake and howl at the moon. Or we'd whip up a full-course meal at midnight, stoned as fuck, and watch horror films all night long. She taught me how to make her family's staple Indonesian curry, which was her way of telling me I was her family now.

She was so loving I didn't care if she was late to everything. Okay, maybe a little. But where she lacked in clocks she made up for in heart and soul.

And then there was Cedi.

Cedi was elusive, silly, and clever. She was Paris Hilton-level clever. She'd make stupid, ridiculous comments that left you wondering, "Are you serious?" But if you were quick enough, you'd catch the glimmer in her eyes that told you she was in on the joke all along. She also had the most infectious, charming laughter. She could use it to get out of anything.

Cedi was blessed with a creative mind, sometimes to a fault. While she could draw, act, and entertain, she overthought everything more than Chavos. For example, I once dragged Cedi and Rupiah to a showing of *Rocky Horror*. We took a couple Polaroids before the show. I didn't look good in any of them except for one, the one of me and Rupiah. I kept that one and offered the others to Rupiah and Cedi. Cedi was offended I didn't want to keep the photo of me and her. I understood her hurt and apologized instantly, but she was convinced I liked Rupiah more because I chose that photo over the others. But the truth was, I was being vain. I couldn't choose one friend over another. Even if I tried, it'd be too difficult. They all offer such different things.

With Cedi, out of all my friends, despite the differences in our families and cultures, she understood what I went through the most as a queer person. She, too, was rejected by her family for being gay. She was also an independent, unmarried woman who moved out of her family's house at age twenty. Her very existence defied Ghanaian custom.

I found so much depth in Cedi it hurt. Perhaps that's what drew us together. We saw the dark in each other's eyes, a single flame that was all too familiar.

The thing with queer culture is when our families shun us, we find family in each other.

Friendship will always be tethered to the concept of family. Say you're close to your brother. You're only truly close when you can say your brother is like your best friend. Or say you're close to your best friend. You're only truly close when you can say your best friend is like your sibling. Family becoming friends and friends becoming family are analogs of a deeper relationship. It is a way to say that a relationship is so deep and real it has passed through some unseeable threshold into another dimension.

Chavos, Rupiah, and Cedi.

They were my chosen family. They were the pruned wallflowers in my garden of snakes.

On a superficial level, it may have looked as if our "diversities" were what drew us together. To an extent, perhaps this was so. In a predominantly white, straight, rich, cisgender neighborhood, we endured similar experiences, hardships, and prejudices. Chavos was ridiculed for her East Hartford attire and argot. Rupiah was called *Dora the Explorer*. Cedi was bullied for the tracks in her hair. I was mocked for my feminine attire.

People will say it was trauma bonding. But I don't want the depth of our friendships to be shallowed or erased. Perhaps our superficial differences acted as beacons, sure. But they were not why we nurtured our relationships and let them evolve over decades.

When we were together, we felt normal, special, and loved.

I think about them every day. I feel them next to me in my loneliest of hours. I can't bring myself to talk about Cedi yet. As for Rupiah and Chavos, I hope they survived the Ameriqueerocide. I hope they're safe in another part of this world or, at the very least, have Elders who care for them and don't hurt them. I hope they can find little nuggets of joy in the giant sorrows of today.

Fuck, I miss them.

8

The Unpretty

*P*retty is a double-edged sword.

On one end, pretty draws in eyes. I receive the attention others so deeply crave. I can easily make friends and feel confident in my skin and mirror. I can weasel out of a speeding ticket, even though I've never had a car. Oh, and the men! I get to have my pick, right?

On the other end, pretty lets in snakes and deters depth. People look, never listen. Pretty prevents people from seeing that I am more than just a body, and that I can also be kind and clever. Pretty prevents people from reading what I write. Pretty prevents promotions. How could anyone ever be that good-looking and just as smart? No way. Not possible.

Even in the Divided, pretty is such a privilege! Pretty is what establishes you as a Minor, of course.

Those who are not pretty—those poor, fortunate souls—well, they are forced to be the Red.

9

Verlan

Q*ueer people are constantly doubted.*
Our identities are doubted.
Our personalities are doubted.

People consider us too much or overly dramatic and sensitive. They think we're seeking attention and stand out on purpose—that we chose to be this way. Yes, many of us dress, talk, and act differently. And yes, we have niche language and culture. But the heteros—most, not all—are the ones villainizing us. *They* are the ones being overly dramatic, pointing at us, ridiculing us, and drawing attention to themselves. If they just shut the fuck up, we wouldn't be standing out. We'd simply exist.

But because they doubt our exteriors and mannerisms, they begin to doubt other aspects of ourselves. They doubt our intellect, for example. Heteros believe we're stupid for choosing to be this way, and therefore, we must be stupid in general.

When I was a translator at a City Hall in France with my friend, Yuan, the mayor of the city, who was corpulent and not particularly handsome, sat both of us down to welcome us. We exchanged niceties and told him a bit about ourselves. He was showing us around town when he said to me in French, "You speak better French than I thought you would."

This was the first time we had met, the first time we had exchanged words in person. There was no reason for this man to make this assumption about me.

I applied for the internship through my college. When my college chose me and Yuan as the translators, they sent the City Hall our application essays, transcripts, and a copy of our passports. That's it. That's all they got.

I was in the top twenty percent of my class, behind Yuan. We studied the same subjects and both came from Pennsylvania.

I asked what gave him that impression.

He stuttered and said it was because I had used the informal in my application essay. It was a brief essay in which I used the *vous* form and no slang. I reread the essay that night and tried to find where I was being informal. I even asked Yuan to read it. She agreed it was fine.

The only explanation I could find was that he saw my passport and assumed that I could never be intelligent. I do not look dumb; at least, I don't think I do. I'm not a mouth-breather. My eyes are not vacant. My questions are smart, and my responses are thoughtful. The way in which he spoke to me made me feel like I was an idiot. To him, I was just a pretty, feminine boy who picked looks over brains and chose to be feminine rather than "a real man."

He had said none of this to me. It's what I had sensed. I'm aware I'm overthinking.

I get it; stereotypes can be true sometimes. So, he made those assumptions. And when he was surprised I had not met his expectations, he vocalized it. But it was not the compliment he thought it was. Instead, it made him look like a presumptuous ass.

Yes, it's rewarding being the underdog, but it's also tiring to have to prove to people that I have a brain and that what I have to say is worth hearing. I'm tired of heteros projecting. I think they see how clever we are. Lesbians, gays, non-binary people, trans men and women, all of us in the queer community. They see us, fear us, and then doubt us. And because they're the majority, we lose credibility.

Whatever the majority believes, it must be true, right?

The Ameriqueerocide happened and is still happening, yet we're still here, under their noses, beneath their very sheets. If we still exist, we are clearly clever enough to cheat the system. We have always existed all over the world, in every corner of history, and we will continue to exist exactly the way we are.

10

Ageism

*E*lders *implemented the Bill because they feared the youth taking control.* They felt their power slipping and had to grasp it before it vanished. They wanted tradition, a euphemism for laws that benefit them.

Minors wanted to regulate guns, give women personal autonomy, switch to sustainable resources, put an end to for-profit prisons, provide all citizens with free healthcare, and give power back to the people... We wanted so much. We wanted better for ourselves, each other, and our children. *They* did not. They consider us unholy because we want to modernize outdated laws. We believed in reality, not a fantasy epic about a man in the sky.

People never change, not because They can't, but because They don't want to.

And so, to stop us, the rich conservatives flocked together and wrote up the Bill. It was passed, and the United then became the Divided.

I want to say I am not an ageist.

There must be older people out there who find all this unjust. Where are they? Are they speaking up?

I don't hear them. I don't see them.

All I see is the older generation economically, mentally, environmentally, and literally fucking my generation.

11

Groceries

*T*here once was a girl named Ariana Ottaviana.

We were born just an hour apart on Thanksgiving Day.

She was born first.

What a difference that one hour made.

We were both born in Pennsylvania to Italian families and under the same stars. Characteristically, we are freakishly similar. Reticent yet outgoing. Type A yet accepting of what's to come. Kind and well-mannered. Passionate and lonesome. We enrolled at the same college and studied the same subjects: literature and languages. You'd think she was my clone. But because of the difference in social class, we grew up in vastly different environments.

Ariana was born as an only child to parents who craved having a baby. The moment she came into their world, they were full. They lived in the pastoral lands of central Pennsylvania in a beautiful house with a library you could simply get lost in.

How I envied that Belle.

During dinner, her parents soaked in her words and listened to her stories, her passions. She loved Shakespeare, anything romantic. Her parents encouraged her to travel, to see the world. They spoke to her in French and German to prepare her for her time abroad. She graduated a year early; I, a semester early. She was the valedictorian of her class and received a Fulbright in Belgium. She was not worried about her finances. She had scholarships, intelligence, and, again, parents who craved a baby.

I wonder where she is now? I do hope she's still in Belgium. Anywhere that's not the Divided. A pretty girl like that... every Elder would kill for a Minor like her.

And then there's me.

I was born into a six-child household. My parents had children before, so when I came along, it was nothing new.

My mother's water broke while she was taking the turkey out of the oven. She made dinner for everyone. She didn't want the food to get cold, so she went alone to the hospital.

When my family sat down for dinner, my siblings dominated the conversation. I lost my voice during those days. I loved stories and languages, too. No one in my family cared to talk about that stuff. My passions were ignored never quelled. I wouldn't let my fire die, so I kept my passions to myself.

I put myself through college on my dime, thank you very much.

Dime? I wish it were a dime.

I had three jobs in college. I received several scholarships, but that's nothing in the grand scheme. So I took out loans. Heavy, burdensome, suffocating loans. I feel like I imprisoned myself.

No, prison is much worse.

But I was still not free.

Bills towered over me. A thousand a month in school loans, most of which was interest. Rent, electricity, water... Some days, I went without groceries.

Before the Bill when we were allowed jobs, I made less than thirty thousand a year. Pathetic, I know.

I had to pick up a second job, but I still wanted to write. I couldn't go back to waiting tables or being a tutor. That was laborious work. Serving was physically draining, while tutoring was mentally draining. I needed a side gig that would allow me time and energy.

What was something that came naturally to me and that many people seemed to want from me? What was the easy way out?

Sex.

When people think of me, they don't think of my kindness. They don't think of my intelligence or resilience. My expertise, loyalty, or generosity. No, They think of sex. People constantly objectify me. I hear it in the way people describe me to others. I see it in their eyes. Though I did not like it, I can't say I hated it either. In fact, I took advantage of it.

There once was this website called *Shopping*. It connected young, broke, and pathetic young adults like me with dirty, old, rich men and women who want to have their way with you.

My sugardaddies never dolled me up in diamonds or took me on trips to Ibiza. No, no. There was none of that.

But I did have groceries!

12

Groom

Shopping groomed me for Minority, I choose to believe.
 Let me clarify: I've never been groomed by a pedophile. That is to say, I've never been lured by an adult who then took advantage of me sexually while I was underage. Some of the age gaps between me and my sugardaddies certainly made it feel like grooming, though. Of course, I was of age and gave consent. But if I were just a tad younger, it would've passed as grooming.

Some of the men I met on that site were fifty to seventy years of age.

I am aware there are companionships and couples who have large age gaps and genuinely love each other. That's why I feel like an ageist when I say, with the age gaps I've experienced, I've always felt like they were taking advantage of me. But I was taking advantage of them, so were they really to blame?

Let me clarify again: I was not a prostitute. That is to say, I exchanged my company for money, not sex. A relationship of sorts had to be built first. Then, it would lead to sex, and my daddies would help with bills.

Writing this feels like dancing on a tightrope.

Is this the truth? Or is it just what I've been telling myself to avoid the shame and guilt?

But what does it matter? Minority is now the Law. Everything I chose to do the Law now makes me do. Makes *us* do.

Though they have their similarities, sugaring and Minority are vastly different degradations. With sugaring, I had control. I chose my sugardaddy. I lived freely wherever I wanted and ended the affair whenever I wished. I also didn't have to have sex if I didn't want to. The daddies might've made me feel like I had to, but I still had a choice. With Minority, I have no control. My Elder chose me. I no longer live freely. I live wherever my Elder puts me. I have no say in the matter. If I ended the companionship, my Elder would "cast me into the red light," a common euphemism for killed by the Red. And if I ran away, the Divided would find me and return me like a lost puppy. Worst of all, I must have sex whenever my Elder wants. Otherwise, he dangles torture over me.

Not death.

Torture.

Most people fear death. That's why it's easy for most Elders to use the Red as a threat.

I do not fear death. Do I want to die? No. But sometimes, when my Elder is on top of me, I think of death.

One time during sex, while he was forcing his limp, little dick down my throat, I bit it.

I bit straight into his cock.

He had to be taken to the hospital. He was fine in the end. I didn't do much damage, only to myself.

When the Divided were told, They ordered the Red to have me publicly stripped and whipped. That's how They normally punish their Minors—in a publicized, humiliating fashion.

How my Elder punished me was worse. He cuffed my wrists and ankles to the bed posts, blindfolded me, and invited his work friends to gangbang me for a week. I was naked and sweating, lying face down in the dark. My diet was restricted to water and—I wish I were joking— cum.

During the first few days of my punishment, I refused to let them put anything in my mouth. When they pried open my jaw, I spat out their cum, disgusted.

But then I became hungry. So, so hungry.

When my stomach churned and begged for something, anything, I opened my mouth, held my breath, and swallowed.

Daddy One

*B*elieve it or not, I loved some of the daddies I've had.

Sugardaddies, not Elders. Before the ratification of the Bill.

I was never in love with them. I've never been in love with anyone, really. Being *in love* means a skip in your walk and a stupid grin on your face. It means going out of your way to make someone feel like the only person in the world. It means thinking of the other person when they're not around. Wanting to come home to them. Talking about them incessantly and obnoxiously so. Going on adventures, but also enjoying tedium together. Thinking about the longevity of the relationship. Is this someone I could bring home to the family? Is this someone I'd be proud to stand next to? Is this someone I could be around every day?

To love someone is to care about their well-being. You can ask how they're doing and genuinely care to listen. But to love is more limited, more conditional, than to be in love.

I've had many, many daddies.

Though I've never been in love with Four and Five, I did love them. I cared about their well-being and wanted to make them happy.

I feel indifferent toward Three, Six, and Seven. I still wish them the best.

Two and One, well… They were trash.

One was my first sugardaddy, obviously.

He was a seventy-year-old environmental lawyer in D.C. I was a government hooker.

The little hair One had was wispy and white. He had a hunch, making him just short of five feet tall. When he walked, he shuffled. He always wore slippers.

He found me on Shopping and was intrigued by my "About Me" section, in which I referenced my love of literature, music, and traveling. I mentioned how I spoke English and French and a bit of Italian. I also mentioned how I lived an active lifestyle, a subtle way to brag about my muscular physique.

Though he said what I wrote in my profile captured his attention, I know the not-so-subtle, naughty pictures of me in a variety of thongs, briefs, lingerie, and leather were what really caught his attention. Those pictures made me look easy, which was important to a seventy-year-old.

I was in my early twenties then, the age you should be carded before entering a club, before being served alcohol, and certainly before meeting up with an older man. One never carded me. He never cared.

He lived in Alexandria in a small house that reeked of moth balls, dog hair, and an old man. There was no escaping the pungent 2-nonenal odor lingering in his carpet.

I spent several weekends with him infrequently over two years whenever I needed the money. This was right after I graduated college and when loan corporations wanted their money back. While I was looking for a full-time job, I had to have some kind of income to meet the thousand-dollar monthly payments. Waiting tables did not pay that kind of money. And even if it did, I would have no energy to search for jobs at the end of the day. Job hunting is a job of its own. No one ever talks about that.

I also didn't have a car, which substantially narrowed my job choices. At that point, they were not choices. They were whatever-I-can-gets.

To save money, I moved back in with my parents after college. They lived in a small Connecticut town. If you wanted to go somewhere, you had to drive. My father gave me three months to find a job, or else I'd have to find somewhere else to live. Every day when he came home from work or his little "business trips," he'd ask me, "Moving out of my house yet?"

Thankfully, because of *my* little business trips, he didn't nag me as often as he would have. For another liar, he sure was gullible. I told my family and friends I was going to D.C. to do translation work. It was a believable lie since I had previously worked as a translator. The trick to lying is to formulate a believable lie, stick to that lie verbatim, and pretend, in social settings, that you are a bad liar. People will think you'll never lie to them and that if you ever do, they'll be quick enough to catch you in the act.

People always believe they are smarter and quicker than they really are.

Even I find I'm not nearly as clever as I think I am. If I were, wouldn't I have a high-paying job? Wouldn't I not be in debt? Wouldn't I at least have a car?

Intelligence, as it has always been, is based on social class. And social class, in most cases, is based on chance. You could be the smartest person in the world, but if you're an immigrant, you won't have the same chances to make a difference in this world as, say, the boss's kid. If you have a disability, you'll still be seen as incapable. If you're queer, you'll be doubted, dismissed, and then forgotten.

The cold, hard truth is that it'll take a miracle to make connections if you're not born into riches.

My father had a lot of ups and downs, financially speaking.

The thought of asking my parents for financial aid was laughable. I learned at an early age I was a financial burden to them.

My mother was a waitress. She had next to nothing. My father, well, needed money for his business trips!

Why didn't I ask my siblings for help? That's a more reasonable question. I had two siblings in the medical field and two working for the government. They had money. If I had asked, they would've said they would've helped me, but they wouldn't actually. My loans were recurring monthly. I'm hundreds of thousands of dollars in debt. It'd be ridiculous to ask them for financial aid. How could I ever expect anyone to cough up that kind of money unless I gave them something in return? People rarely help with matters like medical bills, rent, or student debt. No. Instead, they'll feel better buying you useless shit for Christmas.

Perhaps I'm being ungrateful. Perhaps I wasn't trying hard enough to find a high-paying job. Perhaps the recession was fabricated. Or perhaps I had too much pride to ask for help. I don't know. I just find that borrowing money from people you love can poison the relationship. Even after you pay them back, you will always be in debt to them, and your knowledge of that will always linger. Your indebtedness morphs into something they can throw in your face when times get tough. It gives them power. You're the puppet, and they're the puppeteer.

It's why I decided to sugar. I'd rather accept a hand-out from a stranger than be in debt to a friend.

But I could never tell anyone this. How could I ever make my family and friends understand? If they knew that, instead of going to D.C. to do translation work, I was actually going to suck some lawyer's cock, I'd fear they'd offer help. And bam, poison!

Or worse, they'd find excuses not to help. They'd let me go. They'd judge me but say I'm an adult and can do whatever I want with my body. They'd forge lies about their bankruptcy but continue to travel and live up their lives.

The thing is, I wouldn't blame them. I am my responsibility, not theirs. I can't expect people, even people who love me and say they love me, to extend a helping hand. They should be allowed to live their lives the way they want. I'd never want to burden someone with my shortcomings.

And so, I'd take the train from Connecticut down to D.C. and stay the whole weekend with One.

It was the same shit every time. I'd arrive Friday evening. One would order pizza. We'd "catch up," which meant listening to the seventy-year-old's same old stories. He never asked me about myself, my story, or what I needed the money for. He never cared. For all he knew, I was spending it on drugs.

After dinner, we would watch some stupid movie like *Monty Python* or *The Ruling Class*, and he would go off on a tangent about how movies "are not what they used to be."

He was right.

And thank goodness for that.

We then went to sleep in separate beds. Mine was in the basement.

The first couple of times I went to D.C., I spent Saturdays by myself exploring the city. I went to museums, but only the ones that permitted free entry with a student ID. Mine expired the year I graduated. For sixty thousand a year, the ID should've been valid for life.

After the novelty of the city wore off, I spent my Saturdays in a café, writing. I was addicted to coffee then. It helped impede my appetite, which saved me money.

Coffee also helped me get into the writing mindset. I wrote three books then but never got them published. I suppose it was a blessing that I received sixty-plus rejections. Those stories had proud gay characters, proud non-binary characters, proud transgender characters, happy interracial couples, strong female leads, and minorities galore. If my opinions had been published, I wouldn't be alive today. People with those opinions and those platforms—writers, directors, thespians, television hosts, artists, singers, gatekeepers, whatever—were beheaded. The Divided accused them of "harmful propaganda" and "spreading unlawful ideas." So, They got rid of them.

If I wasn't writing, I was meeting up with other daddies who lived in the area. One time, while I was staying with One, I had sex with three different daddies in one day. I don't remember their names. I just bounced from one daddy to the next. This was at the beginning of my sugaring days. I was naïve and still learning what sugardaddies really wanted.

Alas, I was in D.C. to spend time with One. After ten or so hours of writing in a café or sucking a triad of cocks, I begrudgingly returned to him.

Every time, it was the same.

The moment I re-entered his house, he handed me an enema. He never asked how my day was. He only returned upstairs to cast porn onto the TV. He had four rooms in his house. The first was the basement. The second was his bedroom. The third was his living room. And the fourth was storage. It wasn't normal storage, though. No winter clothes, childhood memories, or family heirlooms… No, none of that. It was a room cluttered with piles and piles of adult films and porn magazines.

He never showed me the room. He also never left me alone in his house, so I never snooped. Well, that's not entirely true. One night, One asked me to take out the trash. I stumbled upon the room. I was confused when I opened the door. Who has so much porn they need a room for it all? It was a criminal amount of porn. The room was so filthy and congested I could barely move around in it. I scanned the piles and shelves and saw he had labeled each of every one of them. One shelf read "bareback." Another read "fisting." One pile read "twinks & twunks." Another read "18–."

When my eyes caught the last label, I backed out of the room, threw away the trash, and stood outside for a minute. I contemplated what to do. I wanted to get out of there right then and there. Fuck my bag and phone, I was ready to run. I was disgusted with that last label and terrified that I had seen it. I also gaslit myself. Did I read the label correctly? It was fine print and across the room. It could've read "18+" or something else entirely. I also didn't see any images in the pile, so it could've had a different meaning, like an orgy of less than eighteen people.

I don't know why I was grasping at straws. I suppose it was because I didn't want to believe it.

If I had listened to my instincts and ran, I would've left my phone behind, which had my address in it. He would've then known where I lived. Well, where my family lived. And if I went inside and retrieved my things and then left, where would I have gone? I didn't have any money, no credit. How would I get a train back to Connecticut? I also—I hate to say it—needed this connection, this money.

So, I returned inside and freshened up in the basement. When I was ready, I went upstairs and found him stroking himself to some frat hazing video. Thankfully, we never kissed and always did doggy. He preferred it that way so he could focus on the television. I preferred it because I did not want to look at him, even before I stumbled upon the room. He was ugly in more ways than one. Most of the time, I'd get off on the fantasy of One being someone else, someone buffer, cuter, nicer. That night though, I froze and waited until he finished.

The sex usually lasted an hour, maybe two. He loved our sex, called me his little boy, and told me I was born for it.

When it was over, I went straight to bed.

My visits with One always ended early on Sundays. He'd give me a banana and ask me how much I think he owed me. He drove me to the station and waved goodbye as I caught the morning train back to Connecticut with my dignity gone, a grand in my pocket, and a secret to hold.

I never reported him to the police. I would've had to explain how I knew the man. The police would not understand the sugarbaby-sugardaddy dynamic and would probably arrest me for prostitution. Also, what if I had misread? Then, all I would've done was turn myself in. And so, I chose to be selfish.

After I had found that room, I never contacted One again. I'm not sure if he knew I had seen the room. Or maybe he sensed something was off the last night we had sex. Either way, I never heard from him again.

13

Titanic

e used to sleep in the same bed.

We had to. All eight of us piled together in a single motel bed. It was all we could afford.

Being the second youngest, I slept at the foot of the bed. In the middle of the night, my older siblings would kick me off—accidentally, they said—and I'd sleep on the itchy, cum-stained carpet. I was fine with it. The floor was more comfortable than their bony shins.

I was ten at the time. My parents had just lost their business and house. My mother's father was also on his deathbed. So, we moved from Virginia back to New York to be with family. All this coincided—the bankruptcy, the homelessness, the death, the bereavement, and the relocation. It was not a series of unfortunate events. It was not a blessing in disguise. No. Instead, it was one mighty sucker punch to my parents— my mother most of all. How could I ever be mad at them?

I think it was the first time in my life that I truly pitied someone or at least understood the hopeless sentiment outside of television and literature.

My aunt and uncle were gracious. They let us live with them for a few months. But there was a family feud. I don't know what happened, nor did I care to ask. We must've gotten on their nerves. My aunt and uncle were just starting a family together. My two cousins were barely two years old at the time. We were imposing.

After the feud, we moved into the motel. I don't remember the name of the motel, only that it was in upstate New York and just off the highway. The walls were a dirty mustard. Cockroaches played dead in the vents, and flies swarmed around the singular toilet. It wasn't fancy, but it was where we lived for the time being.

The TV in the room was ancient. I remember flicking through the channels one day and coming across an adult film. My mother snatched the remote and changed it to a channel playing the beloved *Titanic*. That was the first and last time I had ever seen the movie. As an adult, I could never rewatch it. I correlate it with that time in my life, a time in my life that, for a long while, I had chosen to forget.

My mother had five siblings, my father had one, and their siblings each had spouses. We had five aunts and seven uncles. Two of the twelve helped us, but only for a short while. The others never helped. They knew about our situation. They owned houses. Big ones, too. Their children were grown and in college. Some of them didn't even have children. Whether or not my parents had asked for help, they knew what was happening and kept quiet. If they had cared, they would've offered help without being asked. And if they did offer sanctuary and my parents rejected their help for whatever reason, they should've insisted. We were children.

I'm sure they have their excuses, and I'm sure they are perfectly reasonable.

Opening your doors to six kids and two grown adults is a lot. I don't blame my aunts and uncles. I get it. I just feel bad for my siblings. My younger sister probably couldn't fathom what was happening at the time. My older siblings probably have a better memory of all of this than I do. Yet afterward, they had not once broached the subject. Decades passed, but it never came up. Not even when their days became sunny, and their houses became homes. I wonder if it's because the better the memory of a painful time, the more you choose to forget.

Then there's my mother. I feel for her most of all. She lost so much then and only wanted to give her children a home.

I feel bad for my ten-year-old self, too. He witnessed his aunts and uncles turning their backs on their sister in need. At an early age, he was forced to realize that, even though he loved his siblings and knew they loved him too, he could never expect anything from them, even in the darkest of hours.

People say blood is thicker than water, but what's thicker than blood? Gold. Silver. A thick wallet. You see, money will always prevail and matter more to people, all people, regardless of blood.

14

Born into Wealth

Only wealthy Minors are tapped early for Elderhood.

Wealth is more than just riches, though. Wealth is straight, white, cisgender, Christian, abled, American, and assigned male at birth. If you're anything but, you're shit out of luck.

If you—well, your parents—are rich enough, you could skip out on Minority entirely.

And I do mean rich. Filthy rich.

We call these dirtbags the One Percenters. There are a few queer One Percenters out there, I've heard. And even They take advantage of the Law.

If others can, why can't They, right?

Before the Great Division, I enjoyed being queer.

Queer culture was a beautiful thing. We had fashion, theater, literature, music, drag, ballroom, pride, and even language. We had so much. But after the Great Division, They stole everything. They made being queer difficult, undesirable, and abhorrent.

They knew everything, too. They tracked us, found us, and kept tabs on us. They had our internet histories. If it was a one-time offense, the curiosity was merely innocuous. If it was a repeated offense, we were classified as sinners. Depending on who we were and how we presented ourselves, we were either murdered or subjected to a discreet companionship. We would never be tapped early unless we were a One Percenter.

The thought of putting someone through what I've been through as a Minor makes me sick to my stomach. I don't want to take advantage of someone like that. It's deplorable.

But you either do as the Divided tell you or step into the red light.

The Elders of the Minors who are tapped early for Elderhood help those straight, white, cis boys get hired by the best companies and settled into the coziest houses. That's one perk of being wealthy; you can be whatever you want if your wallet is thick enough.

These boys transition from brief Minors to early-admitted Elders and then go on to do dirty, little things to other Minors that were once done unto them.

It's just one big, never-ending circle.

15

Nine Years Left in the Service

*B*efore I was forced into Minority, I was willingly a sugarbaby for more than three years.

I started sugaring after college. I'm twenty-six now. I have nine years left of Minority until I'm inducted into Elderhood. If I had a say in the matter, I would never become an Elder.

According to Western standards of beauty, I am handsome. There's no need to be humble, oblivious, or compliment-seeking. I am also kind, smart, and thoughtful. Perhaps one day, I will find a Minor who could love me for me. But I can't say I'm not disgusted thinking about my inevitable path to Elderhood.

Sometimes, I get jealous when I see a Minor arm-in-arm with a good-looking Elder. I recognize the double standard. A charming, sexy Elder is somehow more desirable than an ugly, greasy Elder when really neither of them should be desirable because they're both Elders. Rapey, oppressive Elders.

Yet, I still envy those companionships. Like everyone, I am superficial. Looks—among other qualities, of course—do matter.

Sometimes, when my Elder allows me to stroll outside, I find myself gazing at those good-looking Elders and Minors.

Some of them, I thought, looked like they were actually in love.

It was an illusion, though.

No one could actually be in love with someone who requested companionship, right? How could anyone ever fall for someone who, by

Law, forced the love out of them? I don't care if you look like Nyle DiMarco or Eva fucking Longoria. I could never truly love an Elder.

"How was your walk?" my Elder once asked when I returned after my allotted hour.

"It was lovely," I replied, keeping my head low. "Thank you very much for letting me take a walk outside."

"Of course, of course," he said. "I love you."

I looked up into those empty, greedy eyes, gave him a smile, and lied.

"I love you too."

16

Elder X

I *was found not a week after the train incident.*

I hid in my apartment for as long as I could. It's not like I had a place to be anyway. After the ratification of the Bill, every Minor was laid off effective immediately. The economy took a major blow when that happened. But it recovered, eventually. Or so They say.

I didn't have much food in my apartment—granola bars, apples, and peanut butter. But I was running low.

They shut off our water supply to draw us out of our holes.

I was starving, thirsty, and stir-crazy and smelled like shit.

So, I crept out of my apartment one afternoon, expecting most of the Elders to be at work, and went down every back alley I could find until I found my way to the grocery store. Most of the shelves were empty. During the first few days, Minors raided every store and bodega in the country. We stocked up to hunker down.

But after those first few days, the Divided made looting more difficult. They stationed the Red outside every entrance. So, I climbed in through a bathroom window. I saw only one person inside the store—a cashier. I planned to grab as much as I could and climb back out the bathroom window.

But he approached me when I was scurrying through the beverage aisle.

"Hey, handsome."

I dropped a water bottle. *Fuck,* I thought. My heart was beating a mile a minute.

I turned and saw a stout, pale man in his mid-fifties. He was ugly as all hell. Crow's feet tugged at the corners of his eyes. His face was blotchy, and his nose was cratered. He wore a gray suit and carried a briefcase. Typical.

He flashed me a smile. No, not a smile.

A smirk.

I thought about running but saw outside a mass of red camo turning down the back alley.

I straightened and steeled myself. And breathed.

Then came his request. No, not a request.

A demand.

"I find you very attractive," the man said in a rich, I-own-you voice. "My name is X. Enchanté." He kissed the back of my hand with his thin, pimply lips. "Would you do me the honor of accepting my companionship?"

He thought his companionship was an honor. This is what plagues most men: they have a distorted perception of themselves, even the ugly ones.

Another mass of red moved outside the windows. I picked the water bottle off the ground and reluctantly, dispiritedly, nodded my head.

"Good boy," said X. "Now let me help you with those."

He offered me his hand and then his wallet.

II

Auction

17

Diamond

*H*is name wasn't really X.

That would be stupid. I'm only referring to him as X because the Divided emphasize discretion. They practically drilled the habit into us. And by us I mean queer Minors.

Fortunately for me, my work as a sugarbaby taught me the importance of discretion all too well. For example, I never used One's real name, even when we were together. If I needed his attention, I'd call him daddy.

One did the same thing. He called me baby.

The reason why I was so discreet is simple: I was scared. One was a well-known D.C. lawyer. He had the money to do whatever he wanted. I didn't know who he knew, nor did I want to find out. So, I was smart and kept my mouth shut. After One, I habitually used anything but my daddies' real names. I continued the habit with my Elders.

But why not aliases? If I had given them aliases—actual names, not numbers or letters—it would've humanized them, and then they'd feel more real. Perhaps I'd become attached, and I didn't want that. No, no. I didn't want that at all.

The Divided, of course, knew about my companionship with X.

They know everything.

Elders are allowed up to three Minors, while Minors must belong to only one Elder. It is the Law. If a Minor is seen fraternizing with another Minor, Elder, or the Red, then you become a Diamond.

Diamond was my neighbor. She, like I, was a total slut.

Before Minority, I slept around quite a bit. I never wanted to commit. I never felt capable or deserving of love. Typical. I had my daddies, yeah, but those weren't serious. After I became a Minor though, I had to stop whoring around. I feared what the Divided would do to me. I'm already queer. Add whore to the equation and consider me dead.

Diamond, however, was brave. An activist, really. The nights when her Elder was with one of his other Minors, she'd bring other men into her apartment and fuck them all night long.

Her apartment was directly across from mine on the opposite side of the courtyard. Her drapes were always open. She was an exhibitionist. Beautiful and knowing, slim and Italian. I personally loved watching her. I didn't have any pornography, only my imagination. I took the free shows when they came.

One time, she even caught me looking as some buff man ate her out. She gestured to me to join. I wanted to, but I didn't dare chance it.

She got away with it for the longest time. She slept mostly with other Minors. But one time, a Red guard pretended to be a Minor and caught her in the act.

Apart from being queer, a whore is the next worst thing you can be in the Divided.

She was ordered a public whipping, branding, and rape by twelve Elders and—can't forget—community service.

Minors, including myself, revered her after that. We gave her credit for igniting the infamous slut movement.

Despite the torture she endured, Diamond adored her icon status and became a repeat offender. After her third repeated offense—technically like her seventieth, but her third time being caught—the Divided ordered her to be burnt at the stake.

She then became a martyr for sluts. Not a martyr who brought upon an insurrection. No. The Divided wouldn't allow that. As far as I know, They covered up her death, and only the sluts in town knew.

But why do Elders hate whores so much?

I know why. Elders are possessive creatures in denial about their sluttiness. They want fidelity in their companionships, so They say. But really, They just want their spouse and three Minors solely to themselves. They don't like sharing unless it's their dick. They're just as much of sluts as we are, if not more.

They call their companionship loyalty, but ultimately, it's just control.

18

Institutional Misogyny

X was a hotshot investment banker.

He was greedy and arrogant, and I loathed him.

Like every Elder, he had three Minors and a wife.

Elderhood, like many other government institutions, is inherently misogynistic. While Elderly husbands are allowed Minors in addition to their wives, wives are not allowed Minors in addition to their husbands. Single Elderly women, however, are allowed Minors. I was surprised when I first heard that. I would've thought ageism and sexism would've gotten the best of the Divided. I suppose They must've pitied the women.

Elderhood is also inherently classist. If a wife has the money to pay the Divided, they can secretly have a Minor or two for the right price.

I never met X's wife. I didn't know her name. X referred to her only as *Her* and ranted about the woman almost every day. It was exhausting. He called Her lazy and boring and said the boil growing on the back of her neck was disgusting to look at, as though the mole on his upper lip was a gift to the eye.

I think she stopped having sex with him, to be honest.

I couldn't blame Her. He was repulsive. His teeth were yellowed from coffee. His tongue was a sickly white. His belly folded over his penis so you could hardly see it, and his ass sagged in a V-shape. Very unpleasant. Not to mention, he had to take pills to get an erection. This replaced spontaneity with planning and expectations. When he couldn't get hard or when those expectations weren't met, he blamed me. When he blamed me, he beat me.

He slapped and choked me a couple times, but it wasn't as bad as the neighbor down the hall. Sometimes, I'd see him leave his apartment with chunks of hair missing and bruises up his neck. One time, I even saw him being taken out on a stretcher. His Elder had nearly beaten him to death. He's not the only one who suffers like that. Every Sunday, I see at least ten Minors bruised and scarred.

The Elders, when questioned, say their Minors were acting out. Or they weren't trying hard enough, working out enough, or looking sexy enough. These excuses were perfectly acceptable in the eyes of the Divided.

As for X's other Minors, I know nothing about them.

I assume they're women. On the night X and I consummated our companionship, he told me he had never been with a boy. I didn't know if "boy" meant a young man or another man in general. I never asked for clarification. I did not care.

I just wanted to get the sex over with.

But it wasn't that simple. I was X's little experiment.

I have broad shoulders yet a slender body. I'm muscular yet naturally smooth everywhere. I have an evenly shaped waist, a tenor voice, a square jawline, and short hair. I usually sit cross-legged and emanate a boyish, feminine charm.

He forgives himself for his bisexuality by blaming me and my androgyny.

Sometimes, when he's having sex with me, I see the shame unfurl behind his eyes in the reflection of the mirror. The shame becomes more noticeable when the sex becomes more aggressive.

–Oh, and I do mean "when he's having sex with me…" not "when *we're* having sex…" Those are two vastly different dependent clauses.

While the latter implies that sex is consensual, the former does not. I can't necessarily say it was rape because, to an extent, I did allow X to fuck me. But I only allowed him to fuck me because of the Law.

If anything, the Divided raped me.

19

Investments

I used to dream about the day I'd have a kid.

I wanted to name him Leo.

When I was a child, I never saw myself getting married. In my future, I always saw myself as a single, working parent to an only child. I'd drive Leo to soccer practice, theater rehearsal, or both. I'd make him his favorite meal when he was sick—butter chicken. He'd love Indian food. He'd be an adventurous kid. I'd teach him French and Italian, but he'd nag me about learning Spanish with him. I'd read to him every night. His favorite story would be *Where the Mountain Meets the Moon* by Grace Lin. He'd also love *The Lorax*, mainly because I'd read it to him in funny voices. On Saturdays, we'd go hiking or kayaking. On Sundays, we'd have an artistic project, like going to a thrift store and buying a bunch of fabric to sew into a garment. Or we'd give each other a sentence that would be the first line of a short story we'd each have to write.

It's what I had wanted when I was a child. But maybe that's the problem: as adults, we give our children what we always wanted, not what they want.

In this alternate future, I even saw the not-so-pretty parts of parenting, like diaper messes, jumbled calendars, and verbal sparring.

But this future was just a dream, and the Divided woke me up.

How could I ever have a child in a world where, by age eighteen, some geezer will come along and take them away from me, essentially making them their sex slave? They would no longer be allowed in my life. By age thirty-five, my child would become an Elder and take advantage of another child. How could I ever have a child in a world where fidelity, autonomy, love, and freedom do not exist? How could I ever have a child in a world that is dying, a world that makes them feel like a financial burden, a world that is a prison?

I'm not the only one who feels this way. Surely not. I can't imagine any parent being okay with their eighteen-year-old becoming the property of an Elder.

They exist though, parents who are okay with it. I've heard whispers of some Elders—it's always men—becoming parents as a source of income. They impregnate their female Minors, kidnap the baby once born, and send them off to what are called *grooming camps*. Once the baby becomes a Minor, they go up for sale. Elders then come shopping for the best-looking and most in shape. It was a puppy mill but for Minors. And if the Minor is sold, the Elder who had spawned the child would receive a hefty check in the end. Their child was nothing more than an investment.

Deplorable, isn't it?

There were good parents once. After the Bill, they grabbed their children and went into hiding. The Divided found them, of course, executed them, and placed their children into grooming camps.

I've also heard that some parents accepted the inevitable and found Elders for their children, like twisted arranged marriages. While arranged marriages are normal in other cultures, this particular arranged companionship is just fucked up. How can you raise a child and seek out a geezer who would take your eighteen-year-old away from you and fuck them until they're thirty-five?

I hate what I'm writing. It's disgusting and makes everything feel more real. But it is real. It's not my imagination. It's not fabrication. It's really, truly happening, and people are just accepting it.

20

Fairies in Charleston

I tend to overthink.

Most people do, really. I personally ruminate on my hypocrisies. Though hypocrisy is a normal flaw in human design, having one still makes me feel inhuman.

One hypocrisy of mine is how I deal with emotions. I normally experience the extreme of an emotion but only for a moment. And then I'm over it. Most people don't believe me because a) most people get whiplashed by my passion, and b) most people dwell.

Dwelling is a waste of time.

I'm not referring to every emotion though. I bask in moments of joy and peace. Those moments are hard to come by. I'm referring to annoyance, sadness, and anger. I allow those emotions to burn, never fester.

Take my time in Charleston, for example. A group of bros followed me and my friends to a gay bar and called us all sorts of slurs. At that age, I had developed thick enough skin to let those half-baked insults bounce off me, especially the ones that were just truths spoken in a pejorative tone. *Faggot? Yes, I am. And what?!*

But my friends were feeling unsafe and scared. At that age, my friends had become my family. I went into protection mode.

It wasn't until one of the guys called my friend a tranny that I turned around and decked the guy in his throat. He made a guttural noise and fell to his knees.

Drag queens and kings were outside the bar smoking cigs. They came up behind me like some queer fire brigade. They each had a gadget—pepper spray, pocket knives, brass knuckles.

"Do we have a problem here?" said one of the drag performers. He was calm as he brandished his knife.

They helped their friend up and left, muttering more slurs as they went.

I was annoyed, saddened, and angered. But I refused to let them rob me of a fun night. So, I went inside with my friends and the drag performers, got drunk, had a laugh, and danced.

I got over it. More so, I *chose* to get over it.

I have a motto for this type of emotional burning: bridge-water. It's short for, build yourself a bridge, let the water flow underneath, and get the fuck over it. Yeah, we were the subjects of a hate crime. Yeah, we could've notified the authorities. But girl, bridge-water. The night was young.

Ah, those were the simple days. Days of worrying about stalkers and becoming the victim of a hate crime. How lucky was I to have such minuscule worries?

My friend Rupiah used to say that, though she admired how easily I got over things, I needed to learn how to process my emotions better; that it's okay to acknowledge the hurt and find strength in the pain rather than pushing it aside. That's my hypocrisy—at least one of them anyway. I say it's okay to experience these emotions, but I refuse to let them endure for too long.

During the years of the United, that made sense because processing emotions helped the idea of a better tomorrow.

In the years of the Divided, it's better to be numb.

21

Belonging

One day, during one of my walks, I found a pencil.

It was one of those half pencils you'd use when you play mini golf. Big enough to last me a while but small enough to be hidden among the leaves in a gutter.

I looked over my shoulder and saw the Red passing by. I bent over, pretended to tie my laces, and slipped the pencil into my sock.

My heart was racing.

Minors are not allowed pencils. Minors are not allowed many things—phones, novels, musical instruments, pens, paintbrushes, TVs, anything creative or that can be used for communication. They didn't want us dreaming or communicating because dreams become talks of revolution.

Sometimes, if your Elder liked you and had the money, they'd buy you what you wanted on the black market. But the transaction would have to be untraceable. They'd then smuggle the item into your apartment as stealthily as possible.

X never bought me anything. That's why I seized the opportunity and stole the pencil.

When I stood up, I saw a girl with red hair and a freckled face at the end of the street staring at me. She wasn't wearing red camo, the telltale of the Red. Instead, she was wearing the familiar black robes of a Minor.

Minors assigned female at birth wear black robes. Minors assigned male at birth, like me, wear black dress suits.

They were trying to be clever with the coloring. The Red wear red because they're in charge of executions and arrests. Elders wear gray because the color represents age and wisdom. And Minors wear black, perhaps as a nod to *the little black book*.

I think it would've made more sense if the Elders wore black. We're seen as promiscuous, but they're the ones with three Minors and a husband or wife.

Anyway, the girl.

I'd seen her before, naked at the bonfires.

She smiled at me, and I smiled back and became aware of my body. Exchanging smiles with another Minor… even that is against the Law. Smiles spur friendships, and friendships make solidarity, which is the foundation of an uprising.

So, I turned around and returned to the apartment. X was still there, like usual, waiting for my return. He was sprawled out on the bed in the nude, stroking himself. He came over to me and began stripping me of my clothes. My first thought was of the pencil. If he found the pencil, he could turn me into the Red.

Thankfully, he was already hot and bothered. His cheeks flushed—a sign of climaxing. With my pants around my ankles, he bent me over the bed and rammed his little dick into me. Two minutes later, he came.

"Dinner's on the table. I got take-out."

He zipped up his pants and left.

I locked the door behind him and then ran across the floorboard. When I first moved into the apartment, I discovered an empty, hidden compartment under a wooden plank. Over the years, I hid things in it.

There was a burnt piece of paper that must've got caught in the wind after a Sunday ritual and found its way to my windowsill. It was an excerpt of a poem about freedom.

"You shall be free indeed when your days are not without a care nor your nights without a want and a grief,
But rather when these things girdle your life and yet you rise above them naked and unbound.
And how shall you rise beyond your days and nights unless you break the chains which you at the dawn of your understanding have fastened around your noon hour?
In truth that which you call freedom is the strongest of these chains, though its links glitter in the sun and dazzle your eyes."

I don't know what book it came from, and I'm unsure what the poem means. The double negatives confuse me. I reread it frequently though. It's the only piece of literature I have. While I don't fully understand the poet's words, I cherish them deeply. I find a new meaning every time I read it. I think it's about trying to release all earthly desires but remaining mindful of your inevitable inner compulsions so that you may "rise above them" and cultivate a sense of inner freedom and self-compassion. If something doesn't go your way, having that inner freedom and self-compassion can help soften the blow of failure. I've also interpreted it as: life chains us. We are prisoners of our minds. Our goals—what we want most in our lives—are what keep us from freedom itself.

Perhaps none of this is what the poet meant. Perhaps I'm reading too much into it or not at all. Perhaps I'm reading what I want to read or what I need to hear. For most of my life, I've been poor. I've been homeless three times before I became a Minor. Once when I was ten, when my parents lost their business, and we lived in that motel. The second time was when my father threw me out of the house at age sixteen for being queer. The third time was after college. I became a sugarbaby and degraded myself because I was in over my head with debt.

There are many things to fear when you are homeless. You fear the filthy, dangerous streets and the obvious not-having-a-place-where-you-can-eat-sleep-and-call-your-own. You fear your lack of control and freedom. You do things, unspeakable things, just to survive. All my life,

I've equated money with freedom, and my primary goal in life has always been to be free. With that math, all I've been working towards is money.

Why do I put money on such a high pedestal? A pedestal where friendship and knowledge should be? Where peace and health should be? Where love and family should tower?

Why is money so important to me? It's paper. It's really just… paper.

In addition to the scrap of poetry, I have a small collection of pressed flowers.

I wouldn't get in trouble for having these, but I still like having them to myself. I have a couple zinnias, cosmos, and a pansy. I only know their names because my mother used to garden a lot. They remind me of her.

The third and last object in the compartment was a wooden stake. X and I were rearranging the couch one day when the leg of the couch chipped the floorboard. X never noticed, but I did.

Whenever he was gone, I used the headboard of our bed, the windowsill, my nails, and plastic knives to whittle down the piece of wood. I didn't have anything more efficient. Eventually, after weeks of whittling, it became a wooden dagger. I kept it for emergencies, in case I needed to protect myself against X or the Red. Or, if things worsened in the Divided, I'd use it to kill myself.

The Divided extricated Minors from all sharp objects and anything else that could harm us. Knives, scissors, razors. Even the bed sheets were bolted down, so we couldn't hang ourselves with them.

That's it. That's all I have to my name. The scrap of poetry, the pressed flowers, the sliver of wood, and now, a pencil.

They weren't much, but they were mine.

22

Gym, 'Nother Gym

I *spend most of my time working out.*

That's all we're really allowed to do as Minors.

Lift weights at the gym.

Swim in the pool.

Run.

Play basketball or tennis. Only one-on-ones were permitted. Talking while playing was forbidden.

Minors assigned female at birth are allowed to roller skate and tumble, but Minors assigned male at birth are not. I used to love roller skating. But because the Divided declared roller skating "too feminine," I'm not allowed to do it anymore. Similarly, Minors assigned female at birth are not allowed to lift weights. The activity is apparently "too masculine."

I don't mind working out. In fact, I love it. But to work out all the time in between sex gets pretty monotonous after a while, especially since I don't have other activities to break up my day. I wish we were allowed to read, have a job, or pick up a craft to preoccupy our hands and challenge our minds. It's why I've been using napkins to write on. Whenever X isn't home, I sneak the pencil out of the hidden compartment and journal on napkins. Napkins are the only thing I can find to write on. They tear every now and then, but I don't care. It's just something to do.

When I finish journaling or hear X's keys in the door, I stow the napkins into the compartment with the pencil. Now I have one more thing to my name.

Napkins.

While I enjoy working out, it feels weird to have to work out for someone else.

Not weird. Dehumanizing. Dehumanizing to have to maintain a certain physique so as not to be discarded. We must not be less than perfect for our Elders.

The expectation robs us of the enjoyment of the activity itself.

But I shouldn't complain. It could be worse. I could be like the boy down the hall. The one who was taken out on a stretcher. Or I could be living in the apartment building down the street. It's dilapidated and infested with rats and cockroaches. I've also heard those apartments are terribly small and have no air conditioning in the summer months. You just sit there and stew in your filth.

Yes, X is ugly and arrogant and slaps me every now and then, but compared to that, my apartment is practically a penthouse. It's not actually, but it has everything I need and more. I have a couch and a cozy queen bed. I have a full kitchen with plastic cups and plates. I have a running sink and shower. Air conditioning, heating, electricity.

I'm even spoiled with windows! They're barred, yes, but they let in plenty of sunlight!

23

Cat

I once had a cat named Ollivander.

He was a beautiful black cat with golden eyes. I adopted him when he was a kitten. I was in college. He was playful, snuggly, and a little sassy, kind of like me.

I liked having a cat at first. The responsibility, the mental stability, the cute pictures.

Then reality sank in. The ammonia odor, the spraying, the ruined clothes, the kitty litter, the cost. Worst of all, the responsibility.

After a year with the cat, the time came for my semester abroad. I needed to find him a place for the time being. My father refused to let my mother watch after another cat. He had something against pets, or maybe it was just me. I don't know.

Anyway, none of my siblings had steady homes at the time.

Friends were allergic.

Friends of friends were not found.

I had no one.

Unfortunately, like every other page in this horrendous story, this next part is true.

I took Ollivander into a forest where no one could see us. I opened his crate, removed his collar, and walked away.

I bridge-watered.

I don't know why I ever thought that was okay. I told myself that if Holly Golightly can release a cat into the wild, then I can too. When I think back on that day, I'm disgusted with myself. How could I ever be that vile? That irresponsible? That selfish?

I felt like my father. How could I have walked away feeling absolutely nothing?

Well, that's not exactly true. I did feel something.

I felt free.

24

A Trite Trope

I *am not writing to obtain pity or absolve myself of my wrong-doings.*

In fact, this is just my journal. A diary. A way for me to vent and to process things that are happening and have happened to me, including acts I'm committing and have committed.

I'm aware that I'm perpetuating the tortured gay stereotype. I don't mean to. I recognize its harm. I also recognize the power of having a work of art supporting the notion of a queer person living happily ever after. Those stories—those gay stories—are out there. I know so. My older brother Billie is gay. He fell in love with a guy in Switzerland during college. Before the ratification of the Bill, he moved out there and married the guy. The last time we spoke, they were starting the surrogacy process. If he knows what's really happening here, he must be thanking his lucky stars he's there and not here.

I know it's selfish to say, but I wish that were me instead.

No, no. I can't think like that. I'm happy he's not here and doesn't know, truly know, what Minority is. I don't think he would've survived the Ameriqueerocide. I have a masc side I can rely on. It's a perk of being genderfluid. But Billie, he's so noticeably gay he couldn't pass as straight. It's in his spine, wrist, strut, and voice. It's not a bad thing to be noticeably gay. It just makes you more susceptible to hate crimes.

Sorry, not hate crimes.

The Law.

Anyway, Billie has one of those stories. One of those happily-ever-after, gay-as-fuck tales. One that queer people dream about. One that *Disney* could capitalize on.

But this is not one of those stories. I wish it were; I genuinely do. I wish things were simpler. I wish I were ignorant of prejudices, adversities, and abandonment. I wish I had made better decisions in life. I wish my past was a happier story to tell. A story people want to hear and read.

I want that more than anyone else.

So, if there's a tortured gay in this story, I am truly, deeply sorry.

But this is no fairytale. It is real life. My life.

These pages may never be read. And honestly, a part of me is okay with that. I want better for my community or what's left of it anyway.

25

College Is a Scam

At least, American colleges are.

Adults say, "Stay in school, kids." And then, because of societal convention and pressure, They convince their children to pay them hundreds of thousands of dollars.

In the past, the advice of staying in school held actual meaning. But then colleges, universities, loan providers, and banking institutions saw the demand and took advantage.

If I could go back in time and tell my high school self something, anything, I'd tell myself not to go to college. At least not right away. I'd encourage myself to pick up a vocation, save money, travel, learn more about myself, and take time to figure out the next step *I* want to take in life. As young, impressionable minds, we are often persuaded to want something when we don't know what we want.

I love learning; I do. I've always loved literature, stories, characters, languages, and cultures. The first book I ever wrote was called *Cultures*. I know, very clever. I was seven years old when I wrote it. It was bound in orange construction paper and was held together by metallic rings. It was a collection of short stories about characters in cultures around the world going about their days. I read encyclopedias, watched documentaries, and lost myself in the local library. In one story, I had a French character who was a sous-chef at a rococo restaurant, making boeuf bourguignon and coq au vin for judgmental Parisians who may or may not have been based on my parents. In another story, I had a Tanzanian safari guide in the Serengeti, guiding a group of whiny American teenagers who may or may not have been based on my older siblings. In another story, I had a lonely Chinese dragon—who may or may not have been based on myself—living in a chaotic household. They were not good stories. I was a kid, writing about food, animals, and dragons.

As children, we grow up being told we can be whatever we want if we set our minds to it.

But that's not entirely true, is it?

You can be whatever you want if you know the right people, attend the right school, and have the money.

But a major part of growing up that we never seem to talk about is knowing what we can and cannot achieve. Our parents never told us because they wanted us to dream. "They'll know their limitations when the time comes." Not everyone has the vocals to sing the blues. Not everyone has the wit to be an astrophysicist. And not everyone can write.

I've always wanted to be a writer. I've always had the imagination to be one.

When I was a kid, my parents used to buy me toys from Family Dollar. The toys were stuffed monkeys with Velcro on their palms. They were a dollar a piece and looked like it, too. But I liked how they wrapped around my neck like they were giving me hugs. Each monkey had its own name, superpower, quirks, and backstory.

When I was twelve and living in New York, my math teacher asked us to fill in the blanks of a poem that went, "When I grow up, I wish to be a _____." You can guess what I wrote. I'm not sure why we were writing poetry in math class, but we were. My teacher collected those poems and intended to return them to us when we graduated high school. But I moved to Connecticut before she had the chance.

In Connecticut, my English teacher told me my prose was too purple. The next year, another teacher said my writing wasn't good. In my last year, my creative writing teacher told me the subject was not for me.

Because they were my elders—qualified educators—I assumed they were right.

I let myself forget what I wanted to be.

I liked the idea of helping people though. So, I went to college thinking I'd enter the medical field. I took a few science classes, though I knew I'd hate them.

I found my way back to literature, specifically in foreign languages. It was easy for me to pick up another language, but I didn't know what I'd do with that type of degree. So, I chose not to think about it. After graduation, I got an office job. I worked part-time as a barista. And I started sugaring. I made more money as a sugarbaby than I did anything else.

Despite what those Connecticut teachers said about my writing, I started to write again. I'm not sure why. I just did.

It wasn't like I had come across *Cultures* in my mother's basement or those stuffed monkeys in a Family Dollar and was reminded of my childhood passion. No. Perhaps it was some psychological coping mechanism; I had reached a new low in life and unconsciously reverted to the child I once was.

But the poem I wrote in math class… Now that's an interesting story. I had entirely forgotten about it. While my peers received their poems right after high school, I received mine after college. My math teacher found where I was living and mailed it.

When I realized what I was reading, I felt validated. My younger self knew what my adult self did not.

Still, the voices of those Connecticut teachers lingered.

"You lack originality."

"Your writing is not very good."

"You'll never make it."

To encourage myself, I thought of success stories of people rising from hate, adversity, and poverty. Could I be like them? Or have I reached my limit?

I wouldn't say I excel in writing. I excel at nothing really. Nothing except sex. Maybe sex is my calling. People say you should do what you're good at, right?

Maybe for me, it is sex.

It's an intrusive thought, I know.

Maybe I'm just mad at my college.

I didn't need a degree in literature. Though I loved my major, I, like my seven-year-old self, could've learned French independently. I could've traveled, met people, and read whatever I wanted.

Did I learn in college? Of course. Did I make good memories? Most definitely. Did I make friends? Yes. It pains me to say I have regrets. Yes, I challenged myself intellectually and earned a degree. But it didn't help me in the end. Do I have a better understanding of the world? Maybe. Did I have better chances of getting jobs? Not really. Others seemed to think so.

I loathe having regrets. Most people do. I wish I were one of those people who believe things happen for a reason and will always work in your favor. I wish I had that blind, stupid faith.

College was fun and educational, as it should be. But it was also a distraction from the heavy weight of the world. That little piece of collegiate heaven shattered when I left campus and started my loan payments. My days as a sugarbaby helped, but I could never keep up with the bills.

Then I was blessed with Minority. It's the only good thing about being a Minor. Our Elders pay our bills. They must. We're not allowed to have jobs. No need to worry about groceries, rent, or even loans from before the Bill.

It sounds great on paper, but an ugly truth lies behind those stacks of green. My life is in the hands of another. I have no control as to where I wish to veer my life. Not having a job robs me of challenges, accomplishments, and failures. They call it an act of generosity. I call it a heist.

They forbid us from wandering around the grocery store alone. Exploration is a fantasy, and fantasies are dangerous. Our Elders must be present if we're in the store. X has never taken me after the first time we met. He picks up groceries for me, and that is that.

They forbid us from drinking coffee. They believe it'll remind us of work, and They don't want riots on their hands. No, no, that won't do. The only work They want from us is sex. They'll plow us with liquor, most times forcefully, and then take advantage of our wasted bodies.

On my walks, I sometimes catch whiffs of fresh espresso beans from local coffee shops. My mouth waters every time. The smell of coffee is like a whiff of freedom.

While X pays my rent, the apartment I live in is a house of cards. Trust and reliability are outdated words.

He says he's paying off my school loans, but he's probably just paying off the interest. He has three Minors and a wife to care for. Who knows if he has kids? I don't understand how he can afford the things he has. His cars, Minors, houses, and drugs. I know the Divided provide Elders with stimulus checks, and the more Minors an Elder has, the more tax cuts they get. But still, where's the money coming from?

It makes me angry to think about what the government invests in. They'll invest in human trafficking, yet They'll charge their children hundreds of thousands of dollars for knowledge. Knowledge of all things. They should be investing in their children so that our country, our world, can be smarter, right? Better, greener, happier, healthier? No?

Ah, who cares what I think?

I'm just a dumb Minor.

26

Gloria Steinem

I *am no Gloria Steinem.*

I am no muckraker.

This is not an exposé on American universities.

I don't want your pity. What I'm penning is rooted in shame and greed and buried in lies and untold truths. I knew what I was doing when I was sugaring. I never thought college would be a factor and the government a cause. If the United were different, I would've never made that profile. But of course, if people like me could actually afford life, They wouldn't have us. They knew that. So, They did what They did to keep us as their dirty, illicit affairs.

Technically, I am not a sex worker. Sex work is illegal. The Divided call it "companionship." If we refuse to accept their companionships, we die. The Divided does not wish to refer to us as sex workers. Instead, these Elder-Minor companionships exist in a "legally gray area" and "skirt the edge of law."

Whatever that means.

Companionships are never documented, at least publicly. That would look bad from a global perspective. But the Divided still know. They keep records hidden somewhere. How else could They keep Minors in line? Prevent us from whoring around?

For Minors, any relationship outside your companionship is illegal.

Sometimes, I wish an asexual had requested companionship from me. Or a woman. Some women rarely ask their Minors for sexual favors, so I've heard. I wish I had one of those.

But no, I got stuck with X. He's the worst in bed. Every time I ride him, his enlarged nose pores, bad breath, stained teeth, and giant mole repulse me. I hate to fat-shame, but his oblong belly always got in the way, literally. He slapped me a few times for it. Not for fat-shaming. I'd never say something so hurtful. I was smacked because… well, during sex once, he said I wasn't "contorting my body enough" to mold to the shape of his belly.

He disgusted me.

But I also disgusted myself. I was doing despicable things to a man double my age to whom I had no attraction whatsoever. And for what? To live.

I always tried to imagine he was someone else, like Raphael. But it never worked. The stench of his breath and his fat warming my lower back always took me out of the delusion. I'd simply bury my face into the pillows and, with bated breath, pray for him to finish.

Daddy Two

*T*wo was the CEO of a major skin-care line.

I was still living in Connecticut when we met in New York. I found him on Shopping. He had a pot belly and a mustache. I've never liked mustaches. I can grow one, but I hate it. It makes me think of my father.

Though I did not find Two remotely attractive, I did not care. There have been many times when personality, humor, intellect, and spiritual attraction take precedence. So, I gave him a chance. Also, if you're on Shopping, you can't be picky. Money is money.

Two and I met on the corner of Bryant Park. He kissed me abruptly on the lips before exchanging any words. At the time, I was taken off guard. I think he was trying to ease the tension and make himself less nervous about meeting someone off the web, especially off a site like Shopping. But in retrospect, I think it was his way of showing himself he already had me, even before meeting me. He wanted to prove to himself he could do whatever he wanted without any objection on my part.

He said jump monkey. I said how high. Money gives you that power or at least the illusion of it.

He also could've been testing me to see if I were a cop.

I had this one friend in college who was a sugarbaby as well. She was the one who introduced me to Shopping. She warned me of the scammers out there who ask for banking information, promising to deposit large sums of money into your account.

I didn't need her to tell me this. Only an idiot would fall for that.

She also told me horror stories about how she had met with guys off the site who asked if she would sell her body for money and how much it would be for the night. She was a clever girl, though. If she had answered yes with a price and gone to his place to commit the act, she would've been arrested for prostitution. But if she had clarified that she would be paid not for sex but for her time, then she would've technically been sidestepping a legal trap and, therefore, would've been okay. She would be paid for her time, that's all. They'd have a nice meal or see a show. And if the date led to a relationship, sex would be legal. It's essentially a friend helping another friend—a mutually beneficial relationship.

Shopping is a tightrope one must carefully tread. If you went to college in America, you probably already know this. More people are sugarbabies than we realize.

My first weekend with Two was not bad.

He knew this chef in Hell's Kitchen who specialized in French cuisine. He knew I spoke French, so he decided to impress me. We talked all night. He seemed like a nice guy.

He was pretentious though. Yes, yes, I know. Look who's talking, right? Mr. French-is-my-second-language. But let's be real, knowing French is only pretentious in the Divided. Everywhere else in the world, it's normal to speak a second language.

Two was pretentious in a condescending way. For example, when the chef spoke to us in French, Two—knowing damn well I speak French—turned to me and translated what he had said into English.

I mumbled, "Ouais, je sais." Yeah, I know.

While he annoyed me, as a sugarbaby, I've learned to play dumb. If you show your true intellect, your daddy won't want you. There's a reason the word "mansplain" exists. Cisgender men—generally speaking, of course—feel the need to one-up you. It's an insecurity thing. Perhaps they think that if they prove their intellect, it will convince their baby to stay. They'll protect them—us—from all things big and scary.

Oh, I'm as dumb as a sac of rocks. Thank goodness I have such a smart guy to help me understand the ways of life. That's what they want to hear. And that's what they'll pay to hear.

Sometimes, it is clever to play dumb.

After dinner, we walked along the High Line and just talked. Well, *he* talked, to be exact. He talked about his myriad of accolades and impressive career titles, his ivy league education, and all the successful people he knew.

Thanks to sugaring, I became an excellent listener.

That weekend, we had sex. He had a medium-sized dick. Six inches. Not bad. He could never cum while fucking me. To cum, he had a specific method. He would lie on top of me, practically squashing me, and hump me until a dollop of cum puddled on my belly button. It was awkward and a little too vanilla for me. It was bearable though. I've experienced worse.

His familial life was also weird. He said he had a sister and a nephew whom he cared for occasionally. He had a spare bedroom for the nephew. Apparently, his sister was a single businesswoman who wanted a kid and thus got a sperm donor. It was a very specific story, perhaps a little too specific. And then there were the family portraits. In every photo, it was just the three of them, his arm around his sister and his nephew positioned stiffly between them. I think his sister was his wife, and his nephew was his child. I believe it was a lie fabricated so I wouldn't lose respect for him; or he wanted to avoid the awkward conversation, or both. What I do know is he wanted me to put him on a pedestal. I never saw him that way though. I only pitied the man.

I never met his sister or nephew. I was more than okay with that. I never wanted him to meet my family either. How do you explain to your family that you're dating this fifty-year-old man who infrequently helps finance your school loans?

I mentioned the infrequency of the payments because it was maybe every other month I'd see him. My time with him overlapped with my time with One. While One gave me a flat grand every time, Two varied. I think it depended on how much I had gassed him up that weekend or how much he had spent on me while I was there. I never asked him to buy me clothes, take me to fancy restaurants, or go to Broadway. He did that unprompted. I told him I got into sugaring because I couldn't afford rent, groceries, or my loan payments. But he never believed me.

On some visits, I left with six hundred dollars in my pocket. Others, less than two hundred. And when that happened, I was angry. That's how much it was for the train tickets. It defeated the purpose of sugaring. I never expressed my disappointment or anger to Two. I still had to uphold the legal fantasy of being a sugarbaby, not a prostitute. And so, I got a refund on my train ticket and bought a bus fare for less than fifty dollars. The bus took triple, sometimes quadruple, the amount of time to get home, depending on the traffic.

Despite him wasting my time every now and then, I still went back to him, hoping this time would be a six-hundred-dollar visit.

He took me out to L.A. once. He had an apartment along Venice Beach. I knew the trip would be a zero-dollar visit.

At the time, I was working at my uncles' butcher shop to make some extra cash. I lied and said I had another translation gig out in L.A. I got the time off. I considered not going because, well, that wasn't the reason why I was a sugarbaby. I didn't become a sugarbaby to have a luxurious lifestyle and experience the finer things in life. Those were perks. And when I wasn't sugaring or working, I searched for jobs. I needed those extra hours. Then I thought about it… If I can barely afford a train ticket to a neighboring state, when will I ever have the chance to go to California? Would this be my only opportunity? Should I seize it?

I'm happy I did. I haven't been back since. I wish I had stayed. Not with Two. Fuck no! But in California.

Most affairs I have end the same way: they fade out.

There's never any breakup or mutual agreement. I simply leave, and they never call. We keep the book open on an ambiguous chapter in case we ever wanted to pick up where we left off.

Two and I stopped talking after his visit to Philadelphia.

I was living in West Philly then. COVID was on the horizon. I was scared. Everyone was. That fear then mutated into depression. But I didn't want people to worry. When I spoke of my depression, I used its euphemism—sadness.

I've always been told I'm good company. I used to be so happy and optimistic, infectiously so. Even then, my spirit was fighting to win. When he visited me, I was honest about what I was feeling. Perhaps you'll find me stupid for thinking he genuinely liked me, or at least lusted after me. And lust oftentimes is a guise of like.

But he wanted carefree. He wanted radiance. Any type of honesty was an emotional dump on his fabulous, perfect life. He couldn't stand that. Refused to. So, he left that very day and said he wasn't feeling well. We never met up again. He texted occasionally to feign a fading-out effect. He never asked if I got better though.

He didn't care. They never care.

27

Newton's Third Law

I believe in karma, though I don't believe in much.
I've never been one to believe in gods or heaven. I know much about astrology and tarot, though I still don't believe in them. I have no faith in love despite my proclivity for love songs. To me, it's all about confirmation bias. You see what you want to see and find truth in what you want to be true.

But one day, karma will come for the Divided, just like she did X.

X never talked about his emotions.

He never shared his hopes and dreams, fears and worries, or his strengths and weaknesses. If he had, maybe I would've understood. Maybe I could've found a way to forgive him. Maybe I would've even liked him.

But he never wanted to have those talks with me in fear of creating an attachment. He kept me at arm's length so that he could sleep at night and not pity me, so that he wouldn't feel guilty.

X was an underdeveloped character in a book written from another character's perspective. That's what he was.

I knew he was an investment banker. I knew he had a wife. I certainly knew he had bad hygiene. And I knew he had been sexually repressed for quite some time. But that's all I knew about the man. We were in a companionship for almost two years. I should've known more than that. It's sad, really. The person I saw the most I hardly knew at all.

Days with X were days of solitude.

But there are two types of solitude: *aloneness* and *loneliness*. I learned the two thoroughly nuanced words at an early age. When I was living with my conservative parents and loquacious siblings, I chose to be in my head—a safe, comfortable place where I could keep myself company and be my true self. There's also something completely unadulterated about your alone time; it's free from other people's thoughts, preferences, and noise. This is what I like about being alone—the peace.

Loneliness is quite different. To be lonely is to allow your thoughts to become inner demons that rob you of your peace. Before the Divided, loneliness was a stranger to me. He was a heartache—a pain I knew I must let pass.

But when the world changed around me, I changed too.

I can still find inner peace whenever I'm left alone. But when X is around, so is loneliness. I could no longer consider him a stranger.

When X had a heart attack, I felt neither alone nor lonely. Though I had always known it, it was then that I accepted how empty my life truly was. I guess that's the third type of solitude: emptiness.

Thankfully, there is karma. Similar to how bad karma claimed X, good karma will rescue me. At least, I hope she does. I wouldn't blame her if she didn't. I've done many despicable things in my lifetime. Perhaps the bad I've done outweighs the good.

No, no. I can't think like that. I must believe in myself, my soul, and the goodness I've done. And if I believe, perhaps I could rely on karma.

I just have to.

28

Tomorrow

I *felt peace in the air that day.*

I woke up late and alone to the sound and smell of rainfall.

When the clouds cleared, I went on a walk. Leaves were dappled with the beginning hints of autumn. I watched the sun set over the bridge. Though the sky was gloomy in the morning, she wore an elegant pink evening gown just for me.

The trees, the sunset, the sky… The day itself felt cast in a halo.

Moments like these that resemble a dream make me forget I'm alive. These moments never leave me. They push me into tomorrow.

I wonder if X felt the peace that day.

He was horrible to me, yes.

But I sure hope he found peace that night.

29

Poppers & Viagra

*I*t happened not soon after my walk.

A sense of calm followed me to the apartment like leaves at my heel.

I removed my black suit and tie, freshened up, and threw on stockings and garters. The stockings were black net and scalloped, emphasizing my peachy, smooth ass. The garters were lace and attached to a tiny skirt. I looked in the mirror and got a little hard, admiring my bulging muscles in the naughty clothes.

I threw myself onto the duvet and waited for my daddy to come pound me.

I only wore this get-up *for him* and only talked like this *for him*. He liked this stuff. I liked it too, just not with him. At first, I didn't want to put on the stockings or talk that way. I still don't. It's just that after the first beating, I decided to obey.

When he staggered into the apartment that night, I knew he had a few too many. I instantly sighed. *Tonight will be a night of beating.*

Guys—when they're drunk—usually never get hard. And when they can't, they get frustrated and mad, and some have the audacity to take it out on you.

"Heyyyy, babbbyyy," he said in a slurred, ineffectively sexy tone. "You haven't started without me, have ya?"

"No, Daddy. I promise I haven't." I said with my head down and eyes up, crawling toward him on all fours.

"Good. Otherwise, I'd have to teach you a lesson." He hissed in my ear, and I gagged at the alcohol on his breath.

What a grease ball.

I began to unbuckle his pants.

"Hold on."

He stumbled to a locked cabinet—*his* cabinet—while fumbling for the keys.

I've never looked through the cabinet myself, but I've caught glimpses. I've seen bottles of liquor, a bowl of mixed pills, needles, and a big, locked box. I was smart enough not to ask questions.

In the cabinet, he poured himself a glass of whiskey and popped some pills into his mouth. He then waddled over to the bed with a vial of poppers in his hand.

I bent over and let him eat my ass. He loved that, and I didn't mind it.

Eat my shit, I thought.

No, not actually. I had to thoroughly clean down there, or else.

He began slapping my ass. I hated that. It hurt.

He yanked at his penis and muttered under his breath. I could tell he wasn't getting hard. I heard the jangle of his belt slipping out of the loops of his pants. I bit down on the duvet and closed my eyes.

He began spanking me with the metal part of his belt. I was in so much pain I had to choke back my cries.

"Yeah, fuck yeah," he moaned. "Yeah, take that boy."

He was getting off on this.

He pulled back my hair—I hated that too—and began raw-dogging me.

I heard him inhaling the isoamyl nitrate. I peered over my shoulder and saw his face redden. I feigned a moan as he began to pound harder. His small dick felt like a finger. I guess I should be thankful his dick wasn't ten inches or overly girthy. Imagine ramming that into me without easing me open.

When he came, I leaned against the headboard, ashamed, and watched him stagger to the bathroom. He fell to his knees and put a hand on the door. I noticed his breath was unusually raspy.

"A–Are you okay?" I asked without getting up.

He fell to the floor and did not move.

When I realized he had died, my first thought wasn't about him, his wife, or his assumed children.

No, it was all about me.

30

The Court Hearing

*T*he justice system changed immensely after the becoming of the Divided. Yet, at the same time, it hadn't changed at all.

I was imprisoned for thirty days after X's death. The judge needed time to review my case, and the pathologist needed time to perform a medico-legal autopsy.

They wouldn't allow me to stay in the apartment. It belonged to the deceased, not me. They wouldn't let me take anything with me either. That meant everything in my hidden compartment was gone.

Prison was horrible, of course.

I remember when I was in college, I read about Norway's prison system and how it focuses on rehabilitation from a social learning perspective. Essentially, Norwegian prisoners take classes to learn routine, responsibility, and right from wrong. To an American, it sounds like heaven. To a Norwegian, it's simply humane.

In the prison system of the Divided, we focus on cruel and unusual punishment. The prison I was sent to was overcrowded, dark, cold, filthy, and dangerous. We were treated like animals. When you're treated like an animal, you behave like an animal. A platitude, yes, but a true one at that. On my first day, I saw two inmates attack each other over the last moldy apple.

I lost a bit of myself during those thirty days. I can't recall many details, but I do recall missing silence. In the late hours of the night, I heard sobbing, pleading, yelling, and dying. I don't think I ever got one full night's rest.

I also remember the calluses and blisters on my hands. They called it a factory line, but it was slavery. It's not like we were paid for the shoes we made.

If I were Black, Latino, or conspicuously queer, I would've been shot the moment the Red raided the apartment.

Some say I was lucky. But it was not luck. It was privilege.

Thankfully, I had the good sense to change out of the stockings and lace and throw on my "manly" suit.

Before I did though, I sat on the bed and considered my options. I could only think of three: two dumb ones and one not-so-dumb one. The first dumb option was to hide the body at night and live the next week or so in peace and solitude. This option would be freeing but ephemeral. Inevitably, I would run out of food and have to go to the store. I could dress in Elder-drag. But I'm so conspicuously young I wouldn't make it past the entrance without being noticed. Not to mention, X's office and wife would eventually notice his disappearance. His other Minors and I would then be called in for interrogation. And I didn't like the idea of bringing other Minors down with me.

The second dumb option would be to run away. I'd surely be caught and killed within the hour. And if by some miracle I did make it out of the city, I don't know where I'd go or how well I'd fare in the forest, and that's if I made it through the suburbs unnoticed. And honestly, I don't even know if there's a forest past the suburbs. Yes, I am fit, and when I was younger, I read a lot of novels about characters braving harsh environments and living off the land. But those were just books. I don't know the first thing about living off the land. I don't think I could be as shrewd as Suzanne Collins' Katniss Everdeen, as valiant as Lois Lowry's Jonas, or as strong-willed as Ursula K. Le Guin's Genly Ai and Estraven.

So, I went with my third option.

I changed clothes, left the apartment, and approached the Red officer guarding my building.

"There's been an accident."

For my hearing, the court was mostly empty.

Those present were men and men only—the judge, guards, and lawyers. There was no jury.

Once they hooked me up to a polygraph, the prosecutor began asking me questions. Many questions.

"What were you and your Elder doing the night of his death?"

"I thought this only worked with yes or no questions?"

"Answer the question."

"We were having sex, sir."

"Did you have access to your Elder's cabinet?"

"No, sir."

"Did you prepare his meals?"

"Sometimes, sir."

"Why were there stockings and garters next to the bed?"

They knew why. They just wanted to hear it.

"He liked when I wore them, sir."

"Do *you* like wearing them?"

"I did not like wearing them for him, no, sir."

"But do you like wearing them for yourself?"

I paused. "Yes, I like looking at myself in them, sir."

"Do you find yourself… sexy?"

"Come again?"

What kind of questions were these? The prosecutor never stopped to look or ask the technician whether or not I was lying. It was obvious that my responses didn't matter and that the lie detector was all for show and had no real purpose.

"Do you find yourself sexy?" the prosecutor repeated impatiently.

"Ugh, yes? I-I suppose I do, sir."

The judge, prosecutor, and guards all sized me up at that moment. I felt terribly uncomfortable. But I knew not to let my discomfort show.

The judge then pounded his gavel. He revealed that X had died from an overdose—a combination of alcohol and drugs I've never even heard of. He went on to say a local tavern had footage of X doing lines, popping pills, and tossing back shots at the bar. The footage exonerated me.

Why didn't they start with this? Why was I in prison for thirty days? Why was I interrogated?

"The Minor is free of all charges and is now up for Auction," announced the judge. "Case dismissed."

31

$220,000

T   *his would be the part in the movie when the accused would sigh after being proven innocent.*

Not for me. I was the farthest thing from free.

After the hearing, I was immediately brought to Center City. A public service announcement regarding my Auction was broadcast on loudspeakers across the city. Fliers had also been posted on every window and pole. Pictures of my face and naked body were on the fliers. I was a puppy in need of a new home.

"Two female Minors and one male Minor are up for Auction," the voice on the loudspeaker had said. "The Auction will take place outside City Hall at two p.m. As a reminder: Elders already in possession of three Minors are not permitted to request a fourth. If you would like to discard one or more of your Minors, please put a request in at City Hall."

The voice described my stats—age, height, weight, race, ethnicity, hair color, eye color, vocal range, and everything else you'd find on an overly detailed dating site.

Auctions didn't always exist. When the Bill was first ratified, any Elder could acquire any Minor without paying the government for their new property. But after the initial chaos of when the United divided, the Divided decided to capitalize on companionships. Capitalism, it's what They know best. Since the Ameriqueerocide was at its peak, queer Minors were in high demand.

They knew what they were doing. It was all for money, after all.

Money and sex.

When we made it to City Hall, a Red guard began undressing me.

I've seen the procedure in passing before. I knew not to fight back. I let the guard strip me of my clothes and dignity until I was stark naked.

The guard ushered me onto the stage.

Two other Minors were naked and positioned downstage. One was a tall Korean girl. She steeled herself and didn't glance at me once. The other Minor was a short Ethiopian girl who was holding herself in her arms and whose eyes were watery with fear. She, too, did not glance at me.

X clearly liked having tokens.

When the town clock struck two, a man in a gray suit waltzed onto the stage and greeted the audience with enthusiasm that made me want to punch him. He briefly described our pasts and pointed to our most attractive physical features, like we were cars at a dealership.

The tall girl was first. The auctioneer spoke highly of her perky breasts and flat stomach. According to the man, her only flaw was her height. "A woman who is too tall can make a man feel rather small," he said. Before the ratification of the Bill, she was a professional violinist. She was traveling through the United with a symphony orchestra when the news was released. A bit of bad timing, really.

The man appraised her at $300,000. Her bidding lasted a while.

The short girl was second. The man spoke highly of her large breasts, smooth melanin skin, and meek demeanor. According to the man, her shortcoming was her employment history. She used to be an aerospace engineer. The sea of Elders before us, who were mostly men, groaned. Male Elders do not like intelligent women. They fear them.

The bidding for her started at $150,000.

I was last. The auctioneer poked at my butt and said I had a "fuckable, bubbly ass." He also spoke highly of my well-defined abs and pretty, feminine face. According to the man, my flaw was the acne scars on my back. He completely disregarded my employment record and only mentioned my history as a sugarbaby. Apparently, it was a good thing. It meant I knew discretion and knew it well.

As the bidding started, I zoned out and let my eyes scan the audience. Only a couple Elders assigned female at birth were present. They were closeted lesbians and here for the other Minors.

I then noticed a woman standing at the back of the crowd. She glanced between the two other Minors with a lugubrious, almost envious expression on her face. She then met my gaze, and her face contorted with disgust.

At first, I thought she was another closeted lesbian on the prowl for female companionship. But when she walked away, I noticed a boil on her neck.

It was X's wife.

I know I'm not at fault for X's death or "perversions" or whatever you want to call them, but I felt guilty the moment she and I locked eyes.

"And sold for $220,000 to the Elder in the third row!" said the auctioneer.

Before I could see who had bought me, the crowd began to disperse. A Red guard ushered me off stage and threw clothes at my feet.

As I dressed, I thought about how dehumanizing the Auction was. Throughout the entire process, They never once mentioned our names, nor did the Elders ask.

III

Sluts

32

Elder Y

I was purchased by a guy named Y.
Like X, Y was not his real name.

I was hoping a woman had purchased me. Guess I'm not that lucky. Surprise, surprise. I got stuck with yet another closeted man thanks to my feminine masculinity.

The other two Minors were scooped up while they were still naked on stage and while the crowd was still dispersing. The two Elders who had claimed them walked away with their heads held high, proud of their new, expensive property—young, beautiful women. I was left standing backstage with a Red guard, waiting the appropriate time for my Elder to collect me discreetly.

Finally, once the crowd was good and gone, a man in gray came striding toward me. He bowed to the guard, and the guard left.

"Good day, handsome," he said in a smooth, relaxed tone.

"Good day," I said, keeping my gaze low to show submission.

He gingerly lifted my chin and smiled. His smile was warm and beguiling. X never looked at me that way; his smiles were always thirsty and emotionless.

Like X, Y was pudgy. Y, however, was taller, more muscular, and Black. He also, I soon learned, had a much fatter wallet.

"Let me take you to your new home," he said. "It's downtown, right near everything."

I don't know why he mentioned this. It's not like I could go out and enjoy the nightlife. I wouldn't be able to go dancing at the local club or enjoy an evening show at the theater. No, I'd be Rapunzel, cooped up in a tower, staring at the walls.

We began walking.

While the other Minors left City Hall hand in hand with their new Elders, albeit grudgingly, Y stood an appropriate three feet away from me. PDC—public displays of companionship—were forbidden for the queers.

"I've already signed the apartment lease," he added.

"You were expecting me?"

"The moment I saw your flier, I knew I wanted you."

I didn't know whether I should be flattered or repulsed.

"Besides, I've been wanting a third Minor for a while now."

Repulsed.

"What happened to your previous third Minor?" I asked, already knowing the answer. There are only two things that happen to a Minor. One: they become an Elder themself. Or two: they're discarded.

"What makes you think I had one?" he asked.

"Don't all Elders have three Minors? At least at some point in their Elderhood?"

"Not necessarily."

"But did you?"

He eyed me, then shrugged. "Yes, I did."

"So are they an Elder now, or–?"

He eyed me again, and I realized I was talking too much. It's never good to talk too much, especially as a queer Minor. Talking too much means drawing attention to oneself.

"She uhh… She died." He sounded genuinely sad. Could've fooled me.

"She was a lovely girl. Troubled, but lovely. She was astounding in the kitchen. Do you like to cook?"

I nodded. "I haven't in a while. My previous Elder rarely allowed it. I miss it."

"Well, you can cook for me whenever you like. I love home-cooked meals."

We kept walking.

"So what's your name?" he asked.

I almost tripped, surprised by the question. I'm not quite sure if X ever knew my name. He must've for legal reasons. But he never called me by my name, even to grab my attention. Now that I think of it, he never asked for my name when we first met. I would've remembered. It's rare for a Minor to be called by their name. Names mean you are more than just a body.

"I'm… I'm Dime," I said.

"Dime?"

I nodded. "Just a dime a dozen." I couldn't help but smile. It was a phrase I used often whenever I met someone new. It gave people an easy way to remember me and showcased my self-effacing, charming demeanor.

Why was I trying to charm Y? To start off on a good note?

"Your name might be Dime, but you, my darling boy, are priceless." Y winked.

"$220,000. That's technically a price."

"Well, if it means anything, I would've spent much more if I had to." He stopped in front of the luxury apartments I've seen in passing. "Here we are."

A Red guard opened the front door and greeted Y. I was ignored.

My photo was taken for security purposes and added to Y's file. We hopped in an elevator and rocketed to the highest floor.

"I used to be a professional NBA player. Do you know anything about basketball?"

I shook my head.

"That's alright."

He led me out of the elevator and toward the end of the hall.

"Here's your new home," he said as he unlocked the door.

A penthouse. I have never lived in a more beautiful place. Sweeping, glass windows. Lofted ceilings. Expensive furniture. A full kitchen. A personal gym and pool outside on a balcony. The view was spectacular. I could see the edge of the city. There was plenty of sunlight, and the skies were so blue. Yet, somehow, despite the amenities and attractiveness of the place, I did not care.

Of course, it was a lovely place to live. A gilded cage. And before I lost my body to the Divided, a place like this was what I was working toward and desired most in the world. It's what most people want—a beautiful home. But the place wasn't mine. I hadn't earned it. I had simply moved from one house of cards to another, under a roof that could fold at any time, in a home I could be thrown out of at any moment.

33

Good Days

At the beginning of our companionship, I actually liked Y and thought perhaps I got lucky.

Oh, how I was a fool.

He told me I was a better cook than his other Minors and his wife combined. He loved my fra diavolo mussels, conchiglie alla vodka, tikka masala, empanadas, escargot, gazpacho, massaman puk, and bibimbap. He liked more than just my cooking though. He smiled at the cookie batter smeared on my forehead and giggled at how I lost myself in the kitchen, dancing to my own rhythm. He raved about every little thing, and it flattered me.

I love caring for people that way. I get it from my mother.

By cooking for Y though, I inadvertently began to care about him.

The sex didn't help either. It was incredible. Smooth and sensual, just how I prefer it. He was mindful and kind. He ate my ass better than anyone I've ever been with. He ate it like he was a famished pig. He was enormous too, but not too enormous. It took some getting used to. But when he was in me, I never wanted him out. We used lube to open me up and ease him in. He knew where to kiss, lick, and touch. We flipped multiple positions. Our breathing escalated, and we became more verbal in the end. We came at the same time, every time, with him deep inside me.

In sex, I've always been good at self-control. I prefer coming at the same time as the other person because once They come, it's over. I also like that it's a shared moment of release. Most men I've been with do not have the same mindset, let alone know the meaning of self-control. They either only care about pleasing themselves or, at most, see it as a quid pro quo. To achieve this shared moment of release, communication is paramount. I need to know when they're about to come so I can join. It doesn't have to be verbalized. Most of the time, I see it in their stupid, open-mouthed faces.

Y didn't mind communicating during *and* after sex. In fact, he and I had the most genuine conversations post-coitus. Yes, we discussed how amazing the sex was and how sexually compatible we were. But we also talked about emotions and pain and our cultures and pasts. We even talked about politics a few times. He sympathized with us Minors and said it must be awful to belong to someone else.

A real smooth talker, he was.

He felt he was doing unto us what had been done unto his ancestors. It didn't sit right with him. But still, he did it.

"Do you like music?" he asked me one evening while we sat on the couch, wrapped in each other's arms.

"Yes. Very much. But it's been a while."

"What type of music did you gravitate toward? You know, back when you were allowed such a pleasure?"

"I went through phases. Jazz, pop, rock, alternative, classical, showtunes. The one I always returned to was R&B. All eras too. Old school 60s, 90s, 2000s. Anything with soul, rhythm, or bounce. Think Sade, Maxwell, SZA, Lauryn Hill, Alicia Keys, Snoh Aalegra... Who else? Tinashe, Erykah Badu, Ariana, Prince, Aaliyah–"

I stopped myself, realizing I hadn't talked about my passions in a long, long time. I've learned in recent years it does not do to speak too much.

Y held his tongue to his cheek and grinned at my litany of R&B

artists. "I love everything you had just said." He went to the windows and closed the drapes. "Can you keep a secret?"

I looked down with shame. "Discretion is my job, is it not?"

"Of course. Sorry, that was thoughtless." He pressed a button hidden under a cabinet. The kitchen pantry slid to the left and revealed a secret room. "You must never tell anyone. Whenever you come in here, the drapes must always be closed. No one can know."

While his words were cautionary, his tone was threatening. He implied that if the Red find the room, and he goes down, then I go down with him.

The secret room was small and lit with soft, incandescent light bulbs. The intimate, dark setting gave the room a speakeasy vibe. In the center of the room was a vintage record player in mint condition. Behind it was a bookshelf of records. The shelves were bending under the weight of the vinyl.

I was in awe. "I–I haven't heard music in years."

"That doesn't surprise me. You said you like SZA, right?"

I nodded. "Do you have 'Good Days?'"

"I do." He went to the bookshelf and knew exactly where she was. The vinyl case displayed a little Black girl inked in tattoos. "This was very difficult to acquire. Most of the copies have been burned. I had to find it on the black market, of course." He unsheathed the yellow vinyl from its casing and laid it flat on the player. The wheel began to turn, and music poured from under the needle.

"Good Days." It's an alt-R&B song planted in a bed of guitar riffs, watered with synth waves, and pruned with a beat that blossomed and unfurled petal by petal, note by note. I always found the beginning of the song to sound like stars gracefully falling from the sky only to be followed by the layered, dreamy vocals of SZA.

"All the while, I'll await my armored fate with a smile
Still wanna try, still believe in
Good days, always

Always inside

Good day living in my mind."

The song faded, and the record stalled.

"What's wrong?" Y asked. I had tears in my eyes.

"Nothing. It's just… that song. For some reason, it always makes me feel like I'm—like I'm by the ocean."

He spent the whole night showing off his collection, reintroducing me to music I hadn't heard in years.

After "Good Days," he played SZA's *Ctrl* album. We listened to "Time" by Snoh Aalegra. We vibed to Beyoncé's *Lemonade*. "Sorry" and "Sandcastles" had me mouthing along. I'm surprised I remembered the lyrics.

My spirit lifted to Erykah's *Baduizm* and calmed to Tinashe's *Aquarius*. We danced to Doja Cat's *Planet Her*. And I was taken back into time listening to Aaliyah's eponymous album, a time when I was young and free, smoking weed with Rupiah, cruising down winding backroads.

Y let me jump from vinyl to vinyl to hear my favorite, long-lost tracks. I was a child in a candy store, with a sweet tooth for "Appletree," "Bated Breath," "Love To Dream," and "It's Whatever." Though I loved reconnecting with these songs, their meanings and stories panged me. They reminded me of friendship and genuine love—things I'll never know again.

We ended the evening listening to *The Best of Sade*. We snuggled on pillows near the record player and swayed our heads to "No Ordinary Love." He serenaded me with "Your Love Is King." And we made love to "Kiss of Life." He was on top of me by the end of the track, his eyes pouring into mine. We kissed passionately with him inside me, angelic lyrics grazing our ears.

If I had a nickel every time I had sex to a Sade song…

"I'm sorry I don't have more SZA for you to listen to," Y said as I cleaned the cum off my chest. "She had that album *SOS*, I remember. And an EP called *Z*, right?"

"Yeah. She had two other EPs too, *S* and *See.SZA.Run*. They had a glittery, neo-soul vibe. But I could only ever find them on SoundCloud.'"

"Wow, you know way more than I thought you would."

I've heard that before. It essentially meant he thought I looked unknowledgeable and uncultured. Did he really think this was a compliment?

I said nothing and returned to his bookshelf to peruse the rest of the vinyl.

"I like that we can bond over music," said Y. "Sharing music taste is spiritual in a way."

"I see you're also into rock," I said, pointing to *Rumours* by Fleetwood Mac and *Plastic Hearts* by Miley Cyrus.

On his bottom shelf was a box of cigars next to a small collection of books.

"Books!" I said excitedly. "*1984, The Giver, The Left Hand of Darkness, The Hunger Games, Parable of the Sower, Fahrenheit 451*… Nice."

"You've read them?"

"Back when I could, yes. There are a few here I haven't read." I examined a black, starry book. Its cover was illustrated with strange creatures and planets. "Could I read these sometime?"

"Absolutely. Just make sure the drapes are closed. We could get into serious trouble having 'propaganda.'"

I slipped out his copy of *The Handmaid's Tale*. "I burnt a copy of this not too long ago." I flipped it open and began reading.

Y took the book from my hand and returned it to its shelf. "While I give you permission to read my books, I must make one request. I've noticed you've only been going to the gym once a day." He frowned.

"While you do have an amazingly toned physique, if you want access to this room, I expect you to go to the gym twice a day, thrice when I'm not here. Don't want my beautiful boy to lose his abs, do I?"

And there it was—the reality of our companionship crashing over me and washing away the fantasy built in my mind. Despite our compatibility in and out of bed, I am still Y's fine, exotic property, nothing more than just his third Minor.

34

West Philly

I am slaying down Fifth Ave in a custom garment with a box of Channel chocolates in one arm and a bottle of Dom Pérignon in the other.

I carelessly kick rubies with my Balenciagas and skip down the street, where a performer eases the air with his violin. I'm outside my sugardaddy's Manhattan penthouse with his black card safe in my pocket. A bellhop holds the elevator door. A view of the city encompasses me as I rise above the clouds.

Dancing through life, that's how They see me.

When I pass through the threshold, the penthouse becomes a shoebox studio apartment in West Philadelphia. The Chanel chocolates melt into a dead mouse caught in a trap. The bottle of champagne shatters into a cracked mirror I found on the corner of 43rd and Chester Ave.

The custom garment reveals into tattered hand-me-downs and Goodwill finds. The rubies erode into pebbles and dirt carried in from the streets. My Balenciagas become knockoffs, and my skip becomes a drag. The performer's violin imitates the soothing, perpetually beeping fire alarm my property manager refuses to fix.

My sugardaddy's black card becomes my student card. The bellhop retires as a crackhead who follows me home and repeatedly calls me a faggot. Oh, and the city skyline! That becomes a sweeping, smelly view of a trash receptacle just outside my first-floor window.

It was and is all an illusion.

This was my reality when I was a sugarbaby. People assumed I had everything. In truth, I was a twenty-something with nothing to my name.

Most people have at least something to their name. That is why they can never see that having nothing often gives you everything. It gives you freedom.

I had to walk two miles carrying groceries in the dead of summer, even if it rained. I had no car. I was far from everything. My apartment was so small I had to shuffle around my twin-sized bed. I was broke and alone.

But I had the cemetery down the street. I'd go there and read book after book to the Morrises. The Morrises were a couple buried together in the far corner of the cemetery. I know Morris is a pretty lame name, but something about that corner called to me.

I think it was the silence.

Cities brim with noise. But this cemetery—specifically next to the Morrises—offered me the space to be at peace. It wasn't exactly quiet; I heard police sirens and fire trucks every now and then. But most of the time, it was silent. Maybe a bird or a squirrel and once a doe.

The patch of grass was the softest and most secluded in the whole lot. I'd lie beside the Morrises' and sunbathe, stretch, or journal.

I spent my years in West Philly mostly writing. Some days, I even distracted my hunger with writing. I couldn't afford much food, so I consumed words, thoughts, and stories instead. I know that sounds dramatic, but when you focus so much on your craft, you forget other things in life, like time, family, and even hunger.

I owe a lot to West Philly, really. It had its charm. I never thought I would miss that shoebox of an apartment—ever.

Now, in the years of the Divided, I know those years in my early twenties were a time when I was most free.

Not because I was young, sexually active, and not tied down. But because I had nothing at all.

35

Possessive

There were things Y forbade, reminding me time and time again we were not in a relationship.

Unlike X, Y did not let me go on walks alone. He preferred that I didn't go at all. But I easily become stir-crazy and irritable, even for sex. He fucked me regardless. But he preferred it when I was actually into it and gave a little life. So when I asked to go on walks, he joined me. But because this spurred judgmental, homophobic looks from people in town, he eventually hired a walker—a Red guard who would take me on walks as if I were a dog. She and I never spoke. She merely stood a couple yards behind me and watched. After dozens of walks, she got lazy and occasionally let me wander on my own. She told Y she was with me the whole time.

Because Y knew I had mostly been with men, my walker had to be a woman. Y had quite the jealous streak. And when he became jealous, he became possessive and mean.

For example, because I loved to cook, he used to take me to the grocery store to peruse the aisles for inspiration. Those who were shopping were either Elder men with their wives, Elder men with their Minors assigned female at birth, or Elder women by themselves.

When I went with Y, all of them glared at us. They weren't just glaring though. Many closeted Elder men looked at me, my ass, and my pretty face. I could see in their hungry, perverted eyes they were thinking of all the dirty, little things they would do to me if they had the guts to be their true, queer selves.

Y would catch these longing glances from other men. And when we returned home, he would slap me and call me a whore.

Eventually, he did the shopping all by himself.

I was fine with it. I, of course, didn't enjoy the slapping, but I didn't like the glances and glares either. The glances made me feel violated, and the glares made me feel unsafe.

Not to mention, I hated going with Y. I was ashamed to be with him.

"W went missing," Y told me one day.

"V also went missing," he told me another day.

W and V were two Elders who had eyed me at the grocery store. I didn't know them, but Y did.

According to Y, W worked in retail, and V was an architect.

"Poor people," Y said, shaking his head. "They always choose professions that never benefit themselves. It's as if they're asking to be poor."

I bit my tongue.

"Have either of the Elders been found?" I asked one day.

W's body was found buried in Clark Park. V's body washed up in the Schuylkill River.

Schoolkills River?

How's it spelled? Fuck it. Anyway, W and V had both been bludgeoned to death. Investigations were held, and two of their Minors were sentenced to a life of rape.

When a Minor is given a life rape sentence, it essentially means they are bound to a post in Center City, and any Elder who wishes can go up at any time and fuck them, slap them, or do whatever they want to them. Eventually, the Minors would die from causes like hunger, thirst, heat, cold, or general illness. Sometimes, they even will themselves to die. It's called psychogenic death.

W's and V's other Minors and wives were exonerated. The wives became Elders themselves, and the Minors were put up for Auction.

I personally do not believe the Minors who were found guilty were truly guilty. They were scapegoats. I think it was Y. It was the way he smiled when he told me about their disappearances.

Because I feared him killing again, I ensured he and I never again went out in public together. I didn't care if he killed another perverted, rapey Elder. But I did care about other Minors. As individuals who experience the same or similar adversities, we must stick together and protect one another.

I hated seeing other Minors tied to a post like that, being raped every day until death took mercy. Whenever I looked at them, all I saw was myself.

36

Tether

One day, while I was reading a book called Slaughterhouse-Five, I heard a clamor down the hall.

I marked my page, locked the hidden room, and cracked open the front door. At the end of the hall, I saw a girl with red hair in black robes moving boxes into a room.

It was the same girl who saw me pick up the pencil.

Her Elder was not present.

My door creaked, and the girl turned. I reeled back into the apartment.

When Y came home, I asked him about the new neighbors. Normally, I would never ask anything, but our companionship gave me false confidence and misplaced curiosity.

"What neighbors?"

"The red-head at the end of the hall," I said. "Have you met her or her Elder?"

"There's no one else on this floor."

"But I saw her moving boxes…"

"You left the apartment?"

"No, no. I just peeped open the door."

"Good. I don't want you leaving the apartment. Everything you need is here. Food, water, gym. If you need something, just tell me and I'll try to get it. Anyway, what's for dinner?"

My mind was still on the girl. Was Y gaslighting me? Where was her Elder? And how did she have so many things to put in boxes?

"Babe."

"What?"

"I asked what's for dinner?"

"Oh, sorry. Pineapple shrimp fried rice."

He kissed my cheek. "You do so much for me. I should do something for you. Are there any vinyl or books you want me to get you? I can try to find them on the black market. Might take time and money, but you've been such a good boy lately, cooking and cleaning and going to the gym three times a day for me."

I gave it some thought. "Well, there is something I want."

"Yeah?"

"The apartment I was in prior… Do you know if anyone has moved into it yet?"

"I'm not sure. I'd have to check. Why do you ask? You don't want to move back into that grimy apartment, do you? Is this one not good enough?"

"No, this one's perfect. Too perfect really. I just… There's a hidden compartment under the floorboard. There are some personal things of mine in there that I'd love to get back."

"What's in it?"

"Not much. There's an excerpt of a poem I like, a few pressed flowers, napkins, and a pencil." I didn't mention the sliver of wood. It'd be noticeable in the compartment for sure, but it could easily be mistaken for a piece of the floorboard that had somehow fallen in.

I didn't mention the wood because a) I didn't want Y to think I was suicidal, and b) I didn't need it anymore. Y bought knives for me. Real, sharp, metallic knives. I could use those if need be.

"A pencil, you say? Do you write?"

"Sometimes. That's what the napkins were for."

He smiled. "I'll see if I can get into the room and retrieve your things for you."

"Thank you very much."

"My pleasure." He grinned suggestively and led me to the bedroom. "I scratch your back, you scratch mine."

Within the same week, there came a knock on the door.

I was scared. Y wasn't home. No one knocks these days. I looked through the peephole and saw it was the girl.

Against my better judgment, I cracked open the door.

"Hi, neighbor," said the girl. "I made cookies."

I was too stunned to speak.

Up close, I noticed her neck had been branded with a red, upside-down triangle—the symbol of shame for indicted sluts.

"They're chocolate chip," she continued.

"We're–" I faltered. "We're not supposed to speak to each other. Us Minors. We're forbidden."

"Yes, but my Elder's not home, and I saw yours leave this morning. Besides, the Red guard is in the lobby, not up here."

I said nothing in return.

"May I come in?"

"I don't think that's the best idea."

"Well, at least enjoy these cookies. I spent all morning baking them for you."

I accepted the cookies and nodded my thanks.

"I'm Tether, by the way." Seeing I wouldn't say anything, she asked, "What's your name?"

"Dime."

"Dime? What a peculiar name. Well, it was nice meeting you, Dime. I'll see you around."

I closed the door and put the cookies on the counter. A part of me was annoyed that she had put my life in danger like that. Another part of me, I must admit, was impressed. She was committing an act of rebellion simply by speaking to me.

"You made cookies!" Y said later that evening. "Chocolate chip, my favorite!"

Fuck! I forgot to flush Tether's cookies.

Y bit into one. "Mmm, so good. You bake them perfectly every time."

I was already formulating a lie in my head. I was going to say it was a new recipe.

"Yeah, I was in a baking mood today, I guess."

"Mmh." He sniffed the air. "It doesn't smell like it. Where'd you get the basket?"

I froze. "It was in the cabinet. I thought it looked cute."

"I didn't know we had it. Then again, you know the kitchen better than I do." He swallowed a cookie whole. "Oh! I have presents!" He opened his suitcase and pulled out a bag. "Your things."

I pulled out the poem, pencil, napkins, and flowers. Also in the bag were a stack of pens and a journal bound in a mirror.

"I know a couple guys in the black market," said Y. "One of them had a dozen journals to choose from. I thought you might like this one. While I give you permission to write and explore your thoughts discreetly, of course, I don't want you to forget about your looks. Your looks are why I bought you anyway."

I shifted my eyes to my feet.

"I'm sorry, I'm sorry. That's not what I meant. What I meant is your looks are what brought us together. And this journal will never let you forget that. It'll remind you just how beautiful you are." He cupped my chin. "My beautiful, beautiful boy."

But that's the thing. He did mean it. If I had been less pretty, there's no doubt in my mind that he wouldn't have bought me. At least not for $220,000. I would've surely been worth less.

Luckily, I know my worth most of the time. I'm a kind, smart, and thoughtful person. I'm intuitive, brave, creative, and resilient. I have confidence in myself—beauty and brains.

I enjoy compliments, yes, and accept them graciously.

But moments like these—comments and observations centered around only my beauty—make me think perhaps I am on earth for one thing and one thing only.

That's all I am to these people. Some beautiful thing for them to behold, and looks tangible enough to claim. An object, a trophy, a prize.

37

Scars

I *have a total of six physical scars.*

The first is located on my inner thigh and is from when X would dig his fingernails into me as we fucked. I asked him not to apply so much pressure, but that only made him do it more and more forcefully. He liked to hear me yell.

I had bruises from when X and Y slapped and choked me, but those bruises eventually healed and disappeared.

My second scar is on my shoulder from when the Divided whipped me for biting into X's dick.

The other three are from before the Bill.

The third is a group of scars. They're bacne scars from high school that have been cratered, picked over, and browned so deeply into my skin they look like sunspots. My back is the only part of my body I am ashamed of. I've always wanted to cover them with tattoos or get laser removal or do whatever rich people do to get their skin so clear and poreless. Whenever I'm showering with or changing in front of someone else, I find myself turning my back to the wall so the other person won't have to look at them. During sex, you can't do that. You have to embrace the vulnerability.

A part of me always knew sugardaddies wanted the best. They were paying hundreds and thousands of dollars to go on dates with the sexiest, most eligible sugarbabies in town. If they were spending money on a good-looking boy, they'd get the finest, goddamn it!

Most of the time, I'm fucked spreadeagle. They say they like looking at my face. It's not a lie. I do have a pretty face. But I know it's not the whole truth.

No one likes scars. Scars mean complexities, histories, and sympathy (often forced). People want easy.

My fourth scar is on my forearm.

I got that one from my days roller skating along the Schuylkill. The one day I chose not to wear elbow pads, I fell flat onto my forearms. What luck.

My fifth scar is on my right index finger from when my shower door shattered over me. I was bleeding from head to toe. Crumbs of glass dotted my skin, and water curled into red rivulets. My finger got the worst of it. My physician friend who lived around the corner came and plucked glass out of my skin and hair like ticks. My finger refused to clot. I had to go to Urgent Care.

When my doctor, property manager, and family and friends asked what had happened, no one believed me. In fact, they grinned and eyed me up and down.

"Yeah, sure, okay. I'm sure that door fell all on its own," joked my uncle.

"Are you sure there was no type of 'banging' that occurred within the shower that may have caused the door to 'fall?'" asked my property manager. Each word was hand-plucked.

"You thotty devil, you," Rupiah said with the fattest of grins.

I was annoyed with the narrative. Where was the compassion?

I get it. It was a steamy, wet shower. Why not sexualize the naked, pretty boy? I, myself, am to blame for that. I capitalize on my sexuality and flaunt it greatly.

But even as a kid, adults always seemed to sexualize me.

For example, my last name is Gagliastra. In Italian, the second *g* is silent. In English, the second *g* wants to be pronounced. People get a kick out of the name. There's not only *gag* in the name but also *ass*.

Adults feign maturity. I can't blame them. It's only natural to notice those things. People may have chuckled with the boys in my family, but that was the most they received. With me, my sisters, and perhaps Billie too, people always cracked a joke.

"Does that mean you have a gag reflex?"

"I bet he gags, alright."

Some ignorant shit like that.

The jokes were innocuous. I didn't take them personally. It was just weird receiving them as a kid. These grown-ass adults—mostly strangers, family friends, or relatives on my mother's side of the family—were sexualizing a child.

Of course, when I was a child, I didn't understand the comments. I had to ask Goldie.

"It's just a wisecrack, sweetheart," she told me. "You'll understand when you're older."

The mispronunciation of Gagliastra annoyed me not nearly as much as the sexualization of the shower incident. What annoyed me about that ordeal was that not a week later, the same thing happened to a friend of mine. He was not a conventionally attractive man. He's probably a Red now. When it happened to him, no one thought twice about it. People jumped to his side, saying it must've been a 'faulty installation!'

I find it a double standard.

While his cuts were met with sympathy and defense, mine were met with suspicion and sexualization.

My sixth and last scar is on my neck.

A part of it can be hidden under the collar of my dress shirt.

The scar is of a pink, upside-down triangle. The Divided branded me with the triangle the day I became X's Minor. All queer Minors who survived the Ameriqueerocide were forced to bear the symbol. The pink is quite vibrant. They must've used tattoo ink or something.

I was told the symbol dates back to the Holocaust.

I fainted from the pain that day when the branding iron kissed my skin and marked me with shame.

Cattle, that's what we are.

38

Beaches

*O*nce upon a time, I wore a speedo along the New England shore.

It was more of a thong than a speedo, I'll admit. My ass was plump. My privates were covered, I swear. I looked hot in all that skin. I was happy and free then.

Rupiah was wearing a bikini—a total babe.

We were nineteen or something, sprawled out on a blanket, reading our favorite poetry to one another, dissecting the poet's words, and enjoying our day in the sun. We were listening to the lapping of the waves when a sixteen-year-old lifeguard approached us.

"I-I'm sorry," he faltered, "but uh, I feel awkward saying this, but um… we've gotten complaints regarding nudity." He looked directly at me.

"What do you mean 'nudity?'" retorted Rupiah. "We're wearing bathing suits?"

"I know, I'm just–" he couldn't find the words.

"It's okay, I'll just put on my shorts. It's fine."

Next to us was a large Latino family.

"Nudity?!" said the mother. "The boy's wearing a speedo. Every man in Europe wears them. It's normal. Besides, my daughter is wearing a bikini that goes right up her ass for fuck's sake! I don't see anybody complaining about that!"

"I'm so sorry," said the boy. "I personally do not think this is nudity. It's just that the lady over there keeps complaining."

In a lawn chair a few yards away was a forty-year-old white woman smoking a cigarette, scowling at us, at me.

"It's fine. I already have my shorts on."

Everyone was looking at me. I hated it. I just wanted to lie in the sand with my best friend and read.

"I'm sorry again." The boy left.

Then, the woman ashed her cigarette into the sand and approached us.

"You should be ashamed of yourself," she hissed. "Naked on a family beach?! Disgusting! My boys are trying to have a nice time, and now I have to shield their eyes." She gestured to her two sons building a sandcastle yards away, completely unaware of the situation.

She was a foot away from us.

Rupiah grabbed a handful of sand. "You move one more foot toward my friend, and I'm throwing this sand in your fucking eyes, bitch!"

The family near us—the mother, men, and women—stepped in front of me. The father pulled out a switchblade.

"You best leave," he said.

The woman kept her eyes on me and, in one swift motion, spat at me.

"YOU'RE DEAD!" Rupiah said, throwing the sand into her eyes. The woman howled. "Go choke on a dick and get the fuck out, bitch, before I tear out your crunchy-ass hair!"

She lunged at her.

The woman grabbed her sons and ran away, tearing down their sandcastle as she went.

After that, we spent the rest of our day in peace, believe it or not. I was still in my shorts. It was brisk out anyway. Rupiah and I hung out with the family. They poured us cups of champagne, and we shared a joint with the mother until we said our goodbyes.

It was a whirling turn of events. The day started in a place of comfort and poetry, veered off into hatred and double standards with a sprinkle of violence, and ended with a newfound, drunken friendship.

I wish I could say this was the last time something like this had happened to me.

There was the time when I was followed home in Hong Kong while wearing a feminine blouse. There was also the time when an Uber driver in France refused me service and sped off, calling me a "pédé." And then there was the time in the Bahamas.

My family and I were on a cruise. I was in my late teens then. A spell of bravery had fallen over me. Only later in life did I realize it was not bravery but naïveté. I'm a bit embarrassed by the story. I should've known better.

If I wasn't accepted at home, why on earth did I ever think I'd be accepted elsewhere in the world?

I didn't know much about the Bahamian culture and that homophobia was so prevalent there.

When the ship docked on the island, everyone left the cruise to explore. I forget the name of the island, or perhaps I've repressed it. When we left the ship, we were welcomed by a bunch of vendors selling souvenirs. I was wearing a long, black jumpsuit. It was low-cut, meant to be filled with breasts.

A muscular, feminine boy with a tight ass and pretty face in a silhouette they've only seen on women before threatened their comfort zone and beliefs on how men should dress. To me, it was just a cover-up. Underneath, I was wearing a pink speedo. It was an actual speedo this time, not a thong.

The vendors were all women, I noticed. When they saw me, they cheered. "You look fabulous," they said. "Stunning."

It wasn't until we reached the beach that it happened. There was a gaggle of men by the entrance. When I entered, I felt their glares. My siblings did too.

"Go back to America where you belong, faggot," one said.

"You like man aye bey," snarled another.

I wasn't sure what he had meant by that. But by his tone, I could tell it was hateful.

"You'll be dead before you return to the boat," said another.

Several of them flashed their switchblades. Why does everyone have a fucking switchblade?!

My five siblings, brother-in-law, and two parents were not oblivious. They were as uncomfortable and scared as I was. They circled me, protecting me with their mere presence. I, Dime, put my family's lives at risk.

The men continued to bombard us with homophobic comments. Though much of their argot went over our heads, the aggression in their words was felt.

We tried walking down the beach to escape them, but they followed.

It was a beautiful, sunny day. I just wanted to spend it with my family. Then the palm-fringed island grayed. The soft sand beneath our feet became coarse and cold. Even the turquoise water lost its color.

"Should we go back?" asked Billie.

"Yeah, I don't feel like being on the beach anyway. It's too windy," said Goldie. She tried playing it cool so I wouldn't internalize the situation. She knew me well.

In my head, I was already blaming myself for ruining their day.

None of my siblings made me feel bad about it, though. The only person who made comments was my father.

"You shouldn't have been wearing that to begin with," he said. "You should've at least done some research."

And well, he was right. I should've done my research. I should've quelled my existence. I should've conformed.

"If not for your well-being, at least for your family's!"

Daddy Three

While he fit the bill, I wouldn't necessarily call Three a sugardaddy. Yes, he was sixty. But in ways, our connection was genuine. We cooked together. We watched shows together. He came home to me, and I came and went whenever I pleased. We thought of each other throughout our days and bought each other little things we thought the other would like. He used to write poetry for me, too. It was corny, but I liked it.

I think we could've loved each other.

Though he never liked the title, in my mind, I still considered him a sugardaddy. I'm not sure why. He never paid for my company. He never took me on trips or sugared me in any way, and I never asked. In fact, most of our time together was spent between the walls of his small, suburban house in Delaware.

One reason I consider him to have been a sugardaddy is that I lived with him for months on end for free. I'd bring my computer, a suitcase, and a few books and work from his place. Here is someone who has a house and is opening their door to me but is not asking me to pay rent. He says he cares about me. I don't believe it. No one could ever care for me that much. No one cares for anyone that much. He wasn't after me. He was after my body, and if not my body, then an antidote to his loneliness.

I would've stayed longer with Three if it weren't for the suburbs of Delaware. I didn't hate the state. It was just that there was nothing to do there. Three had four cars but never let me use one to go hiking, into the city, or to the gym. The only forms of activity I had were running and biking through boring, flat developments.

That's another reason why he was a sugardaddy in my eyes—he didn't trust me. Trust is a key ingredient in successful relationships, so they say. Every affair I've had with a sugardaddy required distrust just as much as it did discretion.

Another reason—a reason that shames me—could be the ageism in me, the ageism that seems to be in everyone else too.

A family friend once said over dinner how she had a gay cousin who was dating someone double his age. She let her relationship with her cousin dissolve because she refused to understand. Could a young, good-looking man truly be in love with a much, much older man who happens to be more financially stable? No way. Impossible. There must be another reason, right?

I was the only one to defend her cousin. My siblings and mother just sat there and played with their food.

Did I internalize this woman's judgment and everyone's complicity? Did I become one of them? Why did I see Three as a sugardaddy? Why did I feel I had to provide companionship for a place to sleep? Why couldn't I accept our connection and just love him? I easily could have. And if he had asked me to live with him, then that would've been secondary.

But I was young and foolish and focused on the wrong things.

He was kind and patient. He was good-looking too. Fit and thin. He had smile wrinkles and winsome blue eyes. We treated each other equally. If anything, I spent more money on him than he did on me.

Apart from the older age, the financial stability, and the loneliness, the only "daddy" thing about him was his inability to keep an erection. Honestly, we rarely ever had sex. We had consensual sex in the beginning, yes, but he never got off on it. Once I realized he was only fucking me for me, I never asked for it, even though I did crave the intimacy and passion. He could've been asexual. Or a side. Either way, he never wanted penetration. We simply did not match. We cared deeply for each other nevertheless.

Something about him was off. I think—and I only think this because of my experiences—that something may have happened to Three when he was a child. Not all children who are taken advantage of become asexual adults. I, myself, am not an asexual person. Have I begrudgingly used sex to get by in life? Yes. But I still enjoy the act, depending on the person. And with people I'm not attracted to, I still have an imagination.

As I grew up, I became aware of my signs. It showed in my aggression and depression as a child, my antisocial behavior, my acute self-sufficiency, and my night terrors. Of course, these "side effects" could simply be a fraction of my personality and a natural part of growing up. Correlation, not causation. Three's signs were his self-harm, workaholism, poor performance in school, and—where we overlapped—the night terrors.

One time, in the middle of the night, I woke up to him mumbling in his sleep. "No, Uncle Benny. Don't." He jerked around and accidentally smacked me in the face. It happened so quickly that I jumped out of bed, terrified. I thought something was happening. An intruder. He woke up then, apologized, and held me in his arms until we both fell back asleep.

The following day, I asked him who Benny was. He said it was his uncle, who had passed away a few years ago. That was all he said.

The very same week, I finished rereading *The Perks of Being a Wallflower.*

If you haven't read it, in the end, you learn the main character was sexually abused by his late aunt, and he comes to forgive her because she, too, was abused as a child. "Hurt people hurt people" is the takeaway.

Three and I were sitting on his couch when I finished the book. He was scrolling on his phone with my legs draped over his. I was just sitting there, gazing out the window, ruminating on the author's words like I usually do after a good book.

"Were you ever molested when you were a kid?" I asked randomly. It was a casual question shared over cookies and coffee.

He was taken aback by the question and asked me where it came from. I summarized the book and then repeated the question.

"You don't have to share if you don't want to. The book just had me thinking."

He then said, in the most matter-of-fact tone, "I think I was. My dad's friend. He worked in a hardware store."

I didn't say anything after that. I didn't ask any follow-up questions. I didn't care for specifics. I didn't even care to offer my experience. We just sat there, entwined on the couch, aglow in the afternoon light.

Whether it was our lack of sex and trust or my internal ageism, I never saw a future with Three.

And so, I let whatever we had crumble.

It started with my coming and going. Every couple of months, I would bounce between him and my other sugardaddy at the time, Five. He'll have a chapter later.

Normally, I'd take the train, but Five insisted he'd pick me up. Five was more possessive and had to have known I had another daddy. That's why he insisted; he wanted to know his competition. Not necessarily *who* was his competition, but *what*. Was his house bigger? Was his wallet thicker? Was he giving me more? He must know! He probably thought he'd get to meet this other daddy too. See if he was better looking, younger, more hung? Whatever he expected to see, I refused to let them meet. So, I told Three my father was picking me up, and I told Five I was staying at a friend's.

The timing of my pick-up needed to be perfect. If they ran into each other, how would I explain myself? Is this sixty-year-old man really my "friend?" And is this short, pale, portly man really my "father?" Why did I have two daddies? One wasn't enough? Honestly, neither was. I was taking advantage of them and what they both offered. And I had two because, well, I never knew when one daddy would leave or when one would stop offering me their home. Also, I needed an escape daddy in case one became violent and vindictive or codependent and annoying.

When I told Three my father was picking me up, I could tell he knew I was lying. Liars know liars. I knew he lied when he said his "dad's friend." And he knew I was lying then. When I scrambled out his front door, carrying all my bags and computer at once without help, refusing to make a second trip, I saw his face. He was hurt. Heartbroken, really. He realized at that moment I was never serious about him. I think he always knew that, but it was only then that he accepted it.

I wanted to get out of there before the two met.

When I got to Five's car, Five got out and helped me put my stuff in the truck. He said he was trying to help, but I know he only got out to puff out his chest and intimidate the other male looking out the window.

I told Five over text not to get out of the car. I told him if my "friend" saw him, I'd have to explain myself later. But he didn't listen. I was pissed. He was clearly not my father, and if Three looked out the window, he would see that.

Then I thought, if Three ends things with me, I would be okay. With a body everyone seems to fixate on, a sexuality everyone must explore, I'd easily find another daddy.

But Three didn't end things. We continued to text, and I stayed with him several more times over two years. I could tell he was keeping me at a distance. He never said I love you, not even in a friendly way. He was less romantic, more so than usual. He rarely ever reached out and was okay with seeing me less and less over time.

When I was with him, I, of course, learned more and more about him. I learned he was not close to his dad. When his mother Facetimed him, she politely said hello but called me Three's "little friend," as if we were on a playdate or something. During the summer, Three loved cruising on backroads in his doorless Jeep. He also only listened to his music, never anyone else's. I was always bothered by that. My music taste was far superior to his. I know, I know. I'm very modest. But my taste at least evolved over time as I consumed more music. His taste had stayed the same since high school. He even said so. Another thing about him that bothered me was that, in his sixty years of living, he had lived on the same street his entire life. Though he was old and tall, he never really grew at all.

I can't say the reason why we ended things was because we didn't share each other's taste in music or because he lived in one place his entire life. While they were true statements, they weren't good enough reasons. But they were cracks splintering from my coming-and-going and lies. And when one crack begins, more are sure to come, like his lack of an adventurous spirit, disinterest in travel, and distaste for world cultures. He was too particular about things too. He didn't like fruit with savory food, like pineapple on pizza or mangos on tacos. He asked me to clean the shower with a squeegee after every shower because he didn't like water spots. He asked me not to put my toothpaste on the bathroom sink because he was afraid it'd stain the countertop. He also asked me to use separate cutting boards for fruits and vegetables. If I were cutting a vegetable, I had to use the green cutting board. If it were a fruit, I had to use the light green board.

At first, I was okay with his little quirks. I found them cute. I, too, can be particular about things. For example, I can only write if I'm surrounded by no one or a cacophony of noise. I can't be around another person. Either no one or everyone. It's a focus thing.

Anyway, when Three requested I do what he says while under his roof, I did so without question. It was his house. I was a guest, no matter how intimate we were. I'd always be a guest, even if, hypothetically speaking, we committed to each other.

One night, after a particularly bad day for the both of us, I was chopping carrots and tomatoes on the same cutting board. He asked me to use a separate board. I didn't want to dirty another one. Besides, they were both going in the same soup. Did it matter?

We started yelling, projecting our respective days onto each other. I was combative. He was bossy. And we were both stubborn. We fought over nothing. I left him to finish the soup. I stormed away because I was a child. He gave me the silent treatment because he, too, was a child.

I ran upstairs and called Rupiah to vent. Rupiah and Cedi were the only ones in my life who knew I sugared and where I was. Cedi knew because she, too, sugared to pay for school and rent. And Rupiah knew because I knew she wasn't the type to judge.

Anyway, on the call, I said some pretty hateful things about Three. I was in the spare room with the door closed, and Three was downstairs in the kitchen with the oven vent on. There's a likelihood he never heard me. But I was furious and annoyed and chose not to keep my voice down. I can't remember all of what I said. I only remember the most hateful: I called him a disgusting pedophile.

It's a horrible thing to call someone. Libel, really.

I'd like to clarify that not all older men dating someone younger are pedophiles. Love is love and has no age. I get that.

But with Three, my instincts were right.

Not a week later—after I apologized, of course; he didn't because it was his kitchen and he felt he didn't have to—I learned he used to be a police officer and an alcoholic. I intuited his sobriety the first week we spent together. I surmised he was either sober or like me—someone who doesn't particularly care for alcohol.

One night, while watching television, he told me he used to be a big partier. He and his "ex-buddies" and his ex-buddies' buddies would get hammered at his place. During the last party he threw, he made a pass on a guy he had just met. He gave the guy alcohol. When they were drunk, Three kissed and touched him. It wasn't until later he found out that the kid was seventeen. Someone had invited a minor.

The injustice system expunged the sex offense from Three's record. He was an officer, one of them. But he was fired for giving alcohol to a minor. Priorities, am I right?

He also had to take classes.

"What type of classes?"

"Ones that essentially forced me to suppress my 'sexual desires.'" That was all he shared.

After hearing this, my mind whorled. Was I with a registered sex offender? A pedophile? Three was always kind to me despite our occasional bickering. Was I going to let this newfound knowledge alter my perception of him? Should I still visit him? Should I end things? Can people like Three be forgiven?

I also realized that these "classes" could have been the reason for his lack of a libido.

I also remembered Uncle Benny. Was this Three's hurt-people-hurt-people moment? Did he do what he had done because of what had been done to him?

And lastly, I thought, was this even true? Was Three lying to me? I knew he was a liar. Everyone is. Secondly, he could've overheard my conversation with Rupiah and saw his ticket out. I could sense he wanted things to end but didn't know how to do it. In the beginning, he was affectionate. He showered me in kisses and snuggles and enjoyed spending time with me. But in the end, even before I knew about this drunken night, he stopped being affectionate. He was detaching himself from me.

I stayed with him a couple more times after that, but we eventually stopped talking.

Again, I saw no future with Three from the very beginning. I never wanted one, at least with him. I can be sorry I was selfish, and I know I should've forgiven him for his past, but I did not care at the time. I was more focused on myself.

Who will I take advantage of next? Which sad, old sack will be my next victim? And, of course, where will my next home be?

39

Nice, Pretty Things

She always meant well, my mother.

My siblings and I often defended her, saying her heart was in the right place.

She was the type of person to cry while watching *Disney* movies. She was the type of mother who cooked our favorite meals when one of us fell ill or returned home after being away. She prioritized pleasures in life. She loved the sun and autumnal leaves. She loved gardening, sunbathing, and surrounding herself with nice, pretty things. She themed each of our rooms and decorated every inch of the house. She didn't care that the decor was cheap, for what would that matter if it still made her house a home?

She always said her goal in life was to have a large, loving family to come home to. For a long while, she had just that. A husband, children, money in the bank, a house on a lake, and a heart full of love. Her heart never changed despite everything that happened.

Her husband drank, yelled, and cheated.

Her children grew up and came out.

The money in the bank was in a shared account.

The house on the lake became quieter over the years.

The weight of the world grew and grew until, one day, everything just vanished.

The divorce came after my younger sister graduated high school. Like many parents, my father stayed with my mother "for the kids" until the kids could no longer be called kids. In truth, it was never about the kids. His actions conflicted with the sentiment. He threw me out of the house. Was that "for the kids?" He left my sister stranded in Spain. Was that "for the kids?" He never paid for one damn thing except for the house over our heads.

Dental work? My mother paid for it.

Food? My mother made it.

College? I took out loans cosigned by my mother.

He did the bare minimum, all for a tax reduction. We weren't his kids. We were his legal dependents until we weren't.

But this chapter is not about him.

It's about my mother. She never shared this "for the kids" mindset. She truly thought she and her husband would work it out, that after the kids were gone, they could focus on reviving their relationship.

Who knows who made the right choice? Sometimes, it's best to know when to walk away. Other times, it's best to stay and fight.

All I know is we were way more of a family after the divorce and after my father became estranged than ever before. The first Christmas we spent without him was the best Christmas I ever had in my entire life. He wasn't there to provoke us. Granted, we were grown by then. Still, we were at ease without him. And my mother was there to make it a nice, cozy Christmas.

And unlike my father, she grew to accept her queer children.

I want her to know I still think she was—or *is*—a wonderful mother.

And while I want nothing but nice things to say about her, that wouldn't be the whole truth. I've had issues with her just as much as I did with him. Like every parent, she wasn't perfect.

Every kid needs something a little different from their parents. Billie needed affection. Silv needed space. And Goldie needed responsibility.

Of course, we all needed a little of everything, but some needed more of something than others. That's just character, how we're born and grow to be.

My mother had six kids and was only one person. She could only offer so much. I don't blame her for not providing the reliability I needed.

It was little things, really. I needed someone to drive me home after theater rehearsal. She saw it as needing a chauffeur. I saw it as someone supporting a passion of mine. While I recognize it was selfish of me to expect someone to be there for me, I also recognize it was a reasonable request, one asked well in advance. Instead of breaking her promise, she should've just said no. But she never knew how, especially to her children.

So, as I grew, I began to think no one would ever be there for me, even if they promised. I'm not saying she was the reason for my self-sufficiency and distrust in others. You can't pinpoint the exact reason for character flaws. And really? Blaming your flaws on your parents? That's so lame. But to an extent, I internalized her unreliability and perhaps became a little like her. That's on me.

If my mother ever read this chapter, she'd be hurt despite the good things I've said about her. She'd be hurt because I was honest. If it were true, she didn't want to hear it. She was the type of person who saw *Disney* movies as reality. She decorated her houses to distract herself from the rotting walls. She knew about my father all those years. Yet, she chose to live in a lie. If she had accepted the truth, her dream of a happy family would've shattered. And it did in the end, but not in the tragic, damning way she had envisioned.

It wasn't until after the divorce that she got what she really wanted.

I'm not sure if she is still alive.

Sometimes I feel her. I see her in the flowers that bloom in the spring. I see her in strangers who wear her perfume. And I see her in my cooking—pastries and stews.

The last time I saw her was in New York. She's probably still there, worried sick about her kids. Or dead from trying to protect Nickel or Penny.

No, I refuse to think about that. Instead, I'm choosing to believe she is sitting by a lake, basking in the sun, and planting nice, pretty flowers.

40

Please, Cedi

*C*edi *deserves more than a chapter.*

She deserves more than the few times I've written about her. She was not a side character. She was a person. She had stories. Stories I could hear over and over. Stories that made me laugh and cry in one sitting. Stories of a complex, resilient woman navigating through a world built for straight, white men. I wish she had the chance to share her story.

I wonder if she went through with it. And if so, was it the right choice?

The first few days after the Bill was ratified, before cell towers were torn down, I received calls from everyone I've ever loved.

When my mother called, she was at a loss for words.

"I–I don't understand, Dime. What does this mean? I just… I don't get it."

Our call felt brief but lasted an hour. An hour of sitting in each other's confusion, anger, and silence.

"Please take care of yourself, Dime. I can't imagine this new regime lasting. It just can't. I love you."

The same day, I received a call from my sister Penny.

"Dime, you need to find a car, a train, a plane, whatever, and come to California ASAP! Bike if you must! People are rioting here, Dime. Courts are being overthrown. Officers are standing down. I don't think the Bill will last much longer, at least here anyway. That's why you need to come. The States, Dime, they're dividing!"

Then I got a call from Rupiah.

"What the actual fuck, Dime?! What in the hell is happening to this country?! Are we about to get fucking raped by wrinkly dicks? I've been hiding in my room. My parents are bringing me food. But I can't hide forever. I have a boyfriend. Does this mean we have to break up? Who the fuck thought of this idea? Did someone go, 'Hmm, I'm in power, but I'm not getting any pussy. How can I take advantage of my status and get the hottest, pinkest, youngest pussy on the market? Oh! Let me just draw up a bill!' Thank god I can pass as white. But my mother, she's so clearly Asian. What if I lose her? Or what if I lose you or Cedi? Fuck, fuck! Forget I said that! I don't wanna manifest that."

Rupiah always ranted like this.

"My parents are thinking of taking us into hiding," she continued. "We're a biracial family. We are targets! But we've been hearing stories about families getting caught and then prosecuted. Life sentences, enslavement, public hangings... It's like we're back in the olden days! Fuck the old, man. And the rich!"

I got another call. It was her. Cedi. She was terrified. I could tell by how shaky her voice was.

"I don't know what to d–do, Dime. Someone already asked me to be their companion. I said no because I–I didn't believe the news. The guy sent the Red after me. I hauled ass down Main Street. Fortunately, there were a lot of people out. It was easy to get away. Everyone was running home. Bodies were piling up on the streets. I–I was so close to being a body. I'm hunkering down in my apartment, but I'm running out of food for me and my cat. I don't know what to do. I'm all alone. I–I don't want to go back to that lifestyle anymore, Dime. I know you know what I mean. I feared for my life during those days! I feared being raped if I said no to a daddy. I feared contracting an STD. I feared being arrested for prostitution. I feared being homeless and broke. I feared moving back in with my abusive father. And now… now I'm scared again. Don't be mad, Dime, but I don't think I can live anymore. I know it was just an attempt before, but this time, I think I'll actually do it."

"No, Cedi, no!" I said. "This regime might not last a month. We have Allies! I'm sure they will come to our aid. Oppressive governments never last. We just have to wait until it's over. My sister says there are protests in California. The justice system is failing–"

"The justice system has always failed us, Dime! Don't you see? We're screwed! Us above everyone else. You know they're going to target queer people. That's all the One Percent have been talking about."

She wasn't wrong. For years, news outlets, streaming services, social media, and other forms of communication have given the wrong people platforms. Some did so because they agreed, while others wanted to initiate debate. Good intentions or not, this only amplified their voices and led to the spreading of misinformation, hateful rhetoric, prejudices, and public aggression.

"Regardless, Cedi, I–" I faltered, "I don't want you to die. I can't imagine a world without you. I need you. You make me happy. You make me laugh. You're the only person in my life who actually understands what I've been through. You're my best friend. I–I love you. Please."

I was scared. I was reminded of a similar conversation we had a couple years ago. I had almost lost her then.

She was diagnosed with bipolar II disorder and bulimia back in high school. She often felt depressed and thought she had no purpose in life. She was on mood stabilizers and antidepressants. She was highly paranoid and always thought people, including her friends, were making fun of her, even when we were hyping her up. The only thing that kept her moving in life was her art. She drew every day. She wasn't close to her family and didn't have many friends.

I don't know why, but something in me told me to message her that January day. We spoke over the phone, and she confided in me that, earlier that day, she had searched "how to properly kill yourself" on the internet.

I listened and listened and told her to call me if these thoughts ever returned. Doesn't matter what time or where I am, I will answer. And she did call me, every time.

"Please, Cedi, I don't want you to die," I repeated.

"I won't do it, I swear. I'm sorry, Dime. I'm just really scared."

Though it was her regular promise, something in her voice sounded different this time.

I considered calling Rupiah, who lived in the same state as Cedi, and asking her to be on suicide watch, but she was in hiding. I considered calling a psychiatric hospital, but Cedi would be vulnerable if she left her home. I didn't know what to do.

I kept her on the phone for as long as I could.

I called her the next morning, but she didn't answer. I called again that afternoon. And again that night. Every time, no answer.

The day after that, our phones were turned off.

41

Dead Man Walking

*T*hey followed me home," Y said one day.

I peeked over the balcony and saw Red officers walking away from the building.

"They're racists," said Y. "Black Elders don't receive the same respect as other Elders."

It was true. Black Elders have a more difficult time requesting a third Minor. They're usually only allowed two. If they're rich, then they could have a third.

I could also tell Y was treated differently. When he used to take me to the grocery store, the glares we received from others felt mostly homophobic. But sometimes, they felt racist. I know, I know. How does a glare feel racist? Or homophobic? I don't know. All I know is that when others weren't glaring at us for Y flaunting his male Minor, they were glaring at him for something else entirely.

Many Elders are queer.

Some of them are also Black.

Well, *were*. There are new methods of skin bleaching. While the methods are damaging, they make you look like you were born a different, more "tolerable" race. I know. It's fucked up.

The methods are so readily available that anyone can afford it.

Y loved his skin though. In fact, he called himself an Ebony King every day.

"Cooking for your Ebony King?" he'd say.

"Did you work out for your Ebony King today?"

"How about you wake up your Ebony King tomorrow with a blow job, ay?"

While I loathed being bossed around, I did find his racial pride charming and rare.

And the last time we were in a store together, he held my hand. I want to believe it was gay pride, but I know it wasn't. He did it only to tell the other Elders, "Back off, he's mine."

This was why the Red was following him. To be Black and gay during the years of the Divided made Y a dead man walking.

42

The One Percent

*I*t used to be said, *"If you love something, set it free. If it loves you, it'll come back."*

It was an overused saying, I remember. But it has now become obsolete.

Our Elders, men mostly, enjoy trapping their Rapunzels in glorious, lonely towers. They love to confine birds in gilded, blinding cages. But beneath the gilding is always rust.

I can't fight the cage. I can only dream. Dream of being free.

Free from Elders.

Free from debt, class, and servitude.

Free from the shackles of the Divided.

Free from hiding who I am.

That's what I want. I want to stretch my wings. I want to unlock that stupid cage and climb down that fucking tower.

But the thing is, I don't hate the Elders. They're forced into Elderhood just as much as we're forced into Minority. Granted, most of them get off on it.

Still, they're not the ones I hate. The ones I hate are the ones in charge. The Elders I know, they're not the One Percent. The One Percent are the ones who stabbed a stake into the political cracks of what had once been the United. The One Percent are the ones who passed the Bill.

They're the ones who must be overthrown.

43

Ancestors

They walked so we could run.

They were queer but grew up to fear themselves. If they were their true selves, they would have been met with bigotry, hatred, and violence. Under the Nazi Regime, they would have been persecuted and branded with the Pink Triangle. They would have been manhandled and arrested during the Stonewall Riots. They would have been refused healthcare and turned away from establishments during the AIDS Crisis. Before Title VII of the Civil Rights Act and the Fair Housing Act, they could've been fired and evicted based on race, religion, sex, citizenship, sexual orientation, gender identity, and any other branching social determinant.

They watched and fought as their histories were warped and erased and their narratives villainized.

I never learned any of this in school. I learned on my own and from my queer friends. Yet, there's still much I don't know. And it's hard to trust what is out there because histories are often altered to fit the perspectives of those telling them. There were and are many stories that have yet to be and may possibly never be told and written, stories that belong to real human beings, and stories that may never be allowed in schools or on television.

Our queer ancestors have gone through so much as a community at large and as individuals. As queer youth, we must appreciate what our predecessors went through to get us to where we are now. None of us want what they fought for to go to waste. So again, they walked so we could run.

But I am not writing to glorify our ancestors and make everything look pretty with change. That being said, nothing has changed at all, has it? We might not be walking, but we're still running.

For a little while, I did see change. Queer, complex characters— good, evil, and in between—were represented on television and in books. Queer, out-and-proud delegates took up government spaces. I remember Mauree Turner becoming the first out non-binary state legislator in United history. I saw more and more people come out of the closet. And it wasn't just forty-year-olds who were "old enough to know." Young adults were coming into themselves as well. Most queer people, including myself, know about their queer identity at an early, early age. Over time, with social and political progress, more and more younger people felt comfortable and safe enough to come out. Take me and my siblings, for example. My older brother Billie came out at age twenty-one. I came out when I was sixteen. My younger sister Penny didn't feel the need to come out. She just existed.

From what I had seen, the age of coming out decreased over time. Our voices were being heard, taught, and written. We were finally making progress, *were* being the operative word.

Despite all the representation, bigotry and guns continued to enter queer spaces like Pulse and Club Q. Trans and Black lives continued to be targeted. Performers and their drag continued to be banned. Parents continued to abandon their children. Bigots multiplied. Guns multiplied. And then, well, we regressed. People stayed in the closet, and some— those who could, like me—went back into the closet to survive the Ameriqueerocide.

It's just like before. We're branded. We're manhandled. And we're outcasts. History has once again become our present.

I miss being out.

Those years hold my life's truest, most cherished moments.

I want to say they were the happiest times of my life, I do. And in retrospect, especially with everything happening nowadays, they were objectively the happiest times of my life. But I can't truly mean that because it did not feel that way at the time. I was broke and homeless and selling my body just to get by. I lied to people I loved and daddies I despised. And I was foolish enough to believe those lies myself. I worked myself to the bone. I was focused too much on money, security, and freedom. I chose the wrong things over real love. I missed out on life and often forgot to stop and breathe.

But I'll never forget what it really meant to just be. To be my authentic, queer self. To find family in friends. To chase desire and passion. Those moments are snapshots in my mind, a treasure saved for rainy days.

I'm pissed. At a time with knowledge at the tips of our fingers, we never learned a goddamn thing.

44

Cubic Zirconia

*M*onroe. Lewinsky. Queen Anne Boleyn. Now Diamond.
She'll go down in history as the Minor who became a martyr for sluts.

When I think of Diamond, I ask myself, did she always enjoy being a slut? When I was a slut, I enjoyed it sometimes, I admit. It felt good to be desired and topped. But other times, I felt dirty and used. Did she ever feel the same?

On a more sociopolitical note, I also ask myself why I only see her as a slut? A red triangle? What else was she? Was she a lawyer in a past life? An artist? A sibling? As humans, we are all multifaceted. We have family, friends, jobs, hobbies, quirks, and scars. We have so many sides to ourselves, yet when we see someone perform a sexual act or hold themself in an erotic way, sex becomes the only facet we see in that person. We never actually get to know the person behind that floozy façade. We remember less about the person and more about their body.

When I think about Diamond, the Minors she illegally had sex with also come to mind. Were they ever punished? I saw them from my window. Most of them were young men. Like her, they were Minors—another Elder's "property." That meant they were whoring around as well. Yet, they weren't burnt at the stake like she was.

Slut-shaming is a misogynistic act. That's a no-brainer. Slut-shaming is also homophobic. If you're a bottom, you're seen as filthy. A "pig bottom" is the term. But I've met more tops who get around than bottoms. Yet, bottoms are the ones who are slut-shamed. No one says pig top. It's because bottoms are seen as more feminine than tops, which reflects misogyny.

Nowadays, if you're a full-blown slut, you share Diamond's fate. If you go through two Elders before Elderhood, you're branded. If you go through three Elders—say your first Elder dies from cancer, your second dies from a heart attack, and your third dies in a car accident—then you die. The Divided will have you killed. Not because they think you did it. Well, they might, depending on the situation. But they do it because any more than three, you're spoiled milk.

By Law, Minors can be purchased by three Elders at most. Not at the same time, of course. But I've seen Minors who are women being burnt after their second Elder, even though the Law swears they could have a third.

They pick and choose.

Over the years, I learned people's faces. It's only inevitable when you're naked around a firepit every Sunday. You learn bodies too, naturally. I saw pink triangles, red triangles, yellow stars, and other shapes and colors of which I am ignorant.

In addition to their bodies, I also learned which Minors belonged to which Elders and which Minors were already onto their second Elder or, if they're lucky, third.

This is how I learned that the institution of Minority was not only misogynistic and homophobic but also venustraphobic. I don't know if that's actually a word. But I noticed the more beautiful the Minor, the likelier they'd be deemed a slut.

There was this one chick who had a gorgeous face, giant knockers, and a tiny waist. She was burnt after her second Elder.

Another girl who was pretty yet unremarkable and not nearly as curvy went on to live with a third.

Nothing is equal in this country.

It never has been.

If Y dies before I reach Elderhood, I don't know if I'll get a third chance.

I look like a slut. I worked as a slut. I am a slut. But at the end of the day, I pass as a man in their eyes. And we live in a patriarchy. I have privileges women simply do not have. Yet, I don't know if I'll get lucky. Being queer will reduce my chances. Gay sex has always been seen as "revolting" and something to be ashamed of.

But isn't this what They want? Don't They want sluts? Minors They want to use and be used by for filthy, shameful acts?

After the public burning of Diamond, the slut movement was kindled.

The other sluts in town, including myself, wore diamond brooches in honor of her bravery. It must've taken a lot of courage to take that many dicks in the face of adversity.

The brooches were cubic zirconia, of course, but Diamond nevertheless.

Since Minors are forbidden to speak to one another, the brooches were a way for us to say to each other without exchanging words, *I am one of you, and you belong.*

I don't know who made or scattered the brooches. But the day after Diamond died, I found a brooch under a tree during one of my walks. When my walker wasn't looking, I slipped it into my pocket. Later, I looked closer at the brooch and saw it had an engraving that read, *For Diamond!*

At first, I thought it had belonged to Diamond or another Diamond and she or they had lost it. I thought it was pretty, so I kept it. It wasn't until I glimpsed other Minors wearing the same brooch in public that I understood this was an act of rebellion.

When the following Sunday rolled around, I went to Center City in my birthday suit to burn some books.

Several Minors had pinned their brooches to their skin. Blood ran down their chests.

The Red confiscated the brooches and dragged the Minors away. The rest of us were sent home and told not to leave our apartments.

My instincts told me to throw the brooch into Y's hidden room.

The Red must've worked out the meaning of the brooches. They went from apartment building to apartment building in search of rebels. Minors in possession of a brooch were collected, collared, and chained.

Of course, I didn't know what was happening. Y wasn't there to tell me. There was no announcement about the house searches. But I had intuited something was coming.

When they barged in, I got to my knees and held up my hands. They flipped tables and couch cushions, frisked me, and rummaged through drawers. Plants were uplifted. Clothes were thrown to the ground. Clocks and plates broke. They tore the place apart but never found the hidden room.

I got lucky.

I spent the evening cleaning when an announcement was broadcast across the city.

"The Red guards of every apartment building, please escort every Minor in your assigned building to Center City. *Immediately!*"

It had to be about the Minors who were caught. What was going to happen to them? Public whipping? Public raping? Public hanging? Were they going to be burnt at the stake like Diamond?

I joined my fellow tenants outside as if a fire alarm had gone off. The guard to my building did a head count and led us to the crowd outside City Hall.

Around thirty Minors had been collected, though I know I had seen more wearing the brooches. The Minors were on all fours, naked, and positioned on individual turntables. One-third were men, and the rest were women. Their ankles and wrists were cuffed to the turntables. Apples were jammed into their mouths like pigs. Several of them were crying from the humiliation.

The auctioneer walked on stage. He was in gray pajamas.

"This is not where I wanted to be my Sunday evening," he said into the microphone. "Alas, several of you Minors thought it'd be a good idea to wear brooches honoring a whore guilty of treason! Tut-tut-tut… Guards!"

Thirty Red guards walked on stage. They each stood behind a Minor, holding a dagger and a thick, blunt pole. Some of the guards were shaking, which was odd to see. They're normally more tolerant when they stand by.

The auctioneer passed a bowl of a white, chunky glop down the line of Red. "Coat your poles in a generous amount of lard," he ordered.

Each guard greased their poles with a fistful of pig fat.

I wanted to vomit. Several of the guards looked like they wanted to as well.

"Spin."

Each guard spun the turntable so the crowd could clearly see every Minor's anus.

"Now cut."

The guards then took the knife to the anus and cut down to the genitals. Blood leaked from their taints.

The crowd winced. Some had fainted.

The Minors on stage howled in pain and bit down into their apples. They must've been told to keep the apples in their mouths because the few who bit too far into the apple, causing it to fall, were whipped.

"Now the poles."

The guards lifted their greased poles and pushed them into the Minors.

"Anal impalement!" The auctioneer spoke loudly over the cries of the Minors. "This is the price you pay if caught aiding a resistance! These brooches–" He held out a handful of the fake diamonds. "They mean you're a whore, right? Well, if you're such a whore, then I'm sure you'll just love this!"

All thirty of the Minors had died that night.

Most died within the hour. Some lasted a few hours, bless their souls.

Some of the guards wanted it over with. They rammed their poles into their assigned Minors. Those were the guards who took mercy. I saw one guard mouth the words "I'm sorry" to their Minor and, while looking away, jammed the pole through their body in one swift motion.

Other guards slowly pushed their poles into their Minors, perhaps to avoid piercing any major organs right away. They were killing them slowly either to give the Minors time to regret their actions or simply because they enjoyed it.

The death of these thirty Minors would later be called Diamond's Piercing.

When the crowd was sent home, I went straight to Y's hidden room, grabbed my brooch, and chucked it over the balcony.

IV

Home

45

Maudlin

*T*he older I get, the more precious moments become.

Every sugardaddy.

Every Elder.

I've sold my body and risked my health.

I've been spat at, kicked at, and kicked out.

I've met adversity. I know her name and know her well.

Why do I believe heavy moments only exist for you to appreciate the light? Why must I know pain to cherish? Why must we let him pass?

Sugaring was my choice, the path I took. That is no one's fault but mine.

The Divided prevail.

And I sit here now, complicit, a scared little kid who can't even keep a brooch.

Once upon a time, I went to a candlelit string quartet with my friend Chavos.

Two violins, a viola, and a violoncello. They played thirteen Beyoncé songs from Destiny's Child to *Lemonade*. The transition between "1+1" and "XO" put us in our feels. Yes, the songs were slow in tempo, and the strings didn't help, but it was the moment that truly made us emotional. Sharing a beautiful and pure moment with my closest friend listening to our favorite music, music that made us feel belonged… It made me appreciate being alive in a big city with someone I love, doing unique things that persist in memory.

Even now, in the years of the Divided, I still try to find moments like these.

A fresh autumn breeze and yellowing leaves.

Light coming through the blinds and drowning the apartment in a golden haze.

The warmth of the Sunday fires on my cold, naked skin.

Y's music collection. Forbidden songs I've heard before and forgotten, and songs I've never heard but now know and love. A woman named Joni singing about clouds, and a man named Leon crooning about a river.

I even cherish the caring way Y holds me after sex. I always look for these moments. These small, precious moments.

46

Paper Bag Lunches

hen I was in junior high, I had a friend named Geld.
We were good childhood friends. Such good friends that I spent entire summers with her instead of spending time with my family. Her parents let me stay in the spare for months.

At school, she used to bring me lunch because she knew I wouldn't. I didn't have an eating disorder. I was just poor.

Once every three months, my parents would go to a warehouse club and stock up on groceries. Since there were six of us kids, those groceries went by in a blink. I'd have a paper bag lunch for a couple weeks. After that, I had nothing to bring until the next haul.

When we ran out of food, my siblings asked our mother for money. She gave them her waitressing tips. None of us asked our father for money. He always said the same thing. "What, do you think money grows on trees?!"

I was the only one who felt uncomfortable asking our mother for money. Perhaps they did feel uncomfortable, but that didn't stop them. It did me. A part of it was that I knew she didn't have a lot. I felt bad taking what she did have. The bigger reason was that I didn't like how she made me feel when I asked. She always huffed and puffed. I know now it wasn't personal. She was only sighing because she had no money for herself in the end. Of course, my child self took it as *oh, I am a burden.*

Eventually, I stopped asking her for things altogether. And she never offered.

I used to get annoyed that my siblings had no problem asking people for money. I wasn't annoyed with them. I was annoyed with myself. Why couldn't I be more like that? Just beg. That's all you have to do, Dime. Don't feel bad. Just beg.

But I never could.

So I missed out on a few lunches every now and then. Big deal. At least I had dinner waiting for me when I got home. Well, not always. If my mother worked late, we went to bed with bellies full of cereal. My father never cooked. My three oldest siblings were spoiled. My mother didn't start working until they were grown and out of the house. They always came home to food. The three youngest got the short end of the stick. So, I learned how to cook. They were simple meals, meals a fourteen-year-old could make for him and his siblings. Boxed pasta. Eggs. Ramen.

I also had Geld. I never asked her to bring me lunch. She just did.

She was in my French class. That's how we got to know each other. Most people took Spanish because it had a reputation for being an easy A. The French teacher was a strict old lady. No, not strict. Passionate. If you didn't do your homework, she'd shout, "INSUBORDINATION: the refusal to follow a reasonable request!" Verbatim.

Most people dropped the class. Geld and I stayed. The class went from thirty to six overnight.

We first bonded over schoolwork. We were cool kids, obviously. Her mother was a teacher. I used books as an escape. Our shared passion for learning then evolved into a shared interest in shows and music. She brought me to my first *Nutcracker*.

When I moved to Connecticut, she drove from New York to spend time with me. It wasn't a far drive, only two to three hours. But that's forever in teenage years.

Everything changed after I came out of the closet. She wasn't homophobic. In fact, we had a mutual friend who was also queer. When he came out, she was nothing but supportive.

When I came out, it was different. Yes, I was in another state, starting a new life at a new school. But nothing between us had really changed. She was my confidant, someone I talked to every day.

It wasn't until I came out that I saw and heard from her less and less. You see, she had a crush on me. A big one. She told me. She didn't need to. I knew.

She wanted something more, something I couldn't give her. So, she discarded me.

Are friendships supposed to have some degree of sexual attraction? She made me believe so.

Though our friendship faded, my love for her never did, and it never will. At least for that version of her.

I don't care that she walked away. I wouldn't even care if the roles were reversed. I could never, ever, forget those paper bag lunches.

47

Daddy Issues

The father complex is defined as a group of unconscious associations pertaining to the archetype of the father.

The complex usually develops in a child who has a poor relationship with their father. That child then grows up and seeks validation, love, and support in romantic relationships with men who are usually older. I'm not a psychologist, and not every experience is the same, so I won't go too deep.

But shouldn't we seek and receive validation, love, and support for our relationships to be healthy? If so, why does this complex have a negative connotation? Is it because of the age gap? Is the term "daddy issues" inherently ageist? Why is it bad to date someone older than you, assuming you are of age?

When I first started dating and having sex with older men, I thought my attraction toward older men resulted from my unresolved daddy issues. But the older I got, and after I resolved those issues and forgave my father, nothing changed. I was still attracted to older men.

In most cultures, fathers represent a sense of security. Personally, I found validation, love, and emotional security in myself and my chosen family. It was the financial security I never received from anyone.

Fathers are expected to be the breadwinners, the ones who put a roof over their family's heads. Why is this expectation put only on them? The answer is simple: the patriarchy. Men have the most job security. Men earn more than women, at least in this country. I can't help but wonder if women were paid equally and had as many job opportunities as men, would the financial expectation be shared? Would the father archetype instead be referred to as the parental archetype? And the father complex, the parental complex?

And if you think deeper about the father complex, you realize we only ever talk about the complex from the "child's" perspective. What about the "father's" perspective? Why do these old men adopt the father role? Perhaps they have daddy issues themselves, sure. Or control issues. But from my experience with older men, they know about the patriarchy. They are aware of their power and privilege and take advantage of it.

That's why the patriarchy will—unfortunately—always exist. They'll never want to relinquish that power. That's why and how the Divided came to be.

48

D.O.B.

I have always loathed birthdays.

Mine, yes. But everyone else's as well. Expectations get too high. People scramble for plans. Disappointment is inevitable.

My distant family usually gets together for Thanksgiving. Apart from my siblings and mother, only one or two relatives remember that my birthday falls on or around the holiday. I'm more than fine with that. I don't care for attention from people I am not close with. But I can't lie and say it doesn't hurt to be forgotten.

Most people don't like their birthdays because they fear getting old. I don't mind getting old, honestly. I faced a lifetime of adversity when I was a child. I would never want to go back.

Despite everything I am enduring and have endured, I still see life as an uphill climb. Yeah, I was homeless, but at least I was no longer living in a house where my very being was hated. Yeah, I sold my body to dirty, old men, but at least I had groceries. And yeah, I am a Minor, but one day I won't be. While some things get worse, other things get better.

The only thing about getting old that scares me is life passing me by. All I've ever done with my life is struggle. I've struggled with getting jobs, making money, and paying bills. The only times I've traveled have been either through my school or with sugardaddies. Now I'm a Minor, a body, a burden. I should be traveling the world. I should be able to afford rent and groceries on my own. Apart from graduating college, which was just paying an institution hundreds of thousands of dollars for a piece of paper, I haven't done anything substantial with my life. And I'm afraid I never will.

Anyway, birthdays… I've never had a remarkable one. I never try to. It's because of that one birthday I had in Virginia.

I was six and timid. "Nonverbal" was the word my school used. I was in a special speech class. Everyone always asked my mother, "Is something wrong with him?"

I didn't have many friends then. I had a neighbor I was close with. He was a couple years my senior and talked a lot, which worked well with my nonverbal behavior.

It was the night before my birthday. We made a tipi in his backyard with branches and a bed sheet. When it was finished, we slept outside.

Sometime in the night, I woke up to a hand going down my belly.

"Don't worry," he said. "My cousin showed me this."

I sat there, frozen. I had no clue what was happening. I don't think he did either.

For a long while, I had forgotten that memory. It wasn't until I started journaling that I understood what had happened. Though it took years for me to unpack the memory, my body always remembered how powerless it felt.

Interesting, isn't it? How our minds might not recall the details, but our bodies do?

Nowadays, I never exactly know when my birthday is. We're not allowed calendars. Why would a Minor need one? That's why none of these diary entries are dated. I can try to calculate the date based on the issue date of *The Monthly*, assuming we receive the pamphlet the day it's issued. But I don't trust that damn pamphlet.

I can sense when my birthday's approaching. When leaves turn red and fall to the ground, I know it is near.

My last birthday before the Bill was a peaceful one, surprisingly. I called off work and made it a me day. I woke up, made breakfast, went to my favorite café, ordered a couple cappuccinos, and read. I read the whole damn day in that café until the barista told me they were closing shop. Walking along the river, I watched the sun set over the Philadelphia skyline. And I spent the evening eating a home-cooked meal and reading some more.

While it wasn't a particularly remarkable birthday, it certainly was a perfect one.

I think my birthday is next week?

I'm not sure. Doesn't matter. Won't be remarkable anyway.

49

Robbed, Conned, & Grifted

I have been betrayed by three friends in my lifetime, and all three betrayed me for the same reason: Money.

It's always fucking money.

First was Griften. She and I became good friends in middle school. She lived down the street. We hung out every day and stayed friends when my family moved to Connecticut. Our friendship grew and grew well over a decade, throughout college and afterward. Yes, we had ups and downs like any friendship, but I truly thought nothing would get between us.

I was naïve.

See, what had happened was she was also friends with my sister Penny. Penny was sleeping on Griften's couch at the time. Griften decided to break her lease to get a bigger apartment, one with Penny on the lease. Months into living together, Griften never paid the early termination fee on her previous lease. She expected my sister to pay half the fee. Penny wasn't on that lease and never made that promise. Griften felt that because she let my sister sleep on her couch, she had the right to ask her to pay half the fee.

The whole situation reminded me of stories about people who help other people under the guise of selflessness but expect the other people to do something for them in exchange. Griften was like that—selfish.

She called me one day and told me to tell my sister to pay her. Instead, I sent her a third of what Penny "owed." I would've given her the full amount if I had that kind of money. Penny is my sister, after all. I wanted to help in any way possible.

Then Penny told me her side of the story.

I've known Penny since birth and Griften since middle school. I knew them well. More to the point, I knew when they were lying. And from the two calls, I knew Griften was being greedy.

I like money too. But to let money get in the way of a decade-long friendship is some dumb shit. Do I really want to be friends with someone like my father?

… I never heard from her again.

Then there was Connie.

Connie and I became friends in college. Though she had transferred, we stayed friends for half a decade and traveled together to Italy and Hong Kong. We had good memories. I don't know why she did what she did.

One day, I checked my inbox and saw her mother had emailed me saying that ten grand had been taken out of her personal account. She said Connie had sent me this money "with trust and an open heart" and that she expected me to return the missing funds by morning. The email was a threat.

None of this actually happened. Connie was using me as a scapegoat.

Connie called me the next day. Apparently, she had a sugarmama who promised to deposit money into her account if she provided her banking information. Rookie mistake.

She said she told her mother the truth, and her mother apologized to me. Connie never did. I didn't mind that she never apologized. I didn't even mind that she blamed me. But she could've given me a heads-up. When I read that email, I was scared. Was I about to get sued? Taken to court?

They were a filthy rich family. The mother was the CFO of a major insurance company, and the father was a trust fund baby and engineer. Connie wasn't like most sugarbabies. Most sugarbabies sugar because they need to. Connie didn't need the sugar. Her parents paid for her college, rent, and credit card. She sugared because she liked it. She liked the dirtiness, the sex work, the price tag on her body, the discretion, lies, and risk… She liked it all.

I should've taken that as a sign.

Here was another person in my life who did not care about my well-being. She used me like I was only a body and burned a bridge for what?! For money.

… I never heard from her again.

Last was Robbie.

I knew her the least. We became friends when we studied abroad together. After college, we wanted to travel again. She devised an itinerary and asked me to send her money for all the bookings. I sent her two hundred dollars.

You see, she was a single mother to one. I'm unsure what her situation was, but times must've been tough. Tough enough to steal a measly two hundred bucks from a friend.

So yeah, you guessed it… I never heard from her again.

This chapter is not to obtain pity or to call these greedy bitches out. Okay, maybe a little. But it's more so calling attention to money and its control over people.

I know I am not innocent. I was a sugarbaby, for fuck's sake. I used daddies left and right. But I never used friends or family, only strangers.

I pick friends like apples, and only the best become family.

Why did I let these bitches into my life? I thought I had a better judgment of character than that.

Then again, no matter how great your judgment of character may be or how well you think you know a person, whether they're family or friends, people will always use you.

You are either a wallet or a body.

50

Little Rebellions

*O**ne night, the devil visited me in a dream.*

He was wearing gray, and his face was blurred. He tied me to a post outside in the cold and let X, Y, and every daddy I've ever had rape me. I woke up shivering.

I tend to have a lot of nightmares. I always have. When I lived with my family, I went to Goldie for comfort. When I lived alone, I watched drag queens on YouTube until I fell asleep. When I lived with my sugardaddies, I snuggled them. And with my Elders, it is the same. Despite Y's character, I still find comfort in his embrace. I know, it's fucked up.

But on this night, Y wasn't home to soothe me. I went to his hidden room and tried listening to music, but it didn't help. The nightmare was too real. I needed to see another face, another human.

So, against my better judgment, I crept out of the apartment and knocked on her door.

No answer.

I knocked repeatedly until the door opened to a disheveled mop of red hair.

"What is it?!"

"I–I'm sorry." It was the first time we had spoken since she had brought me cookies. "I–I had a nightmare."

"… And your solution was to wake up a total stranger at three in the morning? I thought there was a fucking fire!"

"I know, I know. I'm sorry. This is incredibly rude of me. And I–I know I shouldn't be here. I don't know why I came to you. I just needed to see a face. My Elder's not home, and I know yours isn't either."

She crossed her arms. "How do you know that?"

"When I came back from my walk today, I heard your Elder say he won't see you for a few days."

"You eavesdropped?"

"No. I mean, yes. But accidentally. I was getting out of the elevator when he was saying goodbye to you. That's all."

She said nothing.

"I should go. I–I'm sorry for waking you."

"Well, I'm up now." She tightened her robe. "Come in."

Her apartment looked exactly like mine. Same furniture, same decor, same everything.

"Would you like some ginger tea? It's caffeine-free."

"That would be nice. Thank you."

As we waited for the water to boil, we sat on her couch—my couch—and talked.

"What was your dream about?"

I didn't want to answer.

"… rape."

She nodded. "I've had those."

"Yeah?" I looked around, disinterested. "We have the same apartment, you know."

"Do we now? How odd."

"Why isn't your Elder here?"

"Work trip."

"Same."

Silence.

"Thanks for the cookies, by the way. My Elder loved them."

"Did you tell him I made 'em?"

"No."

Two tired strangers chatting at three a.m. unsurprisingly made stiff conversation.

Her kettle began to whistle.

"Since you're here," she said, shutting off the stove, "from one Minor to another, how are you? Like, really, how are you?"

"I'm okay."

Her gaze told me she wasn't just making conversation.

"The Elder I have now," I added, "is better than the one I had before. He's still not the best though."

"I hear ya. My Elder is so fragile he takes it out on me just to make himself feel powerful." She lifted her shirt, and along her rib cage were bruises, yellow and blotchy.

We went on like this for a bit. We talked about our Elders, who they were, what they did to us, and what they offered. Though she seemed trustworthy, I didn't tell her about Y's hidden room. Some things you don't tell people, especially things that could be taken from you.

"So, what do you think about the Law?" she asked.

"I hate it, of course. Doesn't everyone?"

"Not those who benefit from it." She sipped her tea. "Have you heard that some of the States are still United on the West Coast? And that the Law is banned over there?"

"My sister told me something like that before our phones were cut out. I want to believe it, truly. But people cling to hope like children with imaginary friends."

"Believe it, babe. I know some people. They've told me Oregon and California have aircrafts that pick up groups of Minors from all over the Divided every month and fly them to sanctuary. Elders who were once Minors are hiding pick-up locations and times of departure in *The Monthly*."

She passed me the news pamphlet.

"I never read that junk. It's all fabrication, isn't it?"

Her copy of *The Monthly* was covered in ink. She must've found a pen somewhere, or her Elder must've bought her one on the black market.

"True, but look closely at the letters I circled."

It was a paragraph about Norway and how their prison system was collapsing—a lie.

"You just circled a bunch of letters. Do they add up to a word or something?"

"Yes, but look closer at those letters. Do you see anything different about them?"

I brought the paper closer. Nothing particularly stood out to me. Nothing until I noticed an "i" here was slightly different from an "i" there. Several letters were of a slightly different font from the rest. You would only notice if you had extremely keen eyes. I wouldn't have noticed if Tether hadn't circled them.

On the back of the pamphlet, she had added the letters together.

frickparkpittsburghoctoberthirdfouram

It was gibberish.

Below, she had separated the words into their true meaning.

It read:

Frick Park, Pittsburgh, October 3rd, 4 am.

"We missed it." She frowned. "We would've never made it from here anyway. Don't worry. They'll have other pick-ups. They go all over the Divided, right under Their noses. Last month's pick-up was just outside Miami. And the month before, there were two pick-up locations: Newport and Savannah."

"How do the aircrafts go unnoticed?"

"They have anti-radar technology that keeps their location off other planes' radars and collision avoidance systems. The planes themselves are also made of titanium shells the color of nightshade. It gives the illusion of invisibility. That's what I've heard anyway. I don't know all the details, but I've heard they're super quick, in and out. You have to be there on the dot, or else you just might miss it."

She scratched her neck, and I caught a flash of her red triangle.

"Random question," I said. "Why were you branded? I know the red triangle is the symbol of a slut, but I'm a slut and haven't been branded with it. Why you?"

"My Elder caught me having sex with my previous neighbor. That's why we moved into this apartment. I was indicted for infidelity. Thankfully, I wasn't burnt at the stake like Diamond."

As she dished out more tea, I noticed hair under her arms.

"Aren't you afraid you'll be whipped for that?"

"For what?"

"Your armpit hair."

"Oh, that." She smiled. "I call it *my little rebellion*. Since I don't have any guns or tear gas to fight back, this is my way of rebelling. That, and having sex with a neighbor. She actually made me cum, unlike my Elder.

"He gets livid about my pits, but I don't care. He has no real power."

I didn't say this, but I disagreed. Y absolutely had power—power over me. He could get rid of me with a simple press of a button.

"It's the Divided I'm rebelling against," she continued. "I'm surprised the Red haven't noticed my pits during the Sunday rituals when we're all bare-ass naked. Naked," she laughed at the word. "That word has no weight anymore. Are we naked, or are we just… Minors?"

"There are a lot of words like that, words that have become obsolete since the Bill. Like romance. Nobody knows what romance is anymore."

"Or justice."

We both laughed even though it wasn't funny at all.

"So uh, do you–" I faltered. "Do you really believe the West Coast is saving Minors?"

She nodded and smiled.

And for the first time in a long while, I actually felt—what was it called?—ah yes, hope.

51

Body Positivity

I turn myself on, I admit.

The curve of my hips. My smooth, long legs and bubbly butt. My lacquered, olive skin. My biceps, thighs, and abs. My six-inch cut dick. My pretty face, eyes, and hair. I love every part of me and relish at the sight of myself in the mirror—most of the time.

I thoroughly enjoyed curating my profile on Shopping because it was an act of selling myself, my body, and my words. I used to take photos of myself naked or in slutty garments and use those photos not only to seduce older men but also to jerk off to.

Most will call it narcissism. Others will call it autosexuality. And very few will call it self-love and body positivity. Why not love the body you're in?

It's quite disturbing, isn't it? To be sexually attracted to oneself? Everyone is always perturbed at the thought or at least feigns perturbation.

Yet, no one acknowledges the power of autosexuality. It fills you with self-esteem and eliminates insecurities. It can get you what you want, at the cost of dignity and taste.

Sometimes, I wish I had turned to porn, not college.

I graduated from… Well, who cares? There's no way my college would be proud of me, especially after reading such vulgarity. Besides, I only went there because they gave me the most money. Not real money. More of a discount. They call them scholarships.

While I believe I'm smart, I know I am also attractive. When you're both, people focus on the latter. In their eyes, I'm a whore and nothing more.

They're not wrong about the whore part.

In a society where people do not hold back their opinions, I hear their words and replay them repeatedly in my mind. I believe them to an extent. I'm not intelligent in the literal sense of the word. Am I emotionally intelligent? Yes. I am creative and intuitive and possess common sense. But actual genius? No.

I could never change the world, save lives, or become something impressive and admirable.

So yeah, I find what others say about me true. They must be right. The only good money I've ever made in my life has been from my body, not my brains.

Daddy Four

Not all sugardaddies on Shopping are pedophilic geezers like One or arrogant assholes like Two.

Most of them are, yes. But not all. Some can be nice, genuine, and morally grounded. I believe you could even fall in love with a sugardaddy, and they could fall in love with you in return.

A year before the Bill, I attended a wedding between my friend and her sugardaddy. I could see that they were truly in love despite their age gap and financial differences. That, or they were great actors.

Four was the first of the two sugardaddies I ever loved. I was ashamed to be seen with him though. The shame never vanished, no matter how much I grew to love him. The more I got to know him, the more I cared for him, so it goes.

Four lived in Boston. I had daddies in different area codes to entertain my flight response, to escape one temporary home for another. One was in D.C. Three was in Delaware. Two in New York. Five in Albany. Six and Seven in Rome. I had a French professor in Reims and a few daddies in L.A. and New Jersey, but nothing ever became of those.

Four was in his fifties and worked as a psychiatric nurse. We were an active couple. We ran along the Harbor and frequented the gay gym together. We skied nearly every mountain on the East Coast. He once brought me to the Palisades in Tahoe, which was the most stereotypical sugardaddy expenditure a daddy ever made for me.

Before I met him, he was not a fit guy. In queer culture, we'd call him an otter—hairy, medium height, and thick. I didn't care much about his appearance, to be honest. I didn't care about any of their appearances, really. All that mattered to me was that they were sugardaddies. They would never meet my friends or family, so why would it matter?

Whether it was ageism or fatphobia, I was not physically attracted to Four or any of my other daddies, for that matter. And that was okay. You can't force attraction. What I did find attractive, though, was having sex with dirty men. I can't feel bad about saying that because they *were* dirty. They were cheating on their wives. They were using my underage-looking ass to fulfill their pedophilic, paternal fantasies. They were lying and stealing and boasting and purchasing glorified hookers. How much can you really sympathize with men who do this?

I lived with Four for a few months during the COVID epidemic.

He was a little too obsessed with my physique and wanted it for himself. He soon acclimated himself to my workout routine, though I never asked him to join me on my runs or to the gym. His imitation was flattering, of course. But he was too codependent, and I was too selfish.

My workouts are a time for me to get lost in my mind, my alone time. But he wanted to do everything with me. When I went for runs, he got mad that I went without him. When we ran together, I inevitably ran ahead of him. I had longer legs and had been running since junior high. And so, he got upset that I didn't jog next to him. When I did jog next to him, he got upset that I was listening to music and not talking to him. People who don't listen to music when they work out are maniacs. "If you're talking, you're not running," my couch always said.

Nowadays, I bring the exercise bike and dumbbells in from the balcony, close the drapes, and work out to Y's vinyl collection. It reminds me of the good old days when we had the freedom to bump.

When I lived with X, I had to work out without music. I also had to use the communal gym with all the other Minors in the same apartment building. Since we couldn't speak to one another, we just worked out in the same space in total awkward silence, letting our minds go to waste.

Four was as kind and generous as he was insecure and needy.

I'm a sucker for nice guys.

While he paid for our groceries and took me to the Palisades—a luxurious vacation only people like him can afford—he never actually sugared me with money.

I didn't become a sugarbaby to do rich people things like ski at the top resorts. Those were just bonuses.

One day, when he was trying to plan a couple's trip to Barcelona, I said, "I appreciate that you want to spoil me. I do. It's just this isn't why I became a sugarbaby."

I explained my situation for the umpteenth time—how I didn't have a cosigner to refinance my loans, how my parents never helped, how private loans expect you to pay more than you make.

He didn't believe my motives. "I'm not that type of sugardaddy," he said. "You can stay under my roof and join me on my travels, but I don't give handouts. When I gave handouts in the past, those boys went off and bought drugs and shot up. I don't want that for you."

I don't know where he got this idea that I do drugs. The worst I've done is smoke a joint. I barely like alcohol.

Though Three and Four never paid for my company, I knew daddies like Two and One would. So, I kept my profile up on Shopping.

I also kept Four around. I enjoyed skiing and traveling. But I could tell he wanted someone to love. So yeah, I strung him along.

We did things people in love would do. We went to Sugarloaf Ski Resort and stayed in a lodge with a romantic fireplace. I met his best friends from college. I cooked dinner for him. We spent Christmas together at Cliff House in Maine and got a couple's massage. We opened up to each other about our pasts. We were close.

Our sex was better than the sex I had with One, Two, and Three combined. It wasn't amazing sex, but it was definitely better. We were both vers, so we knew how to make each other feel good. I didn't like topping him. He had a flat ass. I prefer bubbly or muscular butts like mine.

As a sugarbaby, you do whatever your daddy wants in the bedroom. Of course, you have your boundaries.

I definitely wouldn't say I'm vanilla in the bedroom. I like it rough. I like leather, lace, and muscle worship. I enjoy role playing and being pounded and choked a bit. But what I like the most is passion. The more sensual, the better. I rarely got that with sugardaddies. They were always into some freaky shit.

Four was into fisting. I am not.

I never shamed him for liking it. I'm all for sexual exploration and pleasure. We all should be. But my eyes always bulged when he handed me toys the size of my arm. The first time he asked me to fist him, I had a slight existential crisis. Granted, I was blazed. Watching a giant arm-shaped toy go into this little man didn't make sense to me. It was a frightening and mind-boggling sight. But I rolled up my sleeves and got the job done.

It was a lot of work for someone not being sugared.

Whether it was his codependency, financial noncompliance, or intense sexual activities, I, one day, packed up my things and left.

I told him I'd come back, but I never did.

I had that daddy in Albany. Maybe he'd give me what I wanted and what I thought I needed.

I don't know why I stayed with Four for as long as I did. Yes, I cared for him. But I wasn't looking for a future with someone. I was looking to make easy money.

I guess I thought that if I stayed with him long enough, he would fall for me and eventually offer to help pay off some of my loans. While he did fall for me, the latter never happened.

I should've been kinder and left him sooner because, in the end, all I did was break his heart.

52

Intrusive Thoughts

*S*ince *the day I was thrown out, life became less about who I was or what I loved and more about financial security.*

How will I afford life? How will I buy groceries? Where will I be sleeping tonight? All that mattered to me was that I was making money, staying alive, and paying off debt in whatever way possible. Sad, I know.

I grew to be cynical and distrustful. Romance became a fantasy novel and love a lie.

I pretended when I said I love you. I pretended I found bellies sexy. I pretended old, smelly men were my type. I pretended size didn't matter.

I faked a lot of shit, and I hate myself for it. I hate how shallow I am. I hate how I chase after the wrong things. I hate that I went to college.

I lost myself in the rich, bewitching whiffs of sugar. I lost myself in comfortable walks and knock-off shoes. I wandered in the streets for far too long and found myself somewhere I never wanted to be.

I became numb to positive thoughts. I convinced myself that no one would go out of their way to check on me or help me unless I had something else to offer. And I was right.

People said they'd be there for me. But I learned those are just words. When the time came for me to ask for help, times for them became busy and tight.

Unreliability is a quality in all people, myself included.

I learned to care for myself and only myself. Love is a fickle thing. In the end, nothing truly matters.

Perhaps one day, someone will come along and check on me. They'll help bandage my wound and sew up that tear in my shirt. They'll make my favorite meal and play my favorite song. One day, just maybe.

Those people are made from the stuff of dreams.

Every day, I think of home and how I'll never have it.

When I do have a home, I fear losing it. I fear that the home was never mine to begin with. And above all, I fear having to sugar again.

At age ten, I learned that you could have a lovely home and a lovely job, but if you fail at your work, then that home could be taken away from you at any moment. The government will not care if you have six kids. Everything could be taken.

At age sixteen, I learned that people who love you, or at least say they love you, could throw you out at any moment. Simply being yourself could be a reason for hatred. I learned that conditions in love are a reality, and that love is never a sure thing.

In my twenties, while I could not afford a home, I learned I could sell my body to have temporary ones. Everywhere I've lived has been a temporary home. These homes always belonged to someone else, no matter how close I got to that person.

In my mind, I'll always be homeless and poor.

I don't know what home means. When I tell people that, they say the same bullshit, "Home is where the heart is." Blah blah, shut the fuck up.

My heart is in my body. People are convinced that home is cozy and warm. If that is true, then why are the streets so damn cold?

I want to understand, but I can't.

I hope one day I find it—that meaning of home.

53

Three Jobs

*D*id you know you could be sued if you don't pay your student loans? Not always, and not at first, but it could happen.

At first, you start accruing late fees. After your first late fee, you are considered a delinquent and henceforth bookmarked. If they are federal loans, the government could and would withhold your tax refund. Private lenders could and would claim a fourth of your disposable income. And after months of missing payments—for whatever reason, say a recession, maybe?—your loans will go into default. That basically means you'd be fucked. You could lose financial aid, like scholarships, grants, and loans, preventing you from returning to school. Your credit score will plummet. You won't be able to take out a mortgage. Landlords will turn you away. Forget having a home. Oh, and if you have a job that you must drive to, forget it. The car you have, consider it repossessed.

Then, the lawsuits roll in.

Of course, there are loan forgiveness and payment plans and the option to refinance your loans. But loan forgiveness plans depend on the job you have and take a decade to obtain. So that doesn't help in the short term. Payment plans depend on the lender. If you have a private lender, there are no payment plans. That leaves you with the option to refinance your loans, and you do that by taking out another loan with a lower interest rate to pay for the other loans. But you need a cosigner to do that.

The only cosigner I had was my mother. There was no one else I could go to for something so grand. But after the divorce, my mother had very little money. Her co-signature meant nothing. She was making a waitress's income. When I tried refinancing, I was rejected and rejected and rejected. So yeah, I was pretty fucked.

The whole system is created to work against you.

Of course, it doesn't matter now. Elders are obligated to pay our bills. It makes up for all the disgusting things They do to us, right?

Since I was sixteen, I've had to juggle two or three jobs at a time.

In high school, I was a butcher, a server, and a dishwasher. I was paid under the table for all three. I continued to work all throughout college despite the plethora of scholarships I received. I was a French tutor, a movie store clerk, and a server. After college, I began my big boy job in an office but needed additional income. So, I worked as a barista on the weekends. It was still not enough. Not because I'm bougie and had a booming social life, but because I was still not making ends meet. Shocker.

So, I picked up a third job. I became a sugarbaby. Instead of a few extra bucks, it was a few extra grand.

54

Never Bite Feeding Hands

*S*ugaring—*in some twisted, self-debasing way—saved my life.*
I slept with dirty, old men because then at least I had a place to sleep.

I can't entirely detest what I did because it was there for me when nothing and no one else was.

Despite their infidelities, apathies, and daddy complexes, some of the daddies I met were troubled guys who helped me along the way. Their infidelities were upfront and honest. They were aware of their actions and behaviors. Though they had motives, they helped a young person survive.

I must be grateful for that.

I feel like a hypocrite.

In several parts of this diary, I've said I hated my daddies. In other parts, I've said I cared for them. Loved them?

I don't know how to feel or what to believe. Am I falling for my lies? Or have I always just wanted money?

55

Coach

I'm applying for a teaching position," Y said to me one day. "The private school on South Street needs a gym teacher. They don't have a basketball team either. I could start one. You know, for the kids. I don't need the job per se. A former NBA player and you're set for life. But I wouldn't mind doing something in my spare time. All I have now are you and–" The silence meant his wife and two other Minors. "Anyway, I just think it would be fun."

His words were sweet, but his eyes… they said something else.

"Go for it," I encouraged. "I'm sure the kids would love to have a former NBA player as their coach."

"Yeah, but the problem is it'd be a whole day thing. I'd have a lot of kids to teach. And basketball practice wouldn't be until after school hours."

I didn't ask how many kids, but I would've thought it'd be less than "a lot." After the Bill, the population in the Divided decreased immensely. Most Minors, if not all of us, didn't want kids for obvious reasons.

Minors assigned female at birth sought pills on the black market. And if they couldn't get their hands on pills, there were other methods. Though they were dangerous, they were necessary.

It's because of the Handmaid's Act. When the Divided noticed the decrease in births, They forced all Minors assigned female at birth to give birth to at least two children. If they were infertile, their Elder had to report the Minor and decide whether to off them or let them live.

Most Minors assigned male at birth did not have children since their Elders assigned female at birth could no longer bear children. On occasion though, a male Minor would sire a child or two. Those children would be taken to grooming camps.

Childhoods were stolen. Men never learned to be fathers. And women either had children or died.

V

Siblings

56

Least Favorite

y parents accepted three out of six of us kids.
Bless their hearts. They tried so hard.
The other three, well, we were queer. Eventually, they learned to tolerate us. I was the most difficult to tolerate. I didn't make myself smaller or hold back my opinions. I stood up for myself, my friends, and what I believed in, whether it was a losing fight or not. In my parents' eyes, I made it difficult for them to accept me.

"He's not my child," my father told my mother. "No child of mine would wear that shit. I know you cheated."

At the time, I thought I was difficult to love. I know now that some people just have difficulty loving.

Once, when I was living in New York, I went to dinner with my mother.

"Am I the least favorite?" I asked her.

I am not sure why I asked. I already knew the answer. It was obvious in their actions. My parents attended my siblings' sporting events, not mine. They gave all five of my siblings cars for their sixteenth birthdays, not me. Each of them was taught how to drive. I learned through YouTube. My mother also themed each of our rooms when we were infants. Mine was biblical-themed. Barf, I know. But the themes evolved as we became adolescents and teenagers with particular interests. Silv's room was airplane-themed. Nickel's room was baseball-themed. Penny's was beach-themed. I never evolved in their eyes. So, I was displaced wherever there was room.

A part of me wanted her to say, "No, of course not! I don't pick favorites. You're all my favorites."

But she didn't say that.

Instead, she said, "Well, Dime, you kind of made yourself the least favorite. You never made either of us feel particularly needed."

I wasn't hurt. Okay, maybe a little. But she wasn't wrong. I know it feels good to be needed, but I found it difficult to need someone on whom I could rarely rely.

My siblings also wanted their attention. I never cared for it. I had vastly different and more liberal opinions than both of my parents. Of course, I didn't want their attention. Why would I want attention from people whose social opinions and political beliefs I refuse to tolerate?

Since there were so many of us kids, it was easy for me to be left alone. I preferred it that way. Eventually, I got used to being forgotten. I was so out of mind I forgot the appeal of being remembered. So, instead of showing that I needed my parents, I grew to need independence.

57

The Wall

*I*n college, I was in a scholarship program that worked directly with refugees and asylum seekers.

We helped them apply for jobs and translate their résumés. We connected with local and out-of-state refugee organizations. We went to Tucson, Arizona, and Nogales, Mexico, and met with people detained for illegally crossing the border. The detainees told us their stories.

An Italian family of five—two parents and three children—fled religious persecution.

A fifteen-year-old girl fled because she had been raped and held hostage by a gang.

And a twelve-year-old gay and trans boy fled due to the rise of violence toward the queer community. His mother had told him to run.

Their stories were heart-wrenching, the type to spur change and ignite a flame within a person, an activist.

That's exactly what happened too. Several of my peers in the program went on to do amazing work. One moved to upstate New York after college and taught English to middle-aged refugees. Another one volunteered for the Peace Corps. And another continued their education in social justice and law reform and became a civil rights attorney.

The experience affected everyone. Everyone but me.

If anything, I just became more selfish.

I never did anything with that experience. And I'm selfish now for thinking that such an experience should change me.

Did their stories sadden me? Sure.

Did I feel better about myself after the experience? No.

Did I want to change the world? I think I did. I thought I could. But I didn't want it enough.

There were plenty of other things I wanted more. Much, much more.

58

Grand Central Station

*A*s non-binary *people, we endure a lot of bullshit.*
Apart from the genocide and all, we endure obstinacy, specifically an unwillingness to learn.

Take my father, for example. He threw me out because I wore dresses. His reasoning for throwing me out was deeply rooted in queerphobia, an obstinacy to change one's mind about a community of people that happens to include his child.

I tolerate identifiers like boy, son, brother, and uncle. But those words could easily be swapped with person, child, sibling, and… well, there's no gender-neutral option for uncle, is there? Therein lies the issue. With language, especially the English language, we often simplify what we're trying to say. When we become so accustomed to verbal simplification, we also become uncomfortable and resistant to changes in speech. It's human nature to prefer comfort because it offers a sense of security, oftentimes, a false sense of security. We'd much rather think on the fly than take time and effort digging into our puny human brains for a more suitable word.

As someone who knows other languages and has felt linguistically uncomfortable and even incompetent, I know I will make mistakes. Some of the things written in this diary that are okay to say now may very well become offensive over time. Who knows, perhaps some of the things I've already said are offensive now, and I just don't know.

Nomenclature changes, and every piece of art is a product of its time and generation. The key is getting on board with the change.

I don't want to sound too preachy, though. I'm not nearly as perfect as everyone thinks I think I am.

For my pronouns, I accept both he and they pronouns. Personally, I care less about my pronouns because I don't give a fuck what other people call me. That's a growing pain I've outgrown after the umpteenth time being called faggot, fairy, and this and that. People can call me whatever they want. I know who I am. It's why I tolerate words like boy and brother.

But as non-binary people, should we tolerate this treatment? Should we tolerate this general disregard of our existence and all its dimensions? A part of me wants to say no, don't take shit from anyone and demand respect. Another part of me doesn't want to inconvenience anyone or draw that type of attention to myself.

Why else did I keep my shorts on at the beach?

When people come out as non-binary and ask to be called by they/them pronouns, the people they're telling this to usually have the same reaction.

They say we're doing too much and that we're too extra and want to be different. Other queer people say and think it too.

I try not to take these comments personally because I know it's just their obstinacy talking.

I suppose what it comes down to is: are they strangers or are they family?

For my first Pride parade, I went to New York with Rupiah and a couple other girlfriends. Because we were all wearing slutty, gay apparel, we made sure to stick together. Though there were many allies and queer people out and about, there were just as many haters. Haters, traditionalists, right-wingers, deplorables, bigots, closet-cases, conservatives— whatever they want to be called—were there.

We arrived in Grand Central.

The girls and I needed to use the restroom. But I didn't feel comfortable using the men's room because of my outfit. I'd prefer a gender-neutral bathroom, but those are a rarity even in New York. Most of the time, I don't mind using the men's room. It depends on how much I pass as a straight cis male. And that depends on how I'm expressing myself that day.

The girls told me to come with them. As I was washing my hands, a female custodian approached me.

"I don't mind you comin' in here and using our toilets. But you have to at least look the part."

Rupiah looked like she wanted to deck the bitch.

When we left the bathroom, a male custodian approached us.

"That ain't right," he said to me. "You ain't right."

I still remember the disgust and anger on his face. I felt embarrassed, targeted, and a bit scared. But we kept walking.

So yeah, if they're strangers, they can get the fuck out of my face.

If they're family, it just hurts. They should want to know who I am. They don't have to understand. In fact, they'll probably never understand. But compassion is the least they could offer.

Cedi was obstinate. She never understood. Then again, she never tried to understand either. She was queer herself, so her obstinacy always baffled me.

I'm not a gender studies professor or a queer activist. I never signed up to educate Cedi. What I offered her was my experience as a non-binary person. She heard me out, but I could tell from her lukewarm reply and vacant eyes that the topic went in one ear and out the other. She wasn't dumb. No, she was highly intelligent. Instead, she purposefully refused to grasp the concept.

She didn't want to have to evaluate herself and her identity within the gender spectrum. I don't know why she feared or loathed the topic so much. Perhaps she thought it would take away or minimize her womanhood. Or perhaps she was just lazy.

Of course, I wanted my friend to understand me. But I didn't need her validation.

Being thrown out gave me thick skin.

While Cedi did not understand, other people in my life, like my brother Billie, did. Medical practitioners know all about continuing education, so I wasn't surprised by how quickly he had grasped the concept.

When he moved to Switzerland and started the surrogacy process with his husband, he raised an important question.

"What should our children call you? Uncle? Aunt? Something else? We searched for an English, gender-neutral equivalent but couldn't find anything."

Before then, I had never given it any thought. None of my siblings had children yet.

But then an idea came to him. Not me. Him.

"How about your middle initial, Q?"

I liked it. It was simple and cute and sounded like the word "cute." It could also be spelled Queue for those not taken with the single-letter spelling. The verb "to queue" is also ironic; it means "to fall in line." Being non-binary is the opposite of falling in line; it defies order and tradition. And what better way is there to defy tradition than to poke fun at it?

I really appreciated that Billie went out of his way to make me feel loved and understood. He didn't need to, but he wanted to. And that has made all the difference.

Daddy Five

*E*lders—at least X and Y—are similar to sugardaddies but still differ. As someone who has been with both, I can rightfully say that Elders and sugardaddies are ugly in more ways than one. They tend to go after the young and beautiful. They're old, pedophilic, and drunk with masculinity and power. They're liars, cheats, and thieves. They use money to get what they want, and they always do. I wouldn't be surprised if X and Y were sugardaddies before Elderhood. The only real difference between an Elder and a sugardaddy is one is forced onto you and the other you allow onto you. But at the same time, if you were in a tough situation and couldn't afford life, you don't have a choice. So, is there really a difference?

I admit I brought it upon myself. I let Five walk right into my life. Five lived in Albany. I was sleeping on my friend's couch at the time. We found each other on Shopping. He was one of the two profiles located in the Albany area and the only one who had responded to my message. We met at a hotel later that night. He was exactly what I was seeking: gross, fat, round, closeted, married, and completely infatuated with me. Someone like him could never bag a body like mine. I slithered into that hotel room and charmed him. Two snakes, one room.

I knew what he wanted. They all want the same thing.

I stripped, threw myself onto the bed, and lifted my ass. He was a great rimmer, I'll give him that. He wasn't afraid to chow down. Some tops are just so hesitant.

He told me I tasted as sweet as a cherry.

I had him eat my ass for a long, long time. The longer he ate my ass, the less I'd have to look at him.

He was so hideous it made me ashamed. Not because I was with someone so ugly. Well, maybe a little. But because I was taking advantage of such easy prey.

I knew I reached a new low. Yet, I stayed.

Might as well finish, right?

When I was younger, I did not use condoms. I got lucky those times.

We had a semester of health class in the tenth grade. Not a full year. A semester. I personally think health class should be taught in every grade all year round, from middle school up. We should be taught about periods. We should be taught about physical health. Not just P.E. Physical, full-body, anatomical, physiological health, and how to care for our bodies. We should also be taught mental health, body dysmorphia, gender identities, gender fluidity, gender dysphoria, sexual orientations, asexuality, sexual diseases, nutrition, drugs and addiction, toxic relationships and masculinity, queer and Black and Indigenous history, recognizing one's prejudices and microaggressions, recognizing sexual assault, that no means no, how to set boundaries, how to ask for help… There's so much that could be included in the curriculum. Why prioritize geometry and chemistry when respect, health, and wellness are—let's be real— more important?

I learned about condoms and safe sex practices through my queer and female friends at an age that could have easily been too late.

Considering the number of disloyal daddies I've slept with, I'm surprised I never contracted anything. I suppose it's because the daddies I've been with were so ugly no one wanted to fuck them, so they never caught anything.

The night I met Five, we used a condom. His dick deflated like a balloon. They always do. And like every other man who doesn't give a damn, he pulled off the rubber and asked to continue without it even though I had already said no.

He was disappointed, but I stood my ground. I had just met the man. I wasn't on preventative pills. No, not gonna happen.

His dick looked gross. It was a pink and pimply stump. I lied and said I hated blowing. He said that was okay and went down on me instead. Then I lied again. I said I didn't like getting head either. Truth was, I could feel every jagged edge of his teeth. It was painful. He was a soda drinker. Over time, the acidic and sugary carbonation eroded his teeth into tiny daggers.

After our first "date," he was hooked. He messaged me every day. It was annoying, really. I did not like him at all, though I had given him the impression that I did. I didn't reply much. I've never been the best texter, but that's also something I say to people I don't care to text often.

Back when I had a phone, I texted Rupiah nearly every day. I liked her style of texting. She played with words and sayings, shared my references, and purposely misspelled things. She knew how to hold my attention. Most people text in MLA format. That's dull shit. If I wanted that, I'd read a book.

Not to mention, when I saw Rupiah's name pop up on my phone, I smiled. When I saw Five's name, I was reminded of my actions.

Despite my embarrassment, disappointment, and disgust, I continued to see Five.

On our second "date," he gifted me a pile of new books, clothes, headphones, and groceries. I've always said gift-giving is the least important love language, but I think I've only said that because no one has ever shown me that type of love. He bought me books I thought I'd like. He bought me clothes he thought I'd wear. He knew I liked music and cooking. His gifts had thought behind them. It wasn't just money.

Five also offered me a place to sleep. When I wanted to get away from Three or Four, Five booked a hotel for me. I stayed there for months all on his dime.

During that time, I performed for him. I wore the sluttiest outfits. I gave him lap dances. I let him take me to dinner and show me off. They always want to show you off.

I became an amazing typecast actor. I spun my sob story into gold. I told him everything. Told him about the abandonment, the motel room, the parental rejection, the hate crimes, the gender dysphoria, the sexual objectification, the child molestation, all the adversities, true and all. I showed him every scar and bruise and even shed a tear or two. And he used those informative, little anecdotes to humanize me, to help himself better understand why I subject myself to sugaring. Not one of my previous daddies had cared to do that.

He was different. He saw me for who I was and what I had been through. And because of that, I started to actually like him.

After a while, Five expected monogamy from me, as if we could ever be in a real relationship.

It was laughable, really. He was in the closet. I was his dirty little secret. I was not remotely attracted to him, though he didn't know that. He had children my age who knew nothing about me, as far as I know. Oh, and I can't forget, he was fucking married.

I didn't think too much of his expectations. I knew monogamy to him meant bareback sex.

I also knew that if I wanted things to continue with him, I'd have to let him have me the way he wanted, at least occasionally. So, I put my health at risk. For what? A new phone, watch, shoes, tickets to Broadway shows. *Moulin Rouge. Come From Away. The Book of Mormon.* He gave me gift cards to grocery stores. He was a chauffeur whenever I needed one. I never asked for the tangible or experiential, only the financial. He gave me the other stuff because he wanted to. I didn't mind, but they weren't what I needed.

He sent me money. The standard was five hundred. Sometimes, a grand when I expressed the severity of my debt-to-income ratio.

I admit I am a liar, which makes me an unreliable narrator. So whether or not you believe I put that money toward my loans is up to you. I wish I was lying, truly. I wish I had used that money to travel the world. Japan. Brazil. Tahiti! I wish I could treat myself in such grand, luxurious ways.

But one could argue I did treat myself in grand, luxurious ways. I used a dirty man's dirty money to make living a bit easier. How luxurious is that?

I don't enjoy talking ill of Five or Four or even Three, for that matter.

They all helped me when I needed it. They opened their homes to me. They fed me. They listened whenever I opened up.

Five took me to Broadway, a luxury I could never afford. Four took me skiing, a luxury I could never afford. And Three let me sleep in a bed, a luxury I could never afford.

Five pulled out all the stops.

He bought me groceries every day. He got me coffee every morning. He gave me space whenever I needed it, which was every day. I told him I needed it to focus on my work and writing. Though that was true, I also didn't want to be around him—ever.

After weeks in the hotel and bouncing between him and Four, Five decided to rent a two-bedroom apartment opposite the campus of the University at Albany. The building provided a gym, an indoor and outdoor pool, a movie theater, and a communal kitchen. The apartment itself had a kitchen with a peninsula and dishwasher, two bedrooms, two bathrooms with two large tubs, in-unit laundry, and a balcony.

The building also provided a hammock in the garden, a billiards table, a coffee shop, a masseur, and vending machines. The property manager had to provide a lot to their tenants not just because they were "luxury apartments" but because the building itself was secluded just off the highway. I had to leapfrog across the highway to run on the college campus. If you wanted to leave the building, you had to drive. I didn't have a car, so I never left the building except on my runs. The building was in a bubble. *I* was in a bubble. I think that's why Five put me there, so I could never leave him.

He wanted me all to himself.

While I was with Five, my loan provider charged me an extra grand one month.

I called. They said it was because my loans were transferred to a new loan servicer. I didn't understand. All I knew was that I needed to pay twice as much that month, or else my loans would be considered delinquent. I was now in desperate need of money, more so than usual.

I would've used money in my savings, but it was empty. Savings accounts are luxuries.

My credit line was low, and the card itself was already maxed out. Forget that.

I asked Five for help, but he, too, was having financial problems. Something about a "recent investment backfiring."

My loan collector was calling me every day.

I considered contacting one of my previous daddies, but most of those affairs were in their final stages.

So, I redownloaded Shopping.

I usually deleted my profile after every daddy. It made them feel good and tricked them into thinking I thought they were the only one for me. The more I made these men feel good about themselves, the more likely they'd spoil me.

At times, it felt empowering to sugar, truly. *This is my body! I have the freedom to choose how I wish to use it.* I also liked showing off. *I have a great body. Why not flaunt it?* I myself was turned on by my profile. And it felt sexy to be desired by so many. It was a sexual fantasy borderline autosexuality. *All these men crave you, Dime. You're fucking hot.* Then there were times when I felt gross and pathetic, subjecting myself to a life lacking dignity, humility, and class. *Do you not want more for yourself, Dime? Don't you want to be known for your intellect, creativity, and kindness? Not your body?* Sugaring can be dehumanizing, if you let it.

I also deleted my profile because I was afraid that someone I knew would see me, like a relative, coworker, father of a friend, or a college peer also struggling to make ends meet.

This was my double life. I wanted it hush-hush for as long as possible. But I risked revealing my secret every time I curated an eye-catching, salacious profile.

I usually searched for daddies in D.C. and New York. Both were a mere train ride away. I also found the two cities to be the most populated with sugardaddies, at least on the East Coast. When I returned to Shopping, I saw many profiles I had seen before. Daddies I once met, but nothing came of it. Daddies I've chatted with, but we never met. And, of course, new daddies to browse! Hundreds and thousands of cheating husbands and lying fathers. Closeted, toxic men galore! All over the world.

I listed on my profile—between my suggestive photos and age— that I was in Albany. The daddies who liked what they saw would research the price of a train or flight from Albany to wherever they wanted to meet. Daddies rarely ever welcomed me into their real house. It was usually a hotel room. Sometimes, it was a fancy one just to impress me. Occasionally, they brought me to their vacation house, also to impress. But if they did bring me to their real house, it was either because their family was away or because they didn't have one. Live-in situations only blossomed with daddies who wanted me regularly.

Before all that though, the daddies had to fully consider my sugarbaby candidacy. Would I get the job? Do I understand discretion? Do we have overlapping interests? Can I carry a conversation? Would I give them what they really want? Not only would they have to buy my two-way train ticket, but they would also have to pay for dinner and my company. Would I be worth all that money? Am I good-looking enough to cost that much?

Some of them flat-out said I looked "too expensive." I never listed a price on my profile. I couldn't if I wanted to. The site forbade sugarbabies from mentioning anything about money on our profiles. The site would suspend our accounts if we did. To reactivate our accounts, we'd have to watch a ten-minute video about their rules and restrictions.

Some daddies thought I was catfishing them. Those daddies required video calls to verify my identity. Meanwhile, their profiles were always pictureless. No need to add a profile picture. Sugarbabies don't go on Shopping to find attractive sugardaddies. If they did, they're dumb and bound to fail. No, no. Sugarbabies only care about seeing one thing and one thing only: the section in the profile that lists the daddy's level of income. Are they making at least $200,000? $800,000? $1,000,000?

Though I was looking for daddies in D.C. and New York City, the daddies in Albany could see my profile.

Later that evening, Five came home with a sullen pout. He had seen my profile back on the site. We fought for a while. He said he was deeply hurt. I said it was a double standard that he could have a profile, but I could not. I also stressed my financial needs. He told me to get a second job. A "real" second job, not as a sugarbaby or barista. I said I needed those extra hours to myself to write, read, cook, and stay fit. Every second of every day, I was doing something. I've never been much of a lazy person. I wanted to have a nice body. I wanted to eat well. I wanted to exercise my brain and creative juices. Writing was always a priority.

Surprisingly, he understood.

I think he realized I'd spend less time with him if I had a "real" second job. He wasn't an idiot. He knew I was selfish and that I would put my alone time before my time with him any day.

So, we came to a resolution. He told me about this group of men he knew. Once a month, they booked a hotel suite under Five's name and had one giant orgy. Even though they had wives, sometimes they just craved dick. In this case, many dicks. Five told me these men would go wild for "a kid like me," someone so young and beautiful with a perky ass like mine. He said they would pay handsomely, too, all the while abiding by my boundaries.

I slept on the idea. It sounded hot in theory; all these dirty, old men having sex with me in secret, their dicks throbbing inside me, their hands all over me, pleasing me, passing me around. The idea reminded me of this one time in Hong Kong when I went to a bathhouse. I was the only twenty-something there. Everyone else looked to be in their forties or fifties. They were husbands living in a world where having a wife was the social norm. They were businessmen hiding a part of themselves to be taken seriously in the workplace. They were fathers craving a man's touch. Some of them were handsome. Everyone was walking around either naked or in a skimpy towel. *I* was naked. Men gradually swarmed around me in the steam room like fruit flies. One sat next to my right and put his hand on my thigh. Two more came. One stood behind me and rubbed my chest. The other sat to my left and kissed my abs and rib cage. Three more came and got on their knees. One started jerking me off, the other two started sucking my toes. Four more came. Two sucked my fingers, the other two licked my ears. Seven more came and circled me. None of them were touching each other. Instead, they stared dreamily at me, pulled at their dicks, and waited their turn to touch me. I was a rarity among them. They must have me. More and more men came. The three on their knees began jostling each other to suck my dick. Though I was hard as a rock and enjoying being touched and desired by twenty-some people, I became overwhelmed, so overwhelmed I had to get away. Since I was still horny, I looked around at the begging eyes and made my choice. I pointed to a man, grabbed his arm, and pulled him into a private room. I could tell from his face he was shocked that I chose him. Though we didn't share the same language, I knew what he wanted. I climbed onto the sex swing, spread my legs, and, well… had a great time in Hong Kong, that's for damn sure.

While the fantasy remained, the scenarios were nevertheless different. In Hong Kong, it was a non-transactional act of sex. In Albany, I
would be paid. If I agreed to meet Five's "friends," I'd be committing
prostitution and could potentially be arrested. My double life would then
be revealed. I would lose the little shred of dignity I had left. I'd lose people, for sure. Who wants to be associated with a prostitute? I'd also lose
my job and the little bit of honest income I did have. I didn't want to sugar
for the rest of my life. I wanted a better job, which would never happen if
I got caught. I knew this was a possibility the day I started working as a
sugarbaby. To most people, sugarbabies are glorified prostitutes. But
sugaring is technically legal, so I knew I'd be okay. Prostitution is different. There would be consequences if caught. But the consequences
weren't the only thing giving me pause.

In Hong Kong, I chose who got to fuck me. In Albany, I wouldn't
have that choice. I'd have to allow all who paid an entrance fee to fuck
me, whether they were attractive or not. And if I became overwhelmed
or anxious or tired, I'd have to suppress those emotions. I couldn't flee. If
I wasn't enjoying something, I'd have to pretend I did. I'd have to give
my best performance!

After much thought, I decided to do it. I needed to, really.

I set boundaries. There were the no-brainers, like no scat or piss play,
no cameras, no fisting, etc. There were other rules too, but the one I
stressed the most was my condom rule. Anyone who fucks me must wear
a condom. Period.

Five agreed to the rules, sent out photos of my face and body, and
orchestrated the whole orgy. His friends marked their calendars and sent
him money for the hotel.

When the day came, I was nervous as hell. Five and I arrived at nine
a.m. to get the keys to the suite. He was wearing a button-up and pants.
I, bootcut jeans and a tank top. Simple. The hotel receptionist didn't
think anything of us. She gave us the key cards and wished us a good
conference.

"Conference?" I asked Five when we left the lobby.

"The suite is on the same floor as the conference hall. That's what they think the purpose of our visit is for."

The suite was massive. I had never seen one so big. I didn't think hotels provided such large spaces. It had two bedrooms, each with a California king. The living room had multiple couches, a flatscreen, a full kitchen, a long table, and actual space between furniture. In establishments I've stayed in—like the motel my family lived in—the furniture was always crammed together, and you had to wiggle your way around the bed to get to the bathroom.

"To set the mood," Five said as he turned on the porn channel.

As we waited for the others, all of whom I knew nothing about, Five told me he might be jealous watching these guys fuck me. But he said he'd push through it. He knew it was for a good cause.

What a gentleman.

In little to no time, the men came rolling in, as did the dough. Five had informed everyone that cold, hard cash was the only acceptable payment. Leave no trace. A hat was by the door. As men entered, they dropped their bundles into the hat.

When the first few entered, it was a little awkward. I didn't know if we would chat or get right to it. Thankfully, the porn on the screen eased us.

As more and more came, suits were tossed to the ground. Button-ups were unbuttoned. And ties were untied.

I don't know where my clothes went. As soon as they started to undress, my clothes were stripped off my body and thrown somewhere by someone.

It was like I was back in the steam room, but without steam to obscure their faces. I wished there had been steam. Most of them were ugly. I asked for the lights to be dimmed.

"To add a bit of romance," I said.

Dimmed lights give room to fantasy.

Everyone laughed at the idea, either because they knew I was lying or because a scenario like this could never be romantic. They all said I looked so pretty and wanted to see every inch of me. They didn't need to fantasize. They wanted their money's worth, god damn it!

So, I had to look at their faces. Grotesque faces I'd see later in my dreams and for years to come. Men who knew the worst of me.

My arms were on strings.

While the men were fat, old, greasy, and ill-endowed, none of those characteristics were why I thought they were ugly. I mean, maybe a bit. But even if they were conventionally attractive, I would've still found them ugly. They were cheating on their wives and paying someone to have sex with them…

But by those standards, wouldn't that make me just as ugly?

I was fucked everywhere in that suite.

We started in the living room. I was kissed and licked all over. I couldn't tell how many lips, tongues, and hands were on me at any moment. Someone—I don't remember who; I never learned their names—had picked me up and thrown me onto a bed. Some were gentle, and some were rough. Some pitied me. I could tell from their eyes. Yet, they still got off.

Everyone seemed obsessed with my ass.

"I don't usually eat ass, but this one tasted so sweet. You must try," I heard someone say, smacking their lips as if I were wine.

"It's such a cute little boy butt," I heard another one say. "So young."

"You were born for this," another one whispered into my ear.

"You like that, don't you, you little whore," one grunted as he pounded my ass.

Comments like this always fucked me up. I didn't know how to take them.

Someone carried me from the bedroom to the couches. I was in every position—doggy, 69, corkscrew, facedown, standing up, wheelbarrel, cowgirl, reverse cowgirl, and everyone's favorite, missionary. They preferred seeing my face as they dominated me. It made them feel good to have power over someone so pretty.

A line of guys sat on the couch, and I went down the line and rode each of them. A beefy guy lifted me into his arms and bounced me on his dick. He laid me on the table and fucked me on that. Another guy pressed my face into a mirror and made me watch him. Another guy choked me in the shower. Not enough to be bruised, but enough to make him feel powerful. From the shower, we went to the second bedroom.

Some of it I liked. Some of it I did not.

They had me until five. Nine to five was the deal. It gave everyone a chance to have their turn. All thirty-five of them. It gave them time to cum as many times as they'd like. I wanted each of them to leave satisfied. Who knows if I'd have to do this again…

I suppressed my hunger. I drank multiple bottles of water. I was sweating throughout the day.

Lube was everywhere—the couch, the sheets, my hands, my cheeks. Daddies came and went. Several edged themselves, saving their cum for when everyone shot their load onto my chest. Some stayed for a second or third round. In between, they drank whiskies, smoked cigars, and shared laughs.

One guy with a rural, New York accent looked like total white trash—pale and thin with deep-set eyes and a mullet. He pulled out a bag of cocaine and tried snorting a line off my ass. Five stopped him.

"No hard drugs."

I barely noticed what was happening. I was distracted by the dicks slapping my face. Most of them were small dicks—below six inches. Dicks three to five inches long were good to start with but didn't hit the spot. There were a few dicks six to eight inches long. Those felt amazing, especially the thicker ones. Some of the daddies hushed me for moaning so loudly.

Some had a hard time keeping it up. Viagra was being dished out like candy.

There was an Indian guy who had a thick, ten-inch cock. Thank goodness he hadn't gone first. It was a lot, even after being opened. I had to use poppers.

Some tried double dicking me but couldn't fit.

My ass was raw.

Around four o'clock, the guy who had brought the cocaine was getting frustrated. He couldn't stay hard, so he pulled off his condom and tried dicking me down without it. Five was in the mix at the time and pulled the guy off me.

"First, the coke. Now this? Get out!"

The guy was heated. He found his clothes, threw them on, and grabbed a fistful of cash from the hat.

"I'm taking my money back," he said. "You best hope I don't call the cops on you faggots."

"If you do, you go down with us. I have your RSVP and transaction for the hotel," Five said flatly.

The guy left, slamming the door.

"He won't actually go to the police, will he?" *Fuck, I knew this was gonna get out.*

"No, no," a couple of the daddies said.

"He's all talk," one said.

"All talk."

"Empty threat."

They could tell I was scared. They tried quelling my worries but knew the vibes of the room had changed.

"It's approaching five anyway," said Five. "We should get going. Has everyone finished?"

As I washed off in the shower, daddies departed.

Some threw extra money into the hat on their way out, either as a tip or to make up for what had been taken. That was nice of them.

"This was the biggest turn-out ever," Five said as we walked to the lobby.

The receptionist was staring at me as she checked us out.

I can only imagine what she had seen: a trail of daddies exiting the building in groups. Men arriving in proper business attire but leaving with untucked shirts and disheveled hair. A clean conference hall but dirtied hotel room. A young boy not in business attire but in jeans and a tank.

Oh, she knew alright. She'd be an idiot not to.

I didn't care. I was leaving the hotel with a hat full of cash. When we returned to the apartment, we counted. I made ten grand that day. Every cent of it went toward my student loans. The sad thing is, it was only a tenth of my debt.

The cokehead never ratted us out.

We were safe. *I* was safe.

I lived in Five's apartment for a couple more months after the orgy. While I lived there, Five still lived at home with his wife and kids. Over time, he started spending more and more of the day at the apartment, sometimes day after day. If his wife hadn't known then, she definitely knew now. Where else would he be spending all his time? If she was anything like my mother, she tracked her husband down and saw him with a tramp.

Of course, I was ashamed of what I had done. Still am. But I did what I did to survive.

Though Five had done a lot for me, he still annoyed the fuck out of me. He was possessive, passive-aggressive, hobbyless, and unhealthy. He ate junk food. He never worked out. And he compulsively watched the news every second of every day.

I never signed up to live with him. I made that clear from the beginning. I lived with other daddies before and knew that life was not for me. I didn't want to be a houseboy.

I thought the apartment was my space. That's what he promised. He promised I'd have a ton of alone time and that he'd still live with his family. I didn't want to see his face every day or have to lie about why I didn't want to have sex. *Sorry, I have an anal fissure. Sorry, I'm super tired. Sorry, I have a lot of work to do.* He wanted sex every fucking day. I wanted it as infrequently as possible. When long, sexless stretches of time passed, Five became short with me and guilt-tripped me into spreading my legs. I did it just to shut him up. It's whatever. He was paying for the apartment. I owed him sex, at the very least once in a while.

I could handle Five in small doses. All I had to do was fake it, say that I loved him, and act like he was the best sex I ever had. But faking it every day made me feel disgusted with myself. The lengths I'd go to have a roof over my head and food on my plate. Would it be better to starve in the cold than to lie to someone? Of course not. If all I must do to survive in this world is make someone feel special when they are not, then lying can't be so bad.

But when you lie about little things, the lying permeates the rest of your life and other relationships—even the genuine ones—and poisons them. I told my family and friends I found an apartment in Albany. "Why Albany?" they asked. "It was a good price with many amenities," I said.

My family stayed with me over the holidays once. I had Five remove his things from the apartment. I noticed he left a few things behind, like an oversized shirt or shoes too ugly to be mine—things that showed someone else was living there. He didn't forget. He did it on purpose. I used to do the same thing. I'd leave an object behind at a friend's, relative's, or guy's place. It gave me a reason to return. It comes from moving a lot as a kid and leaving places only never to return.

Five had a different reason. He got off on the potential of being caught.

I hid what he left behind and prayed no one would snoop.

Chavos visited me a few times while I was there. She was more confused about how I lived in the middle of nowhere without a car.

"How do you get groceries?"

"I take the bus."

"You carry all those groceries onto the bus? But you cook a lot…"

"I have strong arms."

She didn't seem convinced but didn't press for the truth either.

I think my family knew too but didn't broach the subject. *How can you afford such a luxurious two-bedroom and balcony with your income? How did you get your things to Albany without a car?*

These were questions they never asked.

And if they did ask, I've forgotten my lies.

One day, when Five had returned to the apartment, he asked me how the gym was.

"How'd you know I already went to the gym?"

"You go every day."

"Yeah, but not at a specific time."

"A guess, I suppose. Anyway, how's the book?"

"How'd you know I read today?"

"You read every day."

Though this was true, reading was like working out; I did it whenever I felt like it.

"How were the waffles?"

"Waffles?"

"The waffle machine is still warm. I assume you made some."

He never touched the waffle machine. How would he know it was warm?

I know I am a distrustful person. It's my Venus Scorpio. But distrust protects me. The downside is that I read too much into things.

I found Five's comments suspicious. How does he know I did this already? How does he know I jerked off without him? How is he one step ahead of me? Yes, he was observant, but this felt a little too observant.

My first thought: cameras.

I looked but couldn't find any. So, I ordered a camera detector. I'm not sure if it worked, to be honest. It supposedly used infrared light to detect if there were any lenses in the room. I used it when he wasn't in the apartment one day. I found something in the smoke detector but couldn't tell if it was a camera or not. I covered it with tape, just in case.

Ever since Five started spending more time with me, he brought more and more of his stuff to the apartment. I don't normally snoop through other people's things, even my daddies. But since I was searching for cameras, nothing was off-limits. In one of his bags, I came across a pile of papers. The figure "$500,000" caught my attention. It was a lawsuit. I couldn't read it. Too much legal jargon. I called my friend Cedi, a law student at the time, to explain to me what it was.

She was one of the only two people in my life who knew for a fact I was a sugarbaby. She knew where I was living and my daddy's information. I always shared my location with her. While Rupiah also had this information, Cedi was the only person in my immediate life—as far as I know—who truly knew the ins and outs of sugaring.

Every time I met someone off Shopping, I did my research for safety reasons. I found their socials, searched them on Google, and opened every link that listed their name. I found their accolades, company websites, and the foundations and boards they worked on.

Cedi was exceptionally good at finding people's records, public or not. So, I asked her to read the lawsuit and find out anything she could about Five.

When she did, she called me back and told me calmly yet urgently, "Dime, you need to get out now! I'm on my way."

While I knew something was up with Five, I never expected it to be what Cedi had told me.

I packed my clothes and books and ended things with Five that very day. I gave him a whole sob story and told him I wanted more for myself. I didn't want to leave on his bad side, so I made sure to give him a show.

He was upset I was leaving but understood.

Cedi picked me up, and I stayed with her until I moved back to Philly.

Philly was where I watched the United divide, where I began my life as a Minor, and where I lost the freedom I thought I didn't have.

59

Telephone Bills

I *had always known my father was cheating on my mother.*
I didn't have evidence per se, but I knew. I never met his sidepiece, sugarbaby, or whatever she wants to be called. But I saw his infidelity in the arrogant way he held himself. I saw it in the way he hid his phone from my mother's eyeshot. I saw it in his prolonged business trips. I saw it in the way he came home late at night. I saw it in the way he only hired attractive waitresses. I saw it in the way he made my girlfriends feel uncomfortable. I saw it in the way he drank. And I saw it in the blatant lies he fabricated to make himself look better.

As a kid, I expected people to tell the truth. I was naïve.

My father told his colleagues that he paid for each of his children's college tuition. He wanted to appear as a proper and rich father. He told the lie so convincingly that I knew he could lie about anything.

None of my siblings believed me when I said he was cheating. They knew but didn't want to accept it. They and my mother wanted to live in a fantasy where we were one big, gay family.

Though she didn't completely believe me, Penny believed me the most. She and I were the youngest. We saw the worst of it: the ending. But she, like my other siblings, still idolized my father. He was the breadwinner who worked hard to "put a roof over our heads and food on our plates." He used that line every time one of us fought with him.

It was usually me.

"I put a roof over your head and food on your plate! How dare you disrespect me in *my* house!"

It was always *his* house. *His* home. No matter how hard my mother tried to make where we lived a home, it never felt like one to me. He made sure of that.

The "how dare you disrespect me" line was also something he kept in his back pocket, a verbal dagger he could plunge into his children to demand dominance and silence.

My father was easily disrespected by everything.

"You're a man. Men don't wear dresses. How dare you disrespect me under my roof!"

He always looked like a Tasmanian devil when he got angry. His ears would turn red, and his eyes would go dark.

"You befriend a dyke and bring her into my house? How dare you disrespect me under my roof!"

Cedi and I were only fifteen at the time. We were just starting to understand sexuality. We didn't even know what "dyke" meant.

"I am your elder. I demand respect!"

He always made it about age. But not all older people deserve respect. Respect, like love, is still conditional.

The first real piece of evidence of my father's infidelity was our phone bill.

We were on a family plan together. My father used his card for the monthly payments. Each of us kids, except my little sister, sent forty-five dollars to my father every month. We always paid him on time. But he was a micromanager. He reminded us every fucking day until he saw the money drop into his account.

Greedy bastard. To be in his presence was to make every moment about money.

Long before the divorce, since he kicked me out, I started distancing myself from my father. Though I had forgiven him for what he had done to me, I did not care to reconcile. The only reason why he was still in my life was because of my mother and siblings.

Then, my siblings started distancing themselves from him as well. They had their reasons. Penny, for example, was traveling by herself in Spain to celebrate her high school graduation when my father turned off her cellular data, removed the money she earned from her bank account, and sold her car. She was in a foreign country with no money or cell service. My father said he did what he did because Penny went off gallivanting the world without his permission. I think he did it because Penny went traveling the same year she had brought home a girlfriend. That was her way of coming out, and that was his way to show disapproval.

When my brother Billie was engaged, he intended to take my brother-in-law's last name. My father refused to go to the wedding if he did. To make my family happy, Billie agreed to keep our last name. The ultimatum widened the rift between my brother and father. They rarely spoke after that. When my brother and his husband started the surrogacy process, my father sent Billie an email saying he'd sue them for grandparent rights. Billie was scared and checked with his lawyer. The lawyer said it was an empty threat and that there was no such thing as grandparent rights. But they were two gay men in a homophobic world. The possibility of having their child taken from them was a real threat and fear.

We all had reasons to stop talking to my father. Reasonable reasons. He didn't see it that way, of course. He felt like my mother was pitting us against him during the divorce. But I had just as many problems with my mother as I did with him. The reason why I kept her in my life and not him was because she was a good and kind person. She grew and evolved and bettered herself, whereas my father saw himself as a perfect god without the need for change.

Since fewer and fewer of us stopped talking to our father, the payment of the phone bill was transferred to me. When we managed to get into our account, we found another phone number listed on our family plan. It wasn't any of ours. We didn't know whose it was until we called it. It went to voicemail. The girl on the voicemail sounded young and perky and, according to my mother, was someone who worked for my father.

My mother was crushed, obviously. My siblings, too. I can't say I was surprised. I wish I had been wrong.

After further scrolling, I did some math and noticed a discrepancy. If split evenly among us all, our individual payments came out to thirty-five dollars a month, not forty-five. For years, we had been paying for his hooker's telephone bill.

Ironic, isn't it?

Generational karma.

Not long after, another kid's father would be my daddy, having his children pay my bills.

60

Sharp Pangs We Call Heartbreak

I fear my family reading this.

Of course, they won't. They can't. Reading is forbidden. If the Divided ever found my journal and napkins, They would have me burn them during a Sunday ritual and castrate me for indulging in such a sin.

There are also natural causes. Over time, ink will smear. Water will find them. Pages and lead will fade.

None of it matters. I'm just a pretty face. No one cares what I have to say. They never did, and They never will.

Sometimes, I dream.

I know I shouldn't. Dreams build expectations, and expectations are bound to fail. When those dreams slip away, they take form as dull aches in our chests and, over time, become sharp pangs we call heartbreak. Despite all that, I still dream.

And in my dreams, the Bill is lifted. Reading is legalized and has a resurgence. I become a published, bestselling author.

I have a home, and I call it mine.

But like in every dream, there is always a curveball. Someone in my family picks up my book, reads it, and passes it along. And one by one, everyone I know and love knows all the horrible, filthy things I've ever thought and done.

My life changes.

A fear and a dream twist and collide into one beautiful nightmare. Some dreams never come true, but fears always do.

237

61

Anniversary

A year has passed since your Auction, you know," Y told me one day while kissing my neck.

"For our anniversary, how about you make me my favorite meal and wear that lingerie I love."

It was a command. I knew better than to say no. So, I made him a big Italian feast with the pasta maker he bought me months ago. Afterward, I put on that slutty, schoolgirl uniform and let him have me.

He also wanted cheesecake. So, I made him cheesecake. As we sat listening to music and eating our slices, we heard a pounding on the front door. We jumped to our feet. Was it Tether? Was she okay?

Or did someone hear our music? Was this source of joy about to be taken from me as well?

A swarm of Red then busted into the apartment. I dropped to my knees and was instantly in handcuffs. But Y… Y ran to the balcony.

He was going to jump.

Before he climbed onto the ledge, a guard threw him to the ground and cuffed him.

I had no clue why the Red had raided the apartment.

Or why Y would try to jump.

As I sat alone in a jail cell, still in my costume with my bare ass on a cold, cement bench, I replayed everything I saw before the Red removed me from the apartment.

The guards had flipped tables and rifled through drawers. They confiscated Y's record player, vinyl, and book collection. My things—my pressed flowers, poem, pens, napkins, and journal—were in a box in the hidden room. Y had given me the box a few weeks after he started his coaching position. He said I could use it to store my contraband. My contraband wasn't the only thing in there though. Y had started some sort of DVD collection. The discs weren't labeled, and Y never told me what movies they were. Though he brought home a new disc every week, he never acquired a DVD player or a TV. I assumed he eventually would.

As Y was being dragged out of the apartment kicking and screaming, a Red guard picked up the box and dumped its contents onto the floor. My flowers and napkins fluttered to the ground. The mirror binding of my journal cracked. The guard picked up Y's discs and my pens and put them into plastic bags. Not my journal. No, he must've thought it was just a mirror.

A broken, pathetic mirror.

Hours passed before some man in a gray suit entered the detention center.

"Where're your clothes, son?"

I was freezing.

The man glared at the guard who was watching me. "No one cared to offer the boys pants?!" he yelled.

The guard removed his hand from his pants and fumbled for a pile of clothes on his desk. He tossed me the pile, and I quickly dressed myself.

"Come with me, boy."

The man in the suit led me to a private room and sat me down. No niceties. No introductions. He got right to the point.

"What do you know about these discs?"

He extracted a bag of discs from his briefcase and pushed them across the table.

I shrugged.

"Answer me." His voice was controlled but not rude.

"I-I don't know what they are. I assume they're movies?"

"Not any movie you'd want to watch. Your Elder is a perverted man, you know."

Every Elder is, I thought. *You are too, probably.*

"Your Elder worked as a gym teacher at my little girl's school. He put cameras in the boys' and girls' locker rooms and sold these discs on the black market. Did you know?"

I shook my head.

Would you still care if your daughter hadn't attended that school? Or would you just feign disgust?

"Not surprised. Most Minors are pretty oblivious." He put the discs away. "Your Elder will be beheaded for possession of illegal and harmful propaganda, and by that, I mean possession of music and literature."

"A–Are you serious?"

"Dead."

"But what about the discs? He's not being beheaded for child pornography?"

"Of course not."

I wanted to strangle the man. Apparently, it showed.

"I quite agree with you," he said. "I think he should be hanged for his perversion."

I didn't believe him. Many adults say shit like this, but it's all for show. They still have Minors and sugarbabies who are barely eighteen. They call little boys future heartbreakers and ask their sex partners to wear slutty, schoolgirl uniforms. Adults chase after fountains of youth not just because of vanity but also for perverted pleasure.

"We actually didn't know your Elder had books and music," the man said. "It was a surprise upon breaking in. We're using it as a cover story. The cameras in the school were found by a couple of students. The parents of these students are some of the wealthiest in the city. None of them want this to come to light, so they paid handsomely to use the propaganda card."

It's always money.

"Would the situation be different if it was a poorer school?" I asked.

"He'd still be beheaded for possession of propaganda. It is illegal, after all. But word about a pedophilic gym teacher and former NBA player would certainly make headlines in Elder news outlets."

I never realized Elders had news outlets different from *The Monthly*. I guess I am oblivious.

"What's going to happen to me?" I asked.

"You'll have a second Auction. This will be your third Elder, though. Better pray he won't die on you. You know what happens after your third…

"You're also scheduled to be branded with the red triangle. You're considered a slut now. I read your employment history. I'm surprised you haven't already been branded with the symbol.

"Oh, and since the parents want the story kept on the down low, you won't have a court hearing. In the meanwhile, you'll be permitted to live in the apartment of your previous Elder until, and if, another Elder purchases you. You have a very fine body. I think another Elder will want you. But this is your second Auction within a year. Many Elders will find that awfully suspicious. If you don't get purchased—well, we'll worry about that later."

He made for the door.

"I almost forgot. After your Elder's beheading, you, too, will be punished."

"Punished for what?" My mind went wild. Did they find my journal? Do they know it's mine?

"You knew about his contraband, Mr. Gagliastra, and failed to report him. Tut-tut-tut."

I spent the night at "home."

My journal was still on the ground. It really did look like only a mirror.

I hid it in the dirt of a plant. It was the only place I could think of apart from the no-longer-hidden room.

The next day, a Red guard led me to Center City. There was a crowd of Elders around the stage. A guillotine was center stage. Y was up there naked. His arms and legs were bound to the plank. Instead of his head under the sharp blade, it was his feet.

"They're going to turn him into chuck and feed him to the pigs," the guard said over his shoulder.

"What?"

I had never seen a beheading before. I just thought his head would be cut off, and that'd be that. Done. Easy. Something simple for Elders.

But no. I was wrong.

The guard controlling the guillotine released the lever, and the blade came crashing down and sliced Y's feet clean off. They landed in a bucket. Blood and screams poured out of Y. The guard lifted the blade, pushed the guillotine up and around Y's calves, and released it again.

There went his calves.

Then his thighs.

Then his penis. Not all. Just the tip.

Y was still alive, howling and begging for mercy. Teeth fell out of his mouth from biting down in pain.

When he was just a torso and head, he passed out. I'm surprised he stayed awake for as long as he did. Physiology has always baffled me.

When it was just his head on the plank, the guard lifted the blade for the last time and sliced Y's scalp clean off. His brain fell to the stage like a wet sponge.

Several people in the crowd fainted. Some barfed. And some applauded.

The man who coordinated my last Auction stepped onto the stage.

"THIS IS WHAT HAPPENS WHEN YOU BETRAY THE DIVIDED!" His voice boomed through the crowd as a guard swept teeth and fingers off the stage and into the bucket of blood and dismembered body parts.

"How much blood would a swine slurp up if a swine should slurp up blood?" the guard next to me murmured to the rhythm of the American-English woodchuck tongue-twister. He was swaying his head like a child as if he hadn't just seen a body be turned to chuck.

I looked at him. Like every guard, he was not pretty. His face was red and covered in acne and patchy fuzz.

He looked fourteen.

"And now," the man on stage said aloud, "we're going to show you what happens when you fail to report unlawful activity!"

He looked dead at me.

My legs turned to lead. The fourteen-year-old had to push me up the stairs to get me moving.

I slipped on Y's blood as I crossed the stage. When I joined the man, two guards came up and tore off my clothes. A gag was shoved into my mouth and strapped around my head. My ankles and wrists were tied around a pole so my ass stuck out. The pole was metal and hot from the sun. At night, it'll be freezing. The bright side: at least I wasn't suffering the same fate as the Minors of Diamond's Piercing.

I trained my gaze from the bloodstained stage to the crowd. The men in the crowd were licking their lips.

I knew what was coming. I had seen it before.

62

Makeup

My phone hissed like a snake.

I answered.

It was Silv.

"Dime, you can't post photos of yourself like that. People won't hire you if you do."

The call took place when I was in high school, around the time when I started playing with fashion and when Rupiah started playing with makeup. She painted my face as we watched *Drag Race*. Because I was feeling myself, I posted a selfie.

I told Billie what Silv had said, and Billie was livid yet unsurprised. When they were younger, Silv and his friends locked Billie up in a closet and repeatedly called him a faggot.

I don't know if he ever forgave him for that. Billie saw forgiveness as something contingent upon an apology.

I didn't think much of Silv's call and left the post up.

The hateful comments I received were from family members. The loving comments I received were from friends and strangers.

Ironic, isn't it? The love you're supposed to be born into turns out to be a source of hate.

It was difficult getting hired, I admit.

Was it the makeup? Probably not. But still.

Perhaps he was right.

63

Elder Z

I lost track of how many men were inside me on my first day of punishment. Only six more days, I told myself.

Men came during all hours. Some came at two or three in the morning. Very few women came. They looked like trash, like the woman on the beach who spat at me. But the men… Some of the men didn't look half bad. Did I think this way because women's beauty standards are higher than men's? Or was it because I find dirty men attractive?

Either way, I didn't enjoy what happened to me. Who would?

They branded me that first day.

It hurt just as much as the first time, but I did not faint. This time I got to really take in that burning flesh scent.

The red triangle is positioned just below the pink. The pink had to be on top. It is worse to be queer.

As you can imagine, I didn't catch much sleep those days.

I did catch a cold and a couple of STDs, though. Thankfully, my mother had the good sense to vaccinate me as a child. I was protected against HPV and hepatitis A and B.

And while they're not STDs, I've gotten myself vaccinated and boosted for COVID, the flu, and monkeypox.

Thankfully, the number of visitors petered out over the week.

In between the rapings, all I could do was watch the sun rise and set, and people bustle about the city. The few trees in the city were beginning to brown. I watched leaves fall and get swept up by passing cars for entertainment.

Some Elders passed without looking. Others looked with hungry eyes, either to reminisce or to mentally organize their schedule so they could visit me. How thoughtful.

I saw compassion in very few eyes. Those eyes belonged to Minors.

I thought a lot during those days, particularly of warm and calming memories.

I have never been the type to fondly look back on my childhood. I had repressed so much of myself then that those memories are laborious to reel back. Most of those memories are of me struggling, fighting, stressing, and hiding.

The few good memories I do have are of my siblings.

So, as I stood against the pole, I thought of days when Goldie used to pick me up from school in her red convertible. We'd drive around Radford, get slushies from Sonic, and wear out her Ciara and Britney CDs. Despite our decade age gap, we had so much fun together.

I also thought of Silv. I have this one memory of him reading along to a Jim Dale audiobook. He wasn't the best reader back then, but I remember how determined he was.

Silv and I have never had much in common, so I rarely ever went to him for things. But there was this one time when a car crashed into our house. I was watching a *Studio Ghibli* film near the porch. The car would've hit me if we didn't have the porch. When it happened, I ran to him.

Perhaps I was just a child looking up to my teenage siblings, but Goldie and Silv always made me feel safe.

I thought of Billie, too. Billie was the person I went to for help with my homework. In exchange, he asked me to bag his lunch for him in the mornings or fill his water bottle for track practice. He also came to me when he was sad. One time, he didn't get the role he wanted in the school's production of *Alice in Wonderland*. He wanted the Queen of Hearts and to do it in drag. But our director told him, "This small town is not ready for something like that."

Billie made me feel needed, something I've always struggled to do myself—making others feel needed.

After Billie came Nickel. Nickel was a wild card. Sometimes, he was fun to be around. Other times, I felt like he didn't understood me at all. We used to share a room together. This was his baseball-themed room. Or, "our" baseball-themed room. It was never my room because my mother decorated it to fit his interests. Though nothing about the room said "me," Nickel still made me feel welcomed. When I had nightmares, he'd wake up, turn on the TV, and tell me it was all just a dream.

And then there was Penny. For a long while, I didn't think Penny liked me very much. We didn't spend much time together. When we did, we butt heads.

When we were young, before character differences got in the way, we used to go to the local candy shop. I'd distract the shop owner with charming anecdotes as my sister swiped sour candies and jawbreakers.

We felt guilty about it later, but there's nothing like breaking the law that brings two siblings together.

In addition to my siblings, I also thought of my mother.

I thought of her big, green van she used to drive the six of us in. We called the van "the Green Booger."

Everyone who knew our family called us kids my mother's "six-pack."

She almost had an eight-pack. There were two kids in Virginia she almost adopted. She took care of them for a while, though. One went back to his mother after she got out of rehab, and the other was adopted by my aunt, who was having trouble getting pregnant. He's now my cousin.

That's the thing with my mother. No one quite matched her heart.

Along with my family, I also thought of my friends.

I remembered all the times Rupiah and I kayaked and got high on the lake together.

I remembered all the times Chavos and I spat a Nicki verse while driving to the mall.

And I remembered all the times Cedi and I built puzzles and watched anime together.

Those friendships sound easy, but they weren't always. No love is. They take time and effort to cultivate, through thick and thin.

As I stood there bound to that pole, none of the negative mattered. No. It's the good in people you remember when you need it the most.

Memories welled inside me over my seven days of punishment.

I don't know if any of my loved ones remember these moments the way I do, or even at all. Maybe they cherish them. Maybe they don't.

It doesn't matter.

What matters is the simple things in life. I know, I know, another platitude for you to drown in. But it's true.

The homemade cookies your mother bakes, savor them. Share them.

The songs you listen to, turn them up. Dance harder, sing louder.

The dress you wear in your room, pair it with heels and strut.

The nightmare you have at night, make it a dream.

The board games you play with your friends, play another round.

And the diary you write in, make it a book.

Just because you don't know what home is supposed to feel like doesn't mean you don't have it. Yes, some people will bully and abandon you. But there are kind people out there who will help you pick up your things. And if there's no one, you are someone. You can save yourself.

Every little joy in life is important. They remind us of our will to live and our yearning for more. The Divided know that. They don't want Minors dreaming. They want us naked, gagged, and tied to a post. When my second and final Auction came, I was purchased for half the price as before.

I was not new. I was used.

As the crowd dispersed, I checked my privilege. I, a queer and non-binary person who can pass as a straight, cisgender man, was granted a third Elder.

I, again, was privileged.

While X and Y were ugly, Z was hideous.

He was so hideous that I don't want to describe him. But love can circumvent the shallow. I didn't know who he was. Maybe he'll have redeeming qualities.

Maybe he'll be understanding? Gentle? Kind?

VI

O Captain!

64

The Clinic

*T*he first thing Z made me do was go to the clinic.

"You smell like shit," he said as he dropped me off. "I'll be back in an hour. I'm going apartment hunting. I can't afford the one your previous Elder had you in. It's good of the Divided to extend your stay there until we find you a new one. Bye, kid."

He drove off in his Bugatti.

A Red guard walked me into the building, and the receptionist handed me a clipboard and pen. The pen was full of ink. What a luxury.

I filled out the paperwork as best as I could.

How many sexual partners have you had since your last checkup?

Fuck if I know.

As I waited, I grabbed a copy of *The Monthly*.

It was last month's issue.

"D–Do you have a recent issue of *The Monthly*?" I asked the receptionist.

"We haven't received the shipment yet. Now, please, take a seat."

A few other Minors were in the waiting area. None of us spoke. As I sat there bored, I circled the letters in a different font. *The Minors of Stanford, I hope you're free.*

After Philly, Chavos moved to Stanford to be closer to family. I hope she caught that flight.

Raphael then entered the waiting room.

He took a clipboard and sat next to me.

When my name was called, I left the copy of *The Monthly* next to him.

Daddies Six & Seven

I *once lived in Rome with two Italian daddies.*

Let's call them Six and Seven. Six and Seven were the last two sugardaddies I had before the Bill.

Like Three, Six and Seven didn't pay for my company or help me with my loans, so they weren't exactly sugardaddies. They did do other things to earn themselves the label, though.

Six and Seven were both attractive, middle-aged men. They were a married couple looking for fun. Neither of them spoke English. We spoke only in Italian. I had the essentials down: *buongiorno, ciao, scopami.*

I first met them during my semester abroad when I was gallivanting across Italy. We spent the night together. One thing led to another, and they fell in lust with me. Typical.

After I returned to the United, we kept in touch. I graduated college, started sugaring, and started my first big boy job in an office. Once the pandemic hit, my company moved to remote work.

When I was bumming it at Cedi's, Six and Seven offered to fly me out to Rome. They flashed a golden plane ticket, and my eyes sparkled. I packed my computer, hopped on a plane, and worked from Rome.

At the time, it was a federal crime. Nowadays, I'd be arrested simply for working.

I got fresh espresso every morning.

I frequented museums, absorbed gelato by the gallon, read along the Tiber, and returned home to get plowed by two muscular daddies. You know, Italian shit.

I was their houseboy. I cleaned their house in lingerie and cooked them dinner in only an apron. I know I said I didn't want to be a houseboy, but this was Rome!

My first weekend with them, they took me to a nude, gay-friendly resort. It was lovely, despite what happened.

I must preface: I am blessed with white privilege. I am.

I'm of Italian and Swedish descent. My surname is obviously Italian, but that doesn't mean much these days.

According to stereotypes, my skin is too hairless to be Italian and too olive to be Swedish. I'm not blond. I'm not loud. I'm not this. I'm not that. I'm too much of this and not enough of that.

"Your American blood muddles the purity of Italy," Six told me. It wasn't the first time I heard a comment like this. Most Europeans are nationalistic. They refuse to let Americans feel belonged.

"What else are you?" Six asked.

"I'm not sure."

"Oh, well, you must be something. Cuban? Puerto Rican? Argentinian?"

He phrased it so strangely, that I must be something as if nothing was an option.

Why is American not enough?

Many people—companies, schools, guys at bars—act like they want uniqueness and diversity, but they don't care if you share your world with them or not. No, they'd prefer to make you a poster child to show the world they, too, are open-minded. They won't say it, but they want tokens.

I don't care what they think I am. I know I am white.

If Italians don't want me, that is fine. While I was raised in their Americanized culture, I've never felt much connected to the motherland, even when I learned their language and lived *la dolce vita.*

The queer community is where I have felt most belonged. I can't say I have felt *fully* belonged because many queer people—who prefer the label gay over queer—deny my existence as a non-binary individual. They see me as a gay man. Nothing more, nothing else.

We boast about our inclusivity. Yet, the queer community is much divided. Many gay people want only what they themselves are. Nothing more, nothing else.

At the resort, a group of Polish gays with pink dicks were next to us, talking about us, talking about me.

Seven translated.

"They think your dick looks dirty."

"Dirty?"

"Yes. They're curious why it's so … brown."

The dirty comment was an insult, but the brown part was true. My dick is much darker than the rest of my body. I don't know why. It just is. I've always been aware of the difference in pigment but never found it weird.

And so, on that day, at a resort where shame was not welcome, I covered myself.

In the Divided, uniqueness is not favored per se, but it is—behind doors—sexualized.

No, not sexualized.

Fetishized.

But hey, I can't complain!

At least I'm not the Red. Or the buried.

As for what happened at the resort, well, I was in Rome, for fuck's sake. Sounds like a dream, no?

It was, at first. I was in a city I loved and a country brimming with the culture I was raised in. But a few weeks in, I started to realize Six and Seven were just the same as the daddies across that great blue ocean.

They were pedophilic, arrogant, and controlling.

The first night I got there, they bathed and toweled me like I was a little baby. They got off on it. It was odd. But I was tired and jet-lagged and did not care.

On our second night, they brought me into town and introduced me to their friends. It didn't feel like they actually wanted me to meet them. No, it felt like they were bragging. *Look at this beautiful boy we caught. Can you believe it?* We popped in, I did a twirl, and we popped out. And that was that.

Six and Seven also made comments about pictures I posted on social media. Six told me he didn't like that I posted so many pictures of myself. Pictures of my ass and selfies at the gym or beach. Seven was more direct. He told me I was theirs and needed to stop being a *puttana*. A whore.

I wasn't putting their sexual health at risk. I wasn't sleeping around. I wasn't lying about my status. We used condoms.

As for my posts, it's not like I was posting nudes. Even if I were, it's *my* body.

I called them out on their bullshit. We got into a huge fight. The home quickly became toxic. I knew I needed to leave.

They got a refund on my flight home and told me it was on me now. It's what I deserve, right? For trusting strangers?

They didn't throw me out, but it felt like they could at any moment if I refused.

So, I did what I never knew how to do. I called my brother Billie and asked for help—one of the bravest things I've ever done.

This was a turning point for me.

65

Ask for Water

How about we go back to my place?" he slurred.

His name was Coin. He was a swimmer. Fit, kind, and gay.

Our college was small. To my knowledge, we had about thirty out queer people on campus. I wasn't attracted to any of them or sexually active at the time. I poured that energy into my schoolwork.

Occasionally, I let loose. My way of letting loose was getting high and drunk with my ex-friend Connie. She and I usually got high in the woods and then went to a frat house to get free shots.

Coin was pledging the fraternity.

Midterms had just passed. I drank a little too much. I was slurring my words and stumbling but didn't black out.

Coin was there. He, too, was wasted. He asked Connie if I would be interested. I was either doing a keg stand or ripping a gravity bong.

Coin had an obsessive personality. He repeatedly hit on me, slid into my DMs every day, sent me unsolicited pictures, and even had a friend ask me out for him. Apparently, I'm the intimidating type. I'm not into cowards, so I shot him down. But he didn't take no for an answer. Maybe he thought I would change my mind. So, he kept messaging me.

I'm a ghoster. I already shot him down once. I didn't want to do it again.

Connie told him to go for it, even though she knew how I felt.

That night, he brought me back to his place.

I remember asking where Connie had gone. I didn't know what was happening. It wasn't until he started to undress me that I knew.

He was lying on top of me naked when I asked for a cup of water. I downed it.

What a difference that water made.

While he was in the kitchen, I had enough time to observe my surroundings and realize I was no longer in the frat house. Connie was nowhere to be seen.

The water sobered me enough to ask Coin if we could just go to bed. The water didn't physically sober me. It was mental.

Thankfully, nothing else happened. Around three a.m., I crawled out his window.

I never reported him or told anyone.

I never spoke to him again. That was until several years later when I was living with Three, he sent me a lengthy, thoughtful message. Said he had a lot of time to think about that night. In short, he apologized for taking advantage of me.

I replied with one simple message.

"I had forgiven you a long, long time ago."

66

Star-Crossed

To write this story is to admit the truth.
I've lied so many times in my life that writing has become my way of remembering the truth.

When my daddies and Elders asked for love, I fed them lies. But like every liar, I started believing those lies. I said I love you when I didn't. I tricked my brain into thinking I did. Perhaps I fell for my captors and never truly loved them at all. They never filled a place in my heart, so how could it be called love? I'd rather forget than remember, so why do I write? I left each of my daddies and never looked back. If I loved them, I would've returned, right? But no. No, I only cared about myself.

I wanted money, and daddies wanted me.

But if I'm writing to come clean, I must be honest with myself.

Earlier in this diary, I said I've never been in love. That was a lie. I was in love, once. It was when I returned to Philly after Rome. I moved into a tiny studio apartment in the Gayborhood.

I decided to quit sugaring for good.

I still worked full-time at the company that paid me less than thirty thousand. I picked up hours at a coffee shop. I applied for better jobs every day. Months went by. I heard only rejections. I tried writing during the little free time I had, but of course, that led nowhere.

I was scraping by.

There were times when I thought about going back to sugaring, of course. Weak times when I thought it was the only thing I could do in life, the one thing I'm good at. But sugaring only led me to trouble. I know that now. Sugaring led me to the wrong people and fake love.

Though my daddies said they loved me, I never once believed them. Call it trust issues, whatever. I know in my heart that all they wanted was a cute boy to parade around and get caught with, someone pretty to fuck to make themselves feel less ugly, someone to make them less lonely and perhaps young again.

Each of them said I was mature for my age. Did they only say this to make themselves feel better?

I knew I didn't want that life anymore. No more daddies. Just me. I wanted more for myself. Not to say I wanted less for myself before. Everyone wants more. But in a way, I never felt like I deserved more. I suppose that's why I never put any effort into love. I didn't care to love because I knew I had an abundance of karmic debt noosed around my neck. How could anyone so selfish ever be so lucky? No matter how kind I am to people—even undeserving people—it will never make up for all the poison in my heart. It will never make up for what I did to Ollivander. It will never make up for all the lies I told and all the running and greed and self-absorption.

But I knew I could try. I knew I could try to absolve myself of those immoralities. I knew I needed to quit sugaring, change my behavior, and live a more honest life. I wanted to turn my life around. I wanted to make good, honest money and take care of my damn self. And if real love ever did find me, I'd accept it graciously.

I was twenty-four when it happened.

I was still living paycheck to paycheck. My degree in French lit and econ led me nowhere. I had interviews for better jobs, and by better jobs, I mean better pay. I got to the fifth and sixth rounds of interviews like I was in a video game about to go toe-to-toe with the big boss. But then I received the "Unfortunately" email. They'd say some bullshit like, "We're actually not hiring at the moment" or "We're looking for someone a little more senior."

Work was the same.

The only thing that really changed during that period of my life was me. I was being more vulnerable and honest with people. Blunt, really. I started developing roots in the city. I found my favorite coffee shop, park, and running and biking spots. I found a group of gays to hang out with every Friday over dinner or to watch drag. They were kind and made me feel belonged. I didn't want to screw it up.

I had crushes on all of them.

One guy in the group was named Weston. He was thirty-four at the time. He was handsome, sweet, smart, and thoughtful. He had pampered Lebanese skin and a hockey-player frame. He was quirky, too. He spoke in quotes; you'd only know it if you knew the references. He quoted comedy sketch scenes, television shows, and politicians. I was the same way. And when you know each other's references, sometimes it feels like an insider. I caught most of his references, but some were outside my algorithm. I learned them eventually. Against my will, really. He quoted them every day until they got stuck in my head.

Our first kiss was at a gay bar. I didn't think anything of it, honestly. We were with the gays. By midnight, it was one big, insignificant makeout sesh.

For our first date, I went to his place and made him a home-cooked meal. Spaghetti squash and bruschetta with fresh artisan bread. We drank a bottle of red and ate by candlelight. After dinner, we sat on his couch and talked about life. We drank and played our favorite songs off his speaker. He played Janet and a song titled "Return of the Mack." It had to be the extended mix, he said. I had never heard the song before. When he played it, I knew this man had taste.

I played some Adele, Jhené, and Sade. Sade convinced me to play my sex playlist. It was smooth sailing from there. We started making out. I climbed on top of him, and one thing led to another…

I didn't want to have sex on the first date, but fuck it. I wasn't expecting anything from him anyway. To me, he was just another man wanting what they all want.

While his dick was thick and a perfect eight inches, our first time was not the best. I didn't even cum. He didn't know my body then. Perhaps it was also the wine. He came and thought it was great. I was on a new path of honesty, though.

"It was meh," I said.

He was offended and thus determined to do better next time. And he did. He learned my body and how to make me cum simply from fucking me.

From the third time onward, it was the best sex I've ever had. I might've been young, yes, but I had had sex with many, *many* men. I don't know the exact number. It must be in the hundreds.

Weston was better than all of them.

He was more than that, though. He was loving and tender. A dream, really.

He grew to be my confidant, my best friend. We cooked together and baked olive oil cakes and pistachio cookies. He showed love in his stews, and I in my curries. We gathered friends for brunches and dinners. We danced in the kitchen and listened to rock and R&B. We bonded over shows and vacationed together. I wrote him little notes and hid them in his suitcase. Some of my fondest memories are of us sipping coffee on a Sunday. Simple. Even the not-so-good parts were good. When we hurt each other's feelings and fought, we communicated and apologized. And that makes all the difference.

We fell in love, unfortunately. He met my family, chosen and blood. I moved in. All was well.

But not a year later, the United divided. The Bill was ratified. And all good things came to an end.

Many people will read this and think, "Wow, this person really jumps from one relationship to the next. They don't know how to be alone."

They're wrong. I love being alone. But I can't blame them. I am a whore. I jumped from Albany to Rome to Philly in less than six months.

Yet, I have never considered my affairs with daddies and my companionships with Elders to be "relationships." They were never about deep love. I never used them to fill a void, not to say that's what deep love is about. The affairs were about taking advantage of dirty men and their easy money. The companionships, well, they were pure survival.

Weston was the first person I actually felt like I dated. And he was certainly the first and only person I've ever been in love with.

One time, he and I went down to his family's lake house in Maryland. We both woke up from nightmares, tangled in each other's arms. His nightmare was of a ghost. He was only spooked. My nightmare was of him falling over a staircase. I think I had heard him grumbling in his sleep, and my dream had contorted into a vision of him in pain.

When Weston and I were together, I found it difficult to accept his love.

It was my avoidant attachment style; I craved self-sufficiency.

Love was also not what I had asked the universe for. Love was the last thing on my mind. I wanted a better job. A better home. To be published. More money. More freedom. More travels. A more accepting family. Only then had I expected love to come.

I was annoyed. Why did I find love before everything else? Why did love have to come first? A career and a home meant food and shelter. That, to me, is survival. Love is a privilege. A gift. It's a want, not a need.

I had yet to find a better job. I was still scraping by. When Weston and I went out, he paid for most things, even groceries. I paid for the things I could afford, but the relationship felt lopsided. It reminded me of the days when I was a sugarbaby. I didn't like that. I wanted to take care of myself. I wanted to treat *him!*

But no. No, the universe wanted to test me by resurfacing my intrusive thoughts. Will I ever amount to anything on my own? Will I ever be able to take care of myself? Am I only valuable when I am with a man? And are all relationships just transactional?

I had to learn how to overcome these thoughts. So, I opened up to him about my past. When I told him everything, he was, as usual, so kind and understanding. He said we were in different places in our lives and that it was okay to let someone take care of you. He said I took care of him every time I made him dinner or a cappuccino, did the dishes, or did his laundry. Of course, he was just trying to make me feel better.

I did feel a bit better, but those thoughts never left me. They haunted me every day I woke up under *his* roof, a house *he* was paying for. *It'll never be your home, Dime. Ever.* They haunted me every time we went to the market. *You can barely afford groceries… How pathetic.* And they haunted me every night we went out with our friends. *Does he actually love you, or is he just showing you off? Do you actually love him, or are you just using him for his money?* These were thoughts I fought every day I was with him.

If only I had more money, perhaps these thoughts would vanish, I always thought. I'll never know. The Divided robbed me of ever finding out.

When the Bill was ratified, Weston was in Kansas for a work convention. I still had my apartment. I could've put that money toward my loans. But I've been homeless so many times. I needed a backup plan in case we ever broke up. It was only a few hundred dollars anyway.

While Weston was in Kansas, I was in my apartment. He called when he heard the news. He said all flights had been canceled, and he was determined to find a way back to me. He was scared. We were all scared.

Then, our phones were turned off. I never heard from him again.

He was thirty-four at the time. Thirty-fucking-four. He was a month away from his birthday. If I had an ounce of real luck, he could've been my Elder.

Many couples were torn apart by the Law.

Some physically, kicking and screaming.

Others accepted defeat and cooperated with the Red.

A few, like me and Weston, were never given the chance to end things. We were forced to move on without any closure.

Then there were those who ran away together.

And died together.

How romantic.

67

Thumbless

Z and I haven't spent much time together.

Z refuses to spend time with me until my STDs clear up. I can't blame him. I smell foul. I scrubbed myself raw, trying to shed the odor.

I was given a shot for gonorrhea and antibiotics for chlamydia. Thankfully, it wasn't anything worse. The doctor said the infections would take one to two weeks to clear up. We had to abstain from sex until then.

So, Z kept his distance.

It was nice to spend some time alone in Y's suite before moving to the apartment building down the street. I spent the two weeks working out, journaling, and enjoying the sun on the balcony.

My red triangle was healing just fine. Oh, how I earned it.

The only time Z visited me was to drop off groceries, Neosporin, and my copy of *The Monthly*. Ever since Tether told me about the hidden messages, I've been decoding the pamphlets nonstop. I learned they had stopped in Stanford, Atlanta, Boston, Roanoke, Jacksonville, Annapolis, twice outside New York, and a few other places I can't remember.

When will they come here?

I had grown to be disappointed in the messages. I bet they'll make another stop in New York, Boston, or perhaps both. They are both highly populated cities. I can't be upset. I want other Minors to escape this hell as well. None of us deserve this.

I finished circling all the letters in a slightly different font, grabbed a piece of paper, and strung the letters together.

thewoodlandswestphillydecemberfifthoneam

I separated the words.

The Woodlands, Philly, December 5th, 1 am

I stood up, my heart racing.

I looked at the pamphlet's issue date: *December 2nd.* If today is the same day as the issue date, that means I have three nights until pick-up.

The Woodlands are in West Philly. I used to go there all the time.

I must let Tether know. I should also verify today's date with her.

I looked out the apartment door, saw no one, and ran to Tether's apartment. I knocked on her door, but no one answered. I put my ear to the door and heard nothing.

Maybe she's out for a run.

I went back to my apartment and read the pamphlet over and over just to make sure I had circled the right letters. Later that night, I went back to Tether's apartment. Still no answer.

Where the fuck is she?!

I couldn't go to sleep that night.

I was worried about Tether. I also couldn't stop thinking about the pick-up. What if the pick-up is tonight? What if I miss my only chance to escape? Do I wait until tomorrow to ask Z what the date is? That's if he visits.

I went to Tether's door again and pounded so hard I probably woke up someone downstairs.

I was getting angry, anxious, and impatient.

I paced up and down the hall. It must be around eleven. The sun went down five or so hours ago.

What if I went down to the lobby and asked the building's guard for the date? Would that be suspicious? Would I get in trouble?

I saw no harm in asking, so I hopped in the elevator and went down to the lobby.

The guard stood with her hand on her gun.

"You're not authorized to leave your apartment without the presence of your Elder. Go back upstairs, or else I'll have to report you."

"I'm sorry. I was just wondering, c–could you tell me the date?"

She eyed me. "Why?"

"Umm, I–I think it's my birthday."

"Oh." She checked her watch. "Your birthday is December 4th?"

My stomach dropped.

"–Yes. Yes, it is." Another lie to add to my heap.

"Well, happy birthday then. Now, please, go back to your apartment."

"Right. Sorry. Thank you."

I thought about asking her where the girl in the apartment next to mine was. But that would be too suspicious.

Back in the apartment, I thought out loud.

"I'm in Center City. It's about three miles from here to the Woodlands. If I run at an eight-minute pace, I can be there in under thirty minutes. I must be careful. I can't be seen. The dark will provide me with coverage. It's eleven-ish. Pick-up is at one. I have around two hours, give or take. Where the fuck is Tether?!"

I went back down the hall and knocked again.

"Fuck it, I'll bust it down."

I rammed my shoulder repeatedly into the door, but it didn't budge. It always looked so easy on television. I rubbed my shoulder and gave up. I can't bust my shoulder before running three miles across a city. Besides, if anyone was in there, they would've answered by now.

"One step at a time, Dime."

I returned to the apartment, packed my journal, napkins, and flowers into a drawstring bag, and dressed in all-black running attire.

Then, I remembered the tracker in my thumb. I'd have to cut it off.

Thankfully, when the Red raided the apartment, they left the knives. I went to the kitchen and grabbed the sharpest one. I stuffed a rag into my mouth. In one swift motion, I was thumbless.

It was painful, but I've been through worse.

I wrapped the rag around my bloody stump and went out the door with the knife still in hand.

When the elevator opened, I ran toward the guard like a savage animal.

I was about to pierce her temple when she held up her hands and opened her red camo jacket. Pinned to her chest was a Diamond brooch.

"Get out of here!" she urged. "Quickly! And here!" She tossed me her watch.

I caught it and stumbled out the door, confused.

The watch read twelve.

Fuck, it's later than I thought.

I fastened the watch around my wrist and clutched at the knife.

As I ran through the city, I shied away from as many streetlamps as possible. I took as many back alleys as I could. Running across Broad was difficult. It's such a large street; anyone could've seen me.

I ran faster.

All that training was not for my Elders' pleasure. It was for this moment.

There weren't many drivers out. I saw a few Elders walking around, but I hid in the shadows until they passed.

I approached one of the bridges that crossed the Schuylkill. I was daunted by the open space. There were a lot of lampposts. Cars would easily see me.

So far, I haven't seen any Red.

I was hiding in an alley, waiting for an Elder to pass, when an idea came to me.

"Hey!"

The Elder turned, and I brought the dagger to his head. It pierced his crow's feet and slid through his eyes. I could see my reflection in the bloodied dagger as if his eyes were mine. For a brief and twisted moment, the reflected eyes looked like Tether's.

"I'm so sorry," I said to the Elder as I pushed his naked, twitching body under a dumpster.

I threw on his gray cloak and walked across the bridge as coolly as possible, hoping the passing cars couldn't see my youth under the hood.

When I made it across the bridge, I started running again. I kept the cloak on just in case.

I was running through UPenn's campus now. I saw a lot of Red over there. I also saw other people running in the shadows, I think. Were they other Minors? I didn't stop to check. If they were out there, I'd meet them at the cemetery.

A three-mile run is a cakewalk for me.

I've always been fit, even before Minority. The difficult parts were staying in the shadows and, well, killing a person. Yeah, he was an Elder and probably horrible. But he could've been one of the good ones. I couldn't think about that now.

I finally reached the entrance to the cemetery.

If a plane is going to land here, it will land in the center where there's the most space.

I checked the watch. It was a quarter to one. I threw off the cloak, found a red-brick path, and weaved through a hundred headstones. To my left and right, I saw other Minors doing the same. Most were running. Some were biking. And a few were roller skating. Slay.

I was sweating and consumed with adrenaline disguised as euphoria. I might actually be escaping this hell.

At the heart of the cemetery was a circle of trees and the richest of the buried.

Around thirty Minors were there, catching their breaths and checking on their wounded hands.

I looked around, hoping to see Tether. She wasn't there.

I didn't know the Minors around me but recognized their faces from the Sunday rituals. One was Raphael. He made it.

I made it.

The wind picked up.

A giant Military copter floated down from the sky and landed near us. It came out of nowhere. The copter was so black and quiet that I only noticed it because of the upshift in wind. None of the others had heard it coming either. The silence and massiveness of the aircraft scared us at first. When its mouth opened, no light flooded out, only more darkness.

Some Minors were hesitant as they boarded.

Not me. I ran.

When the door closed, the copter took off into the night.

Lights turned on inside. There were windows, but they were tinted.

"Buckle up, everyone," said a man in green.

He looked fifty. It put us on edge.

"It's okay. You're safe now."

We didn't believe him until the co-pilot looked over his shoulder and said, "Please, trust the man."

He looked our age. So, we buckled up.

I looked out a window and watched the cemetery shrink. I expected the Red to emerge from nowhere and take us back to our Elders. But I saw no sirens. I saw no red camo. Could it be true? Could this really be happening?

The captain of the plane looked like a woman from behind. She had strawberry-blond hair and freckled skin. She handed the controls to her co-pilot and stepped out of the cockpit.

We made eye contact, and I was so amazed I wanted to cry.

It was my sister, Penny.

"Hey, Dime." She smiled, her cheeks shiny with tears. "I knew you'd make it!"

68

Dear Weston,

I am sorry I am trying to forget you.
It hurts too much to remember the good days. Days that passed us by. Days we spent drinking coffee and laughing. Days meandering through thrift stores. Days that make today and every day I have left so gray.

Memories of those days should fill me with happiness, no? Because at least I had them? At least they were once mine? At least I knew what it meant to be happy? So why do those memories fill me with great sorrow?

You should be a bigger part of my story. Not these other men who have taken my body. Not these ugly, classist, pedophilic daddies and Elders.

I don't want you to think I don't think about you. I do, and too often. But every time, I feel guilty and don't know why. I'm not sure if guilty is even the word. Disloyal? Wrong? The word escapes me. But from Elder to Elder and through my days of punishment, every time I glimpse my red triangle, those feelings—that missing word—spoil my memory of you. I can only imagine what you'd think and feel if you had seen me tied to that pole. Just the thought of it crushes me.

To remember you is to acknowledge what I will never have again.

Fuck, I miss you. I'll always miss you.

I hope your month as a Minor was bearable. I hope you can find solace as an Elder. I hope your Minor makes you happy. I know you and know you only have one. You have only what the law requires.

I wish it were me.

I wish we could've hunkered down and waited for your induction.

I wish you had never left.

I wish time never mattered.

And I wish luck was on our side.

69

Feb. 1ˢᵗ, 2028

When I was nine, I went to the optometrist for the first time.

I remember taking my new glasses out of their case and sliding them over my ears as my mother drove me home. I cocked my head onto the window and watched leaves engulf the sides of the highway. I could see each and every leaf for the very first time. Before I had glasses, they were just blobs on stems and trunks. Now, they were individuals, defined in color and shape. But they were still part of a whole. It felt like I was seeing with new eyes.

That's what it felt like when we landed in California, the land of the United.

I reunited with my sister and brother. I know now that some of the most genuine relationships can come from siblings. And if you're lucky, a sibling's love can many times, my case included, save your life.

Penny and Nickel caught me up on everything. They told me about the revolution and the Republic of the West Coast and that the Divided—thanks to the pamphlets and spies—is falling. They apologized for not stopping in Philly sooner. If they were senior enough in the revolution, they would've.

They told me that Goldie has an underground bunker for runaway Minors in upstate New York. She coordinates weekly pick-ups with the Republic. What a badass.

Silv has been unreachable since the Bill. According to records, he lives in Tennessee and is an Elder to three.

Can't win them all.

Penny and Nickel also told me, exacerbating my grief, that I had lost many people. Cedi did, in fact, take her life. Weston tried returning to Philly for me but was shot down for not cooperating. Rupiah and her family were found and executed. And my mother.

She, too, is gone.

I am still coping.

I experience culture shock every day. It's strange walking outside and having freedom. I get triggered every time I see someone who looks like they could be an Elder. I'm learning to break down and unlearn those ageist ideas that the Divided instilled in me.

Having Raphael helps. He understands what I've been through. He's gone through similar if not worse.

He thanked me for leaving the pamphlet next to him at the clinic.

While we both struggle, we've learned how to allow ourselves real love. I've learned how to make people feel needed. I've learned I'm more than just a body. And I've learned how to ask for help.

Raphael and I are not dating. I'm not ready for that. Neither is he. But we're friends. We go to group therapy sessions with the other Minors from Philly. Ex-Minors, I should say.

We talk about our experiences and help each other feel understood and validated. We cry, yell, and choke on our words, but we're getting to a place where we can smile and laugh.

Chavos is also here!

She caught the flight in Stanford. Apart from my siblings, it's nice to have a piece of home.

She, like Raphael, understands the hardships I carry. She lost her sister and both her parents. She's been in California for a month now. She goes to therapy as well.

She found a Latino community a couple weeks after her arrival and introduced me to them. They've been so kind and welcoming. It's nice to feel part of something bigger, something meaningful. They even helped me find an affordable, one-bedroom apartment. It reminds me of my old West Philly studio—simple and small. But it'll do.

We live along the coast. My window is the ocean. She and I often sit along the shore and take in the sunset.

This new life with her is quite truly about the simple things.

There's music around every corner.

Every Sunday, when I eat brunch on my fire escape, I see a performer singing to a crowd down the street. He's always there. Same time every Sunday. And when I go for walks, I see street performers dancing to drums or a guitar. During my first week here, I cried nearly every time I heard music in public. I know that sounds dramatic, but something happens to you when you go from burning music to hearing it.

I also have a calendar. Before the Bill, I remember feeling stressed looking at all my plans. *So much work, so little time.* But now, after going so long without a calendar, I smile at all my empty days, all my empty boxes. *I am free.*

I am now thirty years old. I intend to make these years count.

Nickel helped me find a job at a local bookstore. I also work at a coffee shop for extra cash. Penny has asked me to join the revolution. I think I will, one day. I just need time.

Some days are hard, I admit. And some nights, nightmares come. But despite everything—everything I've seen and felt, everything physical and mental, every obstacle, ache, and fear—I still have good days. I share them with people I love. And when those days don't come, when the good passes me by, I just listen to music and think of my freedoms.

I am free to write. Though, it took some getting used to without a thumb.

I am free to work and drink coffee.

I am free to say no.

I am free to meet people and make friends and free to love.

Those freedoms—*my* freedoms—allow me to have good days, even on bad ones.

Oh, and the books!

So. Many. Books.

My coworker at the bookstore helped me find where the poem about freedom came from. Kahlil Gibran's *The Prophet*. It's even better reading it from cover to cover.

Raphael likes reading, too.

We sit beside each other and read book after book, catching up on lost time and burnt pages. We'll read like this for the rest of our days, for as long as we're in each other's lives, until we reach that final word, wishing and hoping and dreaming and falling into chapter after chapter and characters in love. We'll visit worlds that ease lingering pains and escape to places full of laughter and kindness. We'll overcome the difficulties of yesterday and find strength to enjoy the peace of now and tomorrow.

I will be that protagonist who has a happy ending.

Raphael and I found a queer community together.

They, too, have been kind and welcoming. They take us to musicals, orchestras, and drag performances.

They help us escape our thoughts and memories and nudge us to remember the fun in life. Their brunches and get-togethers remind us of the importance of friendship, food, and culture.

A drag performer I befriended helped me acquire a Republic of the West Coast passport. I used it to fly to the Swiss Alps to visit Billie and his husband. They're doing well.

I finally met my nephews. They are so sweet.

Forgiveness is not contingent on receiving an apology, contrary to popular belief.

Forgiveness is also not the same as reconciliation.

I've forgiven a lot of people in my life. Griften, Connie, & Robbie. Geld. Silv. My daddies and Elders. My mother. My father. Myself.

I forgive for selfish reasons, but that is okay.

I haven't forgiven the Divided yet. They took away my freedom, life, and youth and branded me with shame. I lost my body several times over. That will take years to forgive, especially since They still have power and could come for us at any moment. Perhaps a flame is being kindled inside me right now as I write.

I haven't decided.

But for now, all I want—all I need—is a warm cup of coffee, a book, and a damn good day.

Acknowledgments

I would like to thank Alejandro Baigorri for the simply effective cover design. You brought my abstract vision to life! Thank you, Jessica Raymond, for the succinct critiques and edits. Your expertise was highly valued. Thank you, Istvan Szabo, Ifj, for the painstaking formatting. Thank you to my family, chosen and blood, for the endless support and love. And to all the kind booksellers who took a chance on *The Diary of the Sugarbaby* and invited me to their fabulous stores, thank you very much! You gave me the chance to travel all over "the Divided!" To the Barnes & Noble in Glastonbury, the Barnes & Noble in Annapolis, New York City PrideFest, Little District Books in Washington, D.C., Barbara's Bookstore in Chicago, the Toadstool Bookshop in Keene, the Barnes & Noble in West Hartford, and the Barnes & Noble in Philadelphia, the *Sugarbaby Book Tour* was all thanks to you!

Discussion Questions

1. Why are the characters' names what they are? Dime, Penny, Billie, Rupiah, Chavos, Cedi… What do they all have in common? And what about Dime's sugardaddies and Elders? Why does he call them by numbers and letters and not by their real names or aliases?

2. Who is Tether? What does she represent? And why did Gagliastro choose to call her Tether?

3. What is the author's stance on the American collegiate education system? After reading Dime's diary, should we, as a society, invest in our children's education for posterity?

4. Why did the author choose to make the book part-fiction and part-autobiographical? Which parts of the story felt real to you and which parts felt fabricated?

5. What is the significance of numbers in *The Diary of a Sugarbaby*? Why are there three Elders and seven sugardaddies? How many chapters are in the book? And why did Gagliastro choose to have that amount?

6. What is the significance of colors in *The Diary of a Sugarbaby*? Why must Minors wear black? Why must Elders wear gray? And why must the police wear red?

7. Why does Dime repeat himself so often, especially regarding his place in the world due to his looks? There's a chapter called *Intrusive Thoughts*. What are intrusive thoughts and does this have anything to do with the repetitive nature of the novel?

8. What does Dime's birthday foreshadow? How many of his birthdays transpired throughout the novel? In the Divided, Minors are not allowed calendars. How does Dime know if his birthday is near?

9. How is the plot of *The Diary of a Sugarbaby* reflective of today's social, political, and economic climate? How has the United States improved, and how have we regressed?

10. How does Dime cope with his homelessness? How does he feel toward self-prostitution? How are these two themes entwined? And how do they affect Dime's perspective and definition of home? How would you define home?

11. Who is Penny? What does she symbolize?

12. What does coffee represent in *The Diary of a Sugarbaby*? What about calendars?

13. In chapter 13 *Titanic*, Dime reveals that when he was ten, his family lost their business and house and had to couch-surf with family. After a family feud, they had to live in a motel. How did this spell of homelessness mentally affect Dime in the long term? How was his idea of *love, family,* and *home* altered?

14. Why is Weston called Weston? How is the prefix "West" relevant and symbolic? And why is he only mentioned at the end of the novel?

15. There is a chapter entitled *Gloria Steinem*. Who is Gloria Steinem and how did she inspire Gagliastro's writing?

16. How was the marketing of the book satirical? And why did the author choose to market it that way?

17. Dissect the cover. What do you see? Why is the cover red? How does the abstract design by Alejandro Baigorri reflect the story?

18. Compare and contrast Gagliastro's *The Diary of a Sugarbaby* and Margaret Atwood's *The Handmaid's Tale*.

Afterword

When one writes, one ought to write with intention. Sometimes, the intention should be conspicuous; but that can and may erase the possibility of veiled cleverness. Other times, the intention should be inconspicuous but nevertheless present; this can and may drive the reader to inaccurately believe that the "intention," if identified, is insignificant or arbitrary. Throughout *The Diary of a Sugarbaby*, J.Q. Gagliastro sprinkles both conspicuous and inconspicuous intentions within character names, chapter titles, and pronouns.

The sugardaddies and Elders are the no-name characters of the story. In Chapter 17 *Diamond*, the protagonist Dime states, "[My first Elder's] name wasn't really X. That would be stupid. I'm only referring to him as X because the Divided emphasize discretion." His behavior of not naming his Elders mimics his previous behavior of not naming his sugardaddies. "My work as a sugarbaby taught me the importance of discretion all too well … Why not aliases? If I had given [my sugardaddies and Elders] aliases—actual names, not numbers or letters—it would've humanized them, and then they'd feel more real. Perhaps I'd become attached." During the auctioning of Minors, the names of the Minors are not once mentioned, only their superficial stats, (i.e. height, weight, age, etc.) The lack of names invokes a sense of irreverence. From Dime's experiences as a sugarbaby, he discovered that his daddies never truly cared about him; they never cared to know who "Dime" was. They only wanted a body, somebody to nod along to their stories. Dime calls his sugardaddies by One, Two, Three, Four, Five, Six, and Seven and his Elders by X, Y, and Z and not by their actual names to mimic their irreverent behavior, thus reiterating the idiom "Hurt people hurt people" mentioned in part *Daddy Three* and the idiom "When you're treated like an animal, you behave like an animal" mentioned in Chapter 30 *The Court Hearing.*

One must also note the difference in capitalization. Sugarbaby and sugardaddy are only capitalized when they start a sentence. Elder and Minor are always capitalized. They are proper nouns and reflect the severity of the gerontocratic regime. The words "sugarbaby" and "sugardaddy" are also each spelled as one word throughout *The Diary of a Sugarbaby.* Most credible dictionaries spell each of those words as two words (i.e. "sugar baby" and "sugar daddy"). The purpose of the subtraction of space is to reflect romantic words like girlfriend and boyfriend despite the quasiromantic nature of the sugarbaby-sugardaddy relationship and dynamic.

Apart from Dime's Elders, sugardaddies, Raphael, Weston, and Tether, all character names are related to money. Dime's name and his siblings' names—Goldie, Silv, Billie, Nickel, & Penny—relate to precious metals, a dollar bill, and American currency. The meanings of those names are conspicuous. The meanings of the names of Dime's chosen family—Rupiah, Cedi, Chavos, Yuan, and Geld—are inconspicuous if you are not familiar with world currency and slang. Rupiah is the official currency of Indonesia. This is to pay homage to Rupiah's Indonesian culture and heritage but also to continue this monetary theme. Cedi is the unit of currency of Ghana. Chavos is Puerto Rican slang for money. Yuan is the basic monetary unit of the People's Republic of China. Geld is the German translation for money. In Chapter 13 *Titanic*, Dime expresses an intrusive thought and says, "People say blood is thicker than water, but what's thicker than blood? Gold. Silver. A thick wallet. You see, money will always prevail and matter more to people, all people, regardless of blood." Gagliastro reiterates this point by relating his characters' most fundamental characteristic (their names) to money. The goal of these monetary names is to make the reader ponder why we put money on such a high pedestal. "A pedestal where friendship and knowledge should be?

Where peace and health should be? Where love and family should tower?" (Chapter 21 *Belonging*). Why do we, as a society, put money before family? Or work before family? Should we continue to live that way? How do we balance the capitalist system and mindset?

The character names of Griften, Connie, and Robbie continue Gagliastro's conspicuous intentions and monetary theme. Their names have a thieving undertone. Griften (i.e. "to grift") is given her name because she stole money from Penny with whom she had been friends since childhood. Connie (i.e. "to con") is given her name because when her sugarmama conned her out of ten grand and her parents asked where the money had gone, Connie used Dime as a scapegoat. Connie knew about Dime's financial instability and previous spells of homelessness and saw him as easy prey, a believable lie. In today's social climate, minorities tend to be a scapegoat for many people of privilege and power. Robbie is given her name because she robs "a measly two hundred bucks from a friend" (Chapter 49 *Robbed, Conned, & Grifted*). Throughout Dime's life, he had plenty of people who put money before their relationships. That is why he has "never believed in what people call unconditional love" (Chapter 4 *A Liar, a Cheat, & a Thief*).

Raphael is a reference to the famous Italian painter and architect of the High Renaissance. His work is to be admired not touched. Gagliastro's Raphael was a means to demonstrate Dime's lust. In the authoritarian world of the Divided, queer folk are exterminated as they are seen as filth. However, Dime, Raphael, and many other LGBTQIA+ individuals survive the Ameriqueerocide and are in hiding. "The Ameriqueerocide happened and is still happening, yet we're still here, under their noses, beneath their very sheets… We have always existed all over the world, in every corner of history, and we will continue to exist exactly the way we are" (Chapter 9 *Verlan*). But because the queer community is either eradicated or forced back into the closet, most desires are suppressed for pure survival. All Dime can do is admire Raphael from far, and even then, he must be weary. "I willed myself not to look at Raphael. I could not daydream. If I got a semi in public, I'd be whipped until I bled" (Chapter 6 *The Ameriqueerocide*).

Weston is and was Dime's one true romantic partner before the fall of society. Their first kiss was at a gay bar. Weston was referred to as "loving and tender. A dream, really" (Chapter 66 *Star-Crossed*). The chapter title is a reference to the tragic and unlucky Shakespearean love affair that ends with the demise of both Romeo and Juliet. The character of Weston is not introduced until the end of the novel. In Chapter 68 *Dear Weston*, Dime apologizes to Weston. "I am sorry I am trying to forget you. It hurts too much to remember the good days. Days that passed us by. Days we spent drinking coffee and laughing… Memories of those days should fill me with happiness, no? Because at least I had them? At least they were once mine? At least I knew what it meant to be happy? So why do those memories fill me with great sorrow?" He lies to himself because love hurts, especially in the form of memories. But even in the darkest of times, one must find hope; and to find hope, one must look in places of love. The prefix of Weston's name is "West." In Chapter 50 *Little Rebellions*, Dime learns about the Republic of the West Coast, a place of hope; a place where anyone could live and love freely. In the end, Dime escapes to the West and finds refuge—a euphemism for home. The connection between the name Weston and the Republic of the West Coast begs the question: What does love truly mean?

The intention behind the character of Tether is the most inconspicuous. To tether means to tie (usually an animal) with a rope or chain to restrict its movement. Tether is debatably not a real name. Gagliastro wanted the name to sound real or at least reminiscent of a real name (i.e. Heather). Tether is a Minor like Dime. Minors live a constrictive life and live in "gilded cages" (Chapter 32 *Elder Y*). But the meaning of the name goes deeper than that. In Chapter 36 *Tether*, Dime sees he has new neighbors and asks his Elder, Y, about them. Y claims that no one is on their floor. Tether then illegally pays Dime a neighborly visit and drops off cookies. The reader is led to believe Y is gaslighting Dime, a behavior many patriarchs tend to assume. But why would he do that? In Chapter 50 *Little Rebellions*, Dime enters Tether's apartment and says, "Her apartment looked exactly like mine. Same furniture, same decor, same everything… We sat on her couch—my couch—and talked." Not once in the story did Dime or Y ever bump into Tether's Elder. Tether was also the character who told Dime about the hidden messages in the monthly newsletters for Minors. She claimed she had been decoding them ever since she found out. If that were true, she would've been there at the end with Dime in the chopper. But she wasn't. Gagliastro intended to leave the reader with questions. Who was Tether? Was she ever real? The cookies she gave Dime were real, but did Dime just make those? Was Tether an undercover Republic of the West Coast spy who helped Minors escape? Or was she all in Dime's head? In a world where friendships, family, and partnerships were banned, who could blame Dime if he had an imaginary friend? If she wasn't real, how did he know about the hidden messages? In Chapter 51 *Body Positivity*, Dime claims he is "not intelligent in the literal sense of the word." Could he have been smarter than he had realized? Could he have had more faith in others than he claims to? The character of Tether grounds Dime to reality even if she was imaginary; she tethered him to a place of hope.

The name of the dystopian world in which Dime is forced to live is also important to note. The Divided [States] is the very antithesis of the United States. In Chapter 3 *Autonomy*, Dime states, "Our region of the post-United isn't actually called the Divided. Imagine what the rest of the world would think! No. *I* call it the Divided. You might find the name unimaginative. I find it appropriate." He then uses the capitalized They/Them pronouns to refer to the Divided throughout the story. It is meant to mirror Dime's nonbinary identity in addition to poking fun at our society; a society that villainizes the nonbinary identity (and the queer identity in general). He also uses They/Them pronouns for the Divided so that in moments when the reader thinks Dime is talking about his Elders or daddies, he is actually referring to the Divided. In Chapter 2

Minority, Dime journals, "[Our] bodies belong not to [ourselves] but to Them." Here, "Them" could be the Elders but also the Divided. In Chapter 6 *The Ameriqueerocide*, Dime journals, "They wanted to seem pure and sinless to the rest of the world. But at night, They would welcome a gay, Black boy or a trans, Asian girl into their room and fuck them raw." Again, "They" could be the Elders but also the Divided. Regardless, when Dime says, "fuck them raw," yes, he means it literally but also socio-politically. In Chapter 10 *Ageism*, Dime journals, "People never change, not because They can't, but because They don't want to." Dime is talking about people in general but ties in the capitalized "They" to denote the Divided, emphasizing that it is people in places of power and privilege who do not seek change. In a world full of rich daddies, be a Penny.

~ J.Q. Gagliastro

If you enjoyed *The Diary of a Sugarbaby* by J.Q. Gagliastro, please PLEASE leave a review on any of the following platforms! Reviews go a long way!

Amazon   Barnes & Noble   Goodreads

And if you loved the book, buy some Merch!

And follow J.Q.'s Instagram for upcoming projects and use the #thediaryofasugarbaby and #jqgagliastro to spread the word!

Instagram

Turn the page for a sneak peek into
J.Q. Gagliastro's next novel,

Mercury to the Moon

an illustrated fantasy space odyssey

A Dragon Escapes the Sun

Krimmiel gazed out a dusty window overlooking the purple streets of the planet Mercury. His eyes brimmed with daydreams as sunlight poured onto his shoulders. The Sun was nailed to the sky, its dragons burning fiercely. Their scales and rays illuminated Krimmiel's boyish good looks to the point of unrealistic beauty. Even his slicked-back blond hair and contrasting brown eyebrows seemed too good to be true.

Behind Krimmiel, in an armchair beneath a flickering lightbulb, sat an old human-sized bee named Sin. Sin had seven limbs; six were legs and one a stinger. He also had a furry thorax and two veiny wings and was puffing out colored smoke from his rainbow cigar. One puff was a crimson red and another an icy blue. His body resembled a voluminous evening gown with black-and-yellow stripes and honey drooping from his hoop skirt made of honeycomb. The amber liquid was hardened with age and smelled cloyingly sweet.

Krimmiel was used to the old bee's smell, but sometimes, it did give him a headache like a candle burning for too long.

The two friends were in a musty, poorly ventilated hotel room. It reeked of honey, tobacco, and mothballs.

"I think I'll go for a stroll." Krimmiel coughed over the second-hand smoke. "Would you care to join me?"

"All's well, thank you," Sin replied, his voice deep and raspy. "But could you stop by the Dragon's Belly and pick up some fried butterflies and cherry blossom soup for dinner?" As he spoke, his eyes—which were made of tarnished, ruby gemstones—peered over the newspaper held in two of his pollen-covered limbs. The headline read *KRIMMIEL: A MENACE TO ALIENKIND!*

"Sure, no problem," replied Krimmiel. "Anything *enlightening* they're saying about me these days?" He nodded to the newspaper.

"Just that you 'pose risk to alien-livelihood' and 'are a horrible citizen of Aether,'" quoted Sin. "You really should stop warping wherever you want. They always catch you."

"Not always." Krimmiel grinned, threw on a crop top, and headed out into the blistering heat.

"Oh, and Krimmiel!" Sin hollered, fluttering up from the armchair and dragging his gown to the door.

"Yes?" Krimmiel turned, whipping the chili pepper that dangled from his left ear lobe. The earring was made of glass and glinted in the city lights.

"Could you ask the hotel staff for another lightbulb? The one we have is dying, and I'm having a difficult time reading with my cataracts. I don't know why you booked a room at the Heavenly Hotel…" grumbled Sin. "There's nothing heavenly about it!"

"Hey, I didn't ask you to come," Krimmiel shot back, still grinning. "You came of your own free will, remember?"

"Of course I remember. I wasn't going to let you go to your hearing alone!"

"Besides," Krimmiel pressed on, "we just need a place to sleep. We don't need to live it up in a five-star, Venusian château, do we?"

"Well, it would be nice for a change!"

Krimmiel rolled his eyes. "I'll talk to the hotel staff."

With that, the beautiful man strode into the bright city streets and was engulfed in purple. The lightbulbs in the roads' lampposts were a shade of plum. The sidewalks were the color of wine. Buildings were painted entirely violet. And the parks were wild with lavender and wisteria.

The serpentine dragons of the Sun, which consumed most of the sky, coiled and raged, flickered and smoldered, ceaselessly so. Krimmiel looked unfazed, as though this were a normal sight.

The heavy traffic halted. Krimmiel crossed, glancing from car to car. The alien cars were much smaller than Earthling cars and looked like a hybrid between a Martian rover and a Volkswagen Beetle. The solar panels attached to their roofs flared out into wings, and the logos varied from a blue, crescent moon to a planet with rings.

He passed a boutique selling the latest Lunar boots and wandered down an alley. At its end was a fence and sign that read *Beyond This Point Is the Spider Cavity: TURN BACK NOW!* He veered down another alley and reached a second dead end. *BEWARE: Force Field Ahead*, the sign read.

As he returned to center city, he strolled past two women gossiping.

"Is that the man who almost *exposed* our existence to an Earthling?!" one woman whispered with disdain.

The other woman nodded, alarmed and wide-eyed.

When Krimmiel's gaze met theirs, they squealed and scurried into a shop.

He ignored them and headed toward the vibrantly colored archway that read *The Dragon's Belly*. He hopped in line at a food truck shaped like a pink dragon and watched people in all sorts of outfits bustle around from vendor to vendor, buying Martian snacks, Neptunial seafood, and Earthling cuisine.

"Greetings, sir!" a man said, squinting down at Krimmiel. "How may I help you?"

"May I have two cups of blossom soup and a bag of fried butterflies, please? And can I make that the … *Heliconius charithonia* flavor?" Krimmiel stumbled over the butterfly's scientific name.

"Absolutely." As he put together the order, the man pushed his bifocals up his nose and gave Krimmiel a curious look. "You look familiar, son. Do I know you?"

"I don't believe so." Krimmiel took the food and handed the man an alien coin, which was shaped like a golden star. "Keep the change!"

As he left the marketplace, he noticed several of the vendors were hastily closing shop. At the crosswalk, children were playing on the curb.

"KIDS, GET INSIDE!" shouted a woman from a window, her eyes stamped with fright. "There's a Leonian dragon loose in the city! HURRY UP!"

"That's not funny, Mom!" the little boy hollered, his voice trembling.

"It's not like a house could protect us anyway," replied the girl. "A fire dragon would burn down Violetteville in one breath!"

"Stop it!" The boy bolted inside, blanching and tripping over his feet. The girl chuckled and followed.

As Krimmiel crossed the street, a car came swerving around him, honking and piercing the air with the squeal of brakes. The driver seemed to be speeding away from something. The car did a donut and struck a pole, shattering its windows in a thunderous clap.

Krimmiel fell backward onto the sidewalk, and the soup spilled and scorched him. He gave a yelp, but it was masked by a mighty *ROAR!* He jerked his head toward the end of the street. The searing pain washed from his mind as a fiery beast came barreling down the boulevard. The creature's face lacked flesh and resembled a bony carcass found in the desert. Its feral red eyes narrowed. Its ravening tongue forked like the road. Its scales were like a king's regalia, warm in color—red, amber, and gold. They were beginning to brown, too, a sign of its old age. Its body was aflame, plasmic, and staggered with sharpened wings. In an instant, the laser-like ruby tendrils attached to its head whipped in the air, slashed down lampposts, and incinerated trees. Its body was miles long, so long Krimmiel could not see the end of it. The dragon must have wrapped its tail around hundreds of block corners, tying itself into a skein.

The beast scorched the sides of buildings and melted pavement.

Krimmiel helped the driver out of their car. As the two ducked for cover, the dragon showered the street in flames, coalescing its roar with screams of bloody murder.

The cement became warm in an instant like a saucepan.

Krimmiel covered his head and watched through the gaps of his arms the dragon soaring down the street. As if in slow motion, the dragon's scales did something very strange… They morphed into the image of an eighteen-year-old boy, like a hieroglyphic in a torchlit cave. The boy's feminine looks and caramel hair became but an outline, speckled with stars. Though it was a split second, Krimmiel felt as though time froze.

When the dragon's tail finally caught up with the rest of the dragon, Krimmiel jumped to his feet. "Will you be alright?!"

The driver nodded, still in shock.

Krimmiel then ran after the dragon. As he turned the corner onto a massive square, a squad car zoomed past him, and a crew of men and women in red camo leapt out of the trunk. Ropes of ice and water unraveled from their palms.

At the center of the square, the dragon gathered itself like a spool of thread and shot columns of smoke into the sky. Embers waltzed with the wind.

The crew members managed to cage the animal with their watery and icy ropes. The dragon's scales sizzled like a bucket of water being dumped over a fire.

The dragon roared again. But it wasn't a menacing growl like before. Instead, it was a howl. Its eyes dwindled into a soft amber color—it was pleading.

A final lasso looped around its neck and tightened. The dragon slumped to the ground and slowly lost its flaming exterior.

"STOP IT!" Krimmiel shouted at the dragon catchers. "YOU'RE HURTING HER!"

"GET BACK!" A man in camo pushed him down.

One crew member looked over at Krimmiel and nodded. "Loosen the noose!" she told the man in a commanding tone.

"But it might engulf us in flames!" the man retorted.

"Our orders are to return the dragon to the Sun *alive*," said the woman. "Loosen the noose so it can breathe, soldier!"

Grumbling to himself, the man flicked at the rope. At once, it became lax and brought life back into the dragon.

"Don't worry," the woman said to Krimmiel, "I'll see to it that the dragon is safely returned. Now please, vacate the square before you look like him!" She gestured to a man in a purple suit being lifted into an ambulance. Krimmiel did not catch the man's face but did his arms; they were burnt to a crisp.

Stumbling to his feet, Krimmiel turned the corner and sprinted toward the Heavenly Hotel. When he burst through the door, he found Sin sitting in his armchair, napping. Honeyed drool dripped down his mandibles.

"SIN!"

"What is it?!" Sin jolted awake.

"You'll never believe what just happened!"

In one continuous sentence, Krimmiel told Sin all about the dragon attack. When he finished, Sin said with an air of disappointment, "Ah man, you spilled my soup?!"

"Sin, forget the soup! Something else happened… I—I had another one of those visions!"

Sin's interest was piqued. The bee leaned forward, gravity washing over his face. "Which one?! The one where Cherry dies or the one about—?"

"The boy," said Krimmiel. "He's about to embark on his journey." He wiped sweat from his brow. "I was right, Sin! I was right all along… He's an alien!"

About the Author

J.Q. (Jacob Quentin) Gagliastro is the Swetalian-American nonbinary bestselling author of *The Diary of a Sugarbaby* and *Mercury to the Moon*. They are from Philadelphia and accept he and they pronouns but prefer they. They grew up as the new kid, moving from state to state—VA, NY, FL, MA, PA, and CT. At age sixteen, they were thrown out for being queer. Despite this, they pushed themself through school and earned a BA in French Language & Literature from Allegheny College. They studied language arts in Northern Italy and Angers, France. In France, they worked at the city hall of Fismes as a French to English translator. They then moved to the great city of Philadelphia and returned to their one true passion: literature. Coming from a working-class family of eight, J.Q. always had to support themself. When they couldn't, they became a sugarbaby and sold their body. While *The Diary of a Sugarbaby* is a work of fiction, it is also a horrendous yet bittersweet story about their life and honest experiences as a sugarbaby twisted into a dramatic political satire.

The Diary of a Sugarbaby has become widely known as *THE #1 queer dystopian bestseller*. NYC's Queer Book Club selected it as their October 2024 anniversary read. On August 10th, 2024, Gagliastro appeared on Chicago's WGN TV with journalist Sean Lewis. *The Diary of a Sugarbaby* was featured in *The New York Review of Books*, both April and May issues. Gagliastro developed the sugarbaby merch line and completed an eight-stop *Sugarbaby Book Tour* (NYC, D.C., Chicago, West Hartford, Glastonbury, Annapolis, Keene, and Philadelphia). *The Manhattan Book Review* called *TDS* "*The Handmaid's Tale* on steroids!" *Kirkus Reviews* called it "a frightening novel about an unthinkable future!" And according to *The BookLife Prize*, *TDS* is a "dark satirical work of sci-fi!" Please visit *jqgagliastro.com* and follow *@jq.gagliastro* on Instagram for upcoming projects!

Check out press photos from J.Q. Gagliastro's
Sugarbaby Book Tour!